Emma Helen Blair, James Alexander Robertson

The Philippine Islands, 1493⬜1898
Volume XXXI

Emma Helen Blair, James Alexander Robertson

The Philippine Islands, 1493⧠1898
Volume XXXI

1st Edition | ISBN: 978-3-73407-851-4

Place of Publication: Frankfurt am Main, Germany

Year of Publication: 2019

Outlook Verlag GmbH, Germany.

The PHILIPPINE ISLANDS 1493-1898

Explorations by Early Navigators, Descriptions of the Islands and their Peoples, their History and Records of the Catholic Missions, as related in contemporaneous Books and Manuscripts, showing the Political, Economic, Commercial and Religious Conditions of those Islands from their earliest relations with European Nations to the close of the Nineteenth Century

TRANSLATED FROM THE ORIGINALS

Edited and annotated by EMMA HELEN BLAIR and JAMES ALEXANDER ROBERTSON, with historical introduction and additional notes by EDWARD GAYLORD BOURNE. With maps, portraits and other illustrations

Volume XXXI—1640

The Arthur H. Clark Company
Cleveland, Ohio
MCMV

The Philippine Islands,

1

1493–1898

Explorations by early navigators, descriptions of the islands and their peoples, their history and records of the catholic missions, as related in contemporaneous books and manuscripts, showing the political, economic, commercial and religious conditions of those islands from their earliest relations with European nations to the close of the nineteenth century,

Volume XXXI, 1640

Edited and annotated by **Emma Helen Blair**
and **James Alexander Robertson** with
historical introduction and additional notes by
Edward Gaylord Bourne.

The Arthur H. Clark Company

Cleveland, Ohio

MCMV

3

Contents of Volume XXXI

Illustrations

Preface

The present volume is devoted to a further installment of Aduarte's *Historia*, begun in Vol. XXX—which work will be completed in our next issue. The part here given covers the years 1596 to 1608 in the history of the Dominican order in the Philippines.

Resuming Aduarte's account of the missions carried on by his order among the Indians of Cagayán, in northern Luzón, the pious and devout acts of their converts, and the joy and gratitude of the religious thereat, are recounted at length. In 1596, news comes to the islands of the death of Bishop Salazar in Spain. Aduarte describes in detail the life, achievements, and virtues of that prelate. He was distinguished—not only in the Philippines, but during a long residence in Nueva España—as the friend and protector of the Indian natives. His mode of life was most simple and austere; he was charitable and generous to the full extent of his limited means. By nature choleric and quick-tempered, he trained himself to patience and forbearance; and the slanders of the evil-minded against him only roused his compassion. He was public-spirited, and foremost in all enterprises for the good of the community. To him are attributed the royal grant to the Jesuits for maintaining a school, and the establishment and much of the endowment of the hospital for sick Indians.

Bishop Salazar's journey to Spain enables him to secure for his cathedral important aid, and the division of his diocese, so that its manifold duties may be more satisfactorily performed; soon afterward, he dies at Madrid. During his absence, his see is directed by his vicar-general, Fray Christobal de Salvatierra, to an account of whose exemplary life, valuable labors, and apostolic virtues a chapter is devoted. He protects the Indians, and does much to reform the morals of the Spaniards. Among other things, he compels the Chinese to cease such of their theatrical performances as contain idolatrous and superstitious matter; and obliges the Spaniards to give up attendance at these comedies. It is he who begins the spiritual conquest of the Cagayán region, and he goes on other expeditions; and he assumes charge of the Bataán mission until missionaries come for that field. At his death, he appoints two Dominicans to assume his duties as vicar-general; but they are so opposed by the ecclesiastical cabildo that they resign the office to the latter. Next comes a biographical sketch of the younger Juan de Castro, who is assigned to the toilsome and difficult mission of Pangasinán. In December, 1593, he accompanies an embassy to China; on the return voyage, the ship is wrecked. Castro escapes to land, but soon afterward dies as a result of the shock and exposure thus suffered.

Aduarte recounts, with much detail, the expedition of 1596 to Cambodia, which is accompanied by himself and another Dominican, Fray Alonso Ximenez. Velloso's junk is driven ashore by a storm, and the men, after much privation and suffering, make it over into a shallow oared vessel, and row along the coast in search of water and inhabited places. When reduced to the last extremity, they accidentally find fresh water, and thus are saved, finally making their way to a fort where some Cambojan soldiers are stationed. From these the Spaniards learn that the king who was friendly to them has been driven out by a usurper, and that one of their consorts in the Spanish fleet has reached that country. They join this ship, and soon afterward, learning that the king is plotting to destroy them all, and coming to blows with the Chinese traders who have come to Chordemuco, the Spaniards attack the Cambojans at night and defeat them, killing the usurper of that throne. The Spanish commander Gallinato arrives, and decides to return to Manila; but contrary winds force them to land at Malaca, after twice encountering enemies. Nearly a year later, they succeed in reaching Manila, without other result of their journey "but that of having suffered for the gospel."

In 1596, Fray Bernardo de Santa Catharina is elected provincial; under his rule, the conversion of the natives greatly increases. A new band of missionaries arrives soon afterward, most of whom go to the Cagayán field. In Cambodia Velloso and Blas Ruiz, Spanish adventurers, have aided the lawful king to regain his throne, and they persuade him to send to Manila requesting soldiers and the return of the two Dominican friars. Luis Pérez Dasmariñas offers to make this expedition at his own cost, and Aduarte and Ximenez accompany him. A fierce storm scatters the ships; that of Dasmariñas is driven upon the coast of China, and that in which Aduarte sails is wrecked on one of the Babuyanes group. He sends word of this misfortune to Manila; the governor orders the Spaniards to proceed to China, on which coast they again suffer shipwreck, but find Dasmariñas—who has met a like disaster there, and is enduring great privations. Aduarte has meanwhile returned to Manila; but word of Dasmariñas's misfortune reaches that place, and Governor Tello sends him a ship with aid, and orders to return at once to Manila. Aduarte accompanies this vessel. He goes to Canton, to obtain the viceroy's permission for Dasmariñas's return to Manila; but there falls into the hands of a greedy and corrupt official, who, thinking to extort money from the friar, has him tortured. Finally, Aduarte is placed in prison with the Spanish sailors, but is soon bailed out by a Chinese friend. He makes his escape, and joins Dasmariñas; the latter returns to Manila, but Aduarte's health is so injured that he is obliged to halt at Macao. Fray Alonso Ximenez dies at that place, as a result of his hardships and sufferings in the Camboja expedition; a sketch of his life and virtues is given.

In 1597 another mission arrives at the islands, with Bishop Benavides. The intermediate chapter of the Dominican province is in session, and the new arrivals are therefore assigned to the needy missions; various incidents in those of Cagayán and Pangasinan are related. Biographical sketches of Antonio de Soria and other pioneer missionaries are given. Two of these are sent (1598) on a politico-religious mission to Camboja, with a Spanish officer named Mendoza; they are attacked by Malays, and most of the Spaniards are slain. The rest escape to Siam, but are attacked there also, with further loss of life. Among the dead are the two Dominicans and Mendoza.

At the chapter-session of 1600, Juan de Santo Thomas is elected provincial. The Cagayán missions are extended further into the interior; and the religious zealously pursue and destroy any trace of idol-worship. At the intermediate chapter of 1602, the house of San Juan del Monte, without the city, is established as a retreat for convalescent brethren of the order. At that time occurs a miraculous healing of a friar possessed by an evil spirit; also, a large band of missionaries arrives from Spain, being divinely aided to escape various dangers of pestilence and shipwreck. With these friars all the convents in the province are supplied, and some even go to Japan. Aduarte explains the reason for Dominican missionaries being called to that country, and describes their first establishment, which is in Satsuma.

In 1603 the new king of Camboja asks the Manila government for soldiers and missionaries. Three Dominicans are sent, with a few soldiers as guards, and letters to the king. They are well received; but two of them die, and the factions in that country and the fickleness of the natives induce the remaining friar to return to Manila. In April, 1604, occurs the great conflagration in Manila, and, in the succeeding autumn, the revolt and massacre of the Chinese in and near that city—which have been fully described in previous volumes.

At the chapter of 1604, Fray Miguel de San Jacinto is elected provincial, and several new churches in heathen communities are received. These are supplied with ministers from a new company that arrives that year from Spain. Some account is given of the journey of these friars, with its hardships and dangers—among these being an attack made upon them by hostile Indians at Guadalupe Island, in which six friars are slain and three wounded.

Many of these new missionaries are sent to the Cagayán missions—some to the Itaves Indians, who were considered fierce and untamable by the Spaniards (some of whom, having oppressed the natives, were slain by them) until "the holy gospel declared by the Dominican religious changed them from bloodthirsty wolves to gentle sheep." Aduarte declares that wonderful results were thus achieved, rendering those Indians moral and obedient, and achieving this entirely by kindness and gentleness. The Indians even consent to change their abodes to the mission reductions. The fathers are almost worn out by these tasks, and one dies; but they are encouraged by the wonderful results of their labor and by miracles which the Lord vouchsafes them.

Aduarte presents a long biographical account of Archbishop Benavides, Salazar's immediate successor. He is distinguished in Spain, both as a student and as an instructor. Coming to the Philippines, he immediately undertakes to learn the Chinese language, that he may minister to the men of that nation who come to Manila; and founds a hospital for the poor sick Chinese there. Benavides goes to China (as previously narrated), and afterward to Spain. There he does good service in refuting the opinion prevalent there that conquest must precede conversion, and soldiers clear the way for missionaries. He also procures the recall of a papal brief authorizing the bishops to visit the friars in charge of the Indians, the same as if they were parish priests; and accomplishes other important business, especially in behalf of the Indians, winning golden opinions of his abilities, good judgment, and virtue. Returning to the islands, Benavides takes charge of the diocese of Nueva Segovia, where he labors zealously for the moral improvement of the Spaniards, but most of all for the protection of the Indians from Spanish rapacity. After Salazar's death, Benavides takes charge of the vacant see, and is finally appointed archbishop; but his mode of life is always as simple and austere as that of the poorest friar, and he spends all his income in almsgiving. At his death, he bequeaths the little that he possesses to his brethren, for the founding of a college at Manila. Biographical accounts of other friars are presented. One of these, Jacinto Pardo, dies suddenly, it is supposed from poison given him by hostile Indians. Another, Juan de la Cruz, is a notable linguist.

In 1605, a papal brief (obtained by the Jesuits) forbids any religious to go to Japan except by way of India; but it is revoked three years later. This, in the interim, causes the friar orders much trouble; and Japan, moreover, is greatly unsettled and disturbed by various political matters. In 1606 an intermediate chapter is held at Manila, at which the religious of the order are directed to collect materials (of which Aduarte has availed himself) for a history of the

Dominican province. The great victory of Acuña at Maluco, which occurs about that time, is ascribed to the agency of our Lady of the Rosary, to whom the Dominicans have a special devotion; a confraternity in her honor had been founded in Acuña's army, and the captured town is dedicated to her. In this same year, another company of religious arrives from Spain; one dies before reaching Manila. At this time, a Dominican mission is established in the province of Hizen, Japan.

In 1605 the mission in Pangasinan is extended to the village of Manáoag, farther inland; and, "within a few months, there was not a heathen in the village." A chief in a neighboring village is also converted, to whom a miracle occurs. In 1607, two new churches are established in Cagayán. In Nalfotan the Indians, led by their excellent chief, build a church even before a missionary is sent to them; and all is prospering when a priestess of the old idols stirs up the people, against the new faith, and the villagers take to the hills. Later, they burn the church; but the good chief saves the missionary's life. Another revolt occurs in that province, caused by the cruelty of an encomendero. Troops are sent from Manila; their commander finds that the Indians had cause for revolt, and sends the people of Nalfotan home with their pastor. This mission prospers, and the chief is its mainstay during his life—a function long continued by his pious sister.

The provincial chosen in 1608 is Baltasar Fort. Some account is given of the persecution of Christians in Japan; they are banished from Satsuma, but many find shelter in Nagasaki. The Dominicans accomplish much in Hizen. They also extend their missionary labors among the wild mountaineers of northern Luzón, gathering many scattered hamlets into larger villages, and converting many of their heathen inhabitants. In Ituy they attempt to open a mission, but the Franciscans claim that as their territory; the Dominicans yield, but regret to see these Indians abandoned soon afterward by their Franciscan teachers. In 1609 the general of their order commands the provincials of the mission provinces to report every year the work and achievements of the missionaries, with information regarding the numbers and condition of the order in each province. Several friars die in that year, of whom biographical sketches are presented. One of these, Pedro Rodriguez, has rendered special and distinguished service in the hospital for Chinese at Manila.

THE EDITORS

August, 1905.

Historia de la Provincia del Sancto Rosario de la Orden de Predicadores

(*Continued*)

By Diego Aduarte, O.P.; Manila, 1640.

SOURCE: Translated from a copy of the above work in the possession of Edward E. Ayer, Chicago.

TRANSLATION: This is made by Henry B. Lathrop, of the University of Wisconsin. The present instalment covers pp. 167–384 of book i of the *Historia* (which will be concluded in VOL. XXXII).

History of the Dominican Province of the Holy Rosary

By Fray Diego Aduarte, O.P.

(*Continued*)

Chapter XXXVIII

The advance made by the Indians of this province in virtue, and their attendance upon the sacraments

Even if the religious in this province of Nueva Segovia had done no other good than bringing to an end or preventing so many sins of idolatry as these Indians used to commit, every day and every hour, by adoring the devil and offering him superstitious reverence in all the ways which have already been described, a very great service indeed would have been done to the Lord, to whom all such actions as these are directly offensive. In these idolatrous acts His honor is taken from Him, and His divine supremacy is overthrown and given to His greatest enemy. To prevent one of these offenses to God would be of much more merit than to prevent any homicide whatsoever, for that is a direct offense only against a man; while idolatry is directly against God, and takes from Him His divine honor, which is much more valuable than the life of a man. If this be true, how high is the merit of having prevented the innumerable acts of idolatry which used to be committed daily by those Indians, and having brought to an end the multitude of sins which followed upon this one—constant wars, murders, robberies, drunkennesses which surpassed one another, lewd actions, and all the other vices which were committed—without the rulers of those people concerning themselves the least in them or punishing them, except when they personally were wronged. And this they did, not out of zeal for justice, but as their personal act of revenge, so that they sinned more in the excess of the punishment than the delinquents had sinned in the faults for which they were punished. Now all these evils came to an end, as the result of the preaching of the religious, to the great glory of God. Hence, if they had done no more than this, very great indeed would the service have been which thereby they wrought and continue to work for the Creator of all and the universal Lord. But this was not all; for when these evil growths had been rooted out, there were planted in the hearts of these Indians the opposite virtues. By the aid of the Lord they began so soon to bear flowers and fruit that the first bishop of this province, Don Fray Miguel de Venavides, a holy and most learned prelate, wrote to his Holiness Clement VIII, who at that time governed the church, the following report, in which he gives a faithful account of the establishment of his bishopric, with the accuracy to which his office and dignity obliged him. "This province," he says, "is very new in the preaching of the gospel, for it is only three years since there were ministers of the Order of St. Dominic in it. Before that time

16

there used to be seen now and then a priest in the place where the Spaniards lived. As for preaching to the Indians, there was no idea of such a thing. This province is very near Great China, being distant from it less than seventy leguas; so that now the faith of the Lord appears to be approaching their powerful and great kingdom. The native race of the province is a very spirited one, whom it has cost the Spaniards many efforts and the lives of many men to subdue. As soon as the Order of St. Dominic came into this region, they immediately went to live among the Indians; and they built their churches and houses, which were more like huts built to last two days. They employed upon them very few laborers, and had no teacher or journeymen. The Indians would have died before they admitted them to their villages (and, as it was, there was some difficulty about it), if the good name of those who had been in Pangasinan had not reached these Indians also—who in this way learned how the religious treated the Indians as if they were their own children, and defended them against those who wronged them. When they began to consider the mode of life followed by the religious, their patience and labors, their avoidance of flesh food, their many fasts, continual prayers, great poverty—for the poverty of the Order of St. Dominic here is very great—and the gentleness and love with which they treated the natives, God was pleased that in those villages where there are missionary religious, all the inhabitants desired to be Christians. They have not only become very devout toward God, but very friendly to the Spaniards; thus the religious have put peace and security where they were not before. As a result, in regions where soldiers and garrisons used to be necessary, there now are none, and the country is very peaceful. Every evening the men gather together and recite prayers before a cross, which is usually set up in the plaza of the village, the women doing the same by themselves in another place. Baptisms in the heathen villages are constantly increasing, while those for whom there are not missionaries enough ask for them with all their hearts, and are so desirous to become Christians that we ought therefore to offer thanks to God. [Some chiefs invited the missionaries to their village, saying that they all wished to become Christians. A Spaniard who had command in one village where they were building a church, directed the soldiers to interfere with the work, which would have injured his private interests; but within a short time all those men died horribly. The fathers drive out devils from those who are possessed by them. It is only for lack of missionaries that the whole country is not filled with churches."

The report is very short, and it is therefore necessary for us to expand upon it, making use of the reports of the founders and first missionaries themselves. In addition to what has already been said, they report as follows. Great as was the labor of bringing these souls from darkness to light, they have come to understand their duties, worshiping the Lord with great devotion, and regularly attending His holy sacraments. They go beyond the commandments of God and of His church to do additional works of devotion—especially the women, for they can more easily come to be instructed, and can more easily do what they are told, as they are less occupied than the men are with things to distract their minds and thoughts. Some of them are so devout that they walk always in the presence of God, doing nothing without an inward prayer to Him. In Tular, or Abulug, a village of more than a thousand inhabitants, in which there were more communicants than in the other villages, the religious taught many of them to strive to meditate every day upon some of the mysteries of the rosary. This was an exercise to which the first founder of the province, father Fray Juan de Castro, was very much given, and in which many of his disciples and subjects have followed him. Thus these Indians day by day meditate upon one after another of the fifteen mysteries of the rosary. Other Indians lay aside part of their daily food for charity. Bringing about these results requires from the minister much labor, teaching, assistance, perseverance, and prayer; for without these there is very little or nothing that they can do of themselves, without books or any other guide to direct them. As it is, the Indians have advanced wonderfully—visiting and caring for their sick, especially when they are poor; taking discipline at night in their houses; fasting beyond what they are required; frequenting the churches; and offering their prayers at dawn and at evening. There were some of them who, at the very beginning of their Christian career, went through the fields looking for the little children of poor people who could not take them to town; and, bringing these to be baptized, they acted as their sponsors, making gifts to them afterward of swaddling-clothes or some such thing. Heavy as are the labors of the religious, their joy in them is still greater.

Very great difficulty was found, at first, in bringing the Indians to confess. They regarded it as a shameful thing for them to report to the confessor all the evil things they had done and thought, and they also feared to give the religious power to annoy or blame them by means of their confession. "When a dozen persons were gathered together for their first confession, there was not one of them who was willing to begin, for everyone wished the other to make the experiment. At last the fathers summoned an Indian who came from Pangasinan, and who had longer been a Christian and was better acquainted with the fathers. The Indians asked him many questions about the matter, all of which he answered well, encouraging them greatly; he told them that in his country the Christians confessed without any evil results following. At last one Indian woman, more courageous than the rest, ventured to go to make her

18

confession where the father was patiently waiting in the church—commending the matter to God with all his heart, because it was very plain that the hesitation of the Indians was on account of the fear they felt. She confessed, went away very well satisfied, and, returning to the rest, told them what had happened. They asked her a thousand new questions, especially if the father was angry when she told her sins, and whether he had scolded her. She answered 'No,' and that, on the contrary, he had treated her very kindly and lovingly; so they all determined to make their confessions, and began them heartily." So they come now and make their confessions; and in general it is not necessary to summon them, for they anticipate the confessors, and sometimes even beg that their confessions may be heard, as a penance. They showed the greatest faith and sincerity in their confessions, striving to be reconciled with all their enemies before making their confession. The religious generally encouraged them to make their confessions on the day of their patron saint; and one Indian woman, named for St. Anne, was unwilling to confess on that saint's day. When the father asked her the reason, she answered that she had had a quarrel with one of her neighbors, and that they did not speak to each other; and she begged the father to reconcile them. After he had done that, she very readily made her confession. It frequently happens that a man accused in a court of law denies the accusation, and that the religious is unable to draw anything else from him; while in confession the same man will clearly accuse himself of the same fault which he had previously denied, and will deny again if the same question is asked him on another trial. It not infrequently happens that if they have any ill-will against the religious, or have said anything against him, they confess to that very man, telling him of the ill-will that they have felt against him.]

Chapter XXXIX

The devotion with which these Indians approached the holy communion, and some events which give much glory to the Lord.

[Since the most holy sacrament of the Eucharist is so high and difficult a thing to teach a people whose heathen state makes them opposed to ideas so lofty, the religious in this region spend a great deal of effort upon teaching the Indians this supreme mystery.] At first, only very few and very carefully chosen persons were admitted to the communion, according to the ordinance of a provincial council of Lima, confirmed by the Apostolic See, which in Act ii, chapter 20, says,[1] *Precepit sancta sinodus parochis, ceterisque Indorum praedicatoribus, ut saepe ac serio, de fide huius mysterii eos instituant*; and, later, *Quos autem parochus, et satis instructus, et correctione vitae idoneos iudicaverit, iis saltem in paschate, Eucharistiam administrare non praetermittat*. It is true that the Indians of these regions have much greater capacity than those of Peru, of whom this council spoke; yet because they were so new in the faith, and so badly fitted by their ancient customs for this supreme mystery, the holy communion is not given to them indifferently at Easter, but is given to those whom the minister judges to be properly prepared. At the beginning, greater attention and caution were necessary. Hence, after they had been thoroughly instructed in the mysteries of the faith, and in particular in the doctrine of this holy mystery, and when they showed a desire to receive the holy communion, they were examined as to their lives, habits, and reputation, the most credible witnesses in the village being called in to testify. If they were found prepared, they were admitted to this supreme meal, to this holy table. A week before they communicated, unless they were occupied—and they generally gave up their occupations for this purpose—they went to church and heard spiritual addresses every day. [On these days they prepared themselves with more than ordinary prayer, and rose at midnight to pray and to take their discipline. If they were married, they separated their beds at least on the eve and the day of the communion. Many of the men went to the convent, and followed the hours with the religious. On the day of receiving communion, they followed the same customs as did the members of our order, dedicating the whole day to God, and keeping in it the silence which we observe in our convents on the day when those religious who are not priests communicate. They were taught to say something after mass in order to give thanks to the Lord; for since they cannot read, and have no books, the ministers have to teach them everything of this kind—

especially at the beginning, for afterward there are many of them who teach the others. At the same time, they receive what the minister tells them with greater respect. Many extraordinary examples of piety have been exhibited by the communicants.] In the village of Pata there was an Indian chief, a man of great valor, named Don Francisco Yringan, of whom mention has several times been made. He, being governor there, had as a guest in his house a Spaniard who was traveling that way. He treated him kindly and entertained him as well as he could. The guest, not being content with this, asked him to find an Indian woman, that he might sleep with her; and gave him some trinkets with which to gratify her. But the Indian refused to accept them and to do what the Spaniard asked him, saying that this was wicked and that no one ought to do such a thing, least of all a communicant. This was a reply with which the old Christian ought to have been put to confusion, and which should have made him correct his desires; but it was not so; on the contrary, he grew angry at the answer, and threatened to cane the Indian unless he did what he was told. The Indian turned his back and bending his head said, "Give me as much of a caning as you please, for I am not going to do what you ask." The Spaniard was so intemperate and discourteous that he vented his anger upon him and caned him, the Indian suffering with great patience, as if he had received from God not only faith in Him, but the power of suffering because he refused to offend Him. This is a grace which the Apostle praises, urging the Philippians to esteem it highly; and now it was found in a Philippine Indian. The Indian who suffered this was a man who could have employed lawyers against him who wronged him, though he was alone; and, if he had shouted to his followers, they would have cut the Spaniard to pieces. But, as he was a communicant, he would neither be an accomplice in the sin of the Spaniard, nor would he avenge himself; nor would he even make use of a just defense, as was taught in the counsel of Paul quoted above, *Non vos defendentes carissimi* [*i.e.*, "Not defending yourselves, beloved"]. On another occasion when a great insult was offered to this same Indian, a religious comforted him and encouraged him to patience. The Indian answered: "O father, how good it would be if we all served God with truth. If it were so, that wrong which has been done to me would not have been done. If this thing had happened in the days of our heathendom, it would have sufficed to cause me and my followers to make war to the death against this town; but now that we are Christians, patience!" He said nothing more and uttered not a word of indignation, but passed over his sufferings and endured the insult, although he felt it keenly and was ashamed (though in a very Christian manner). Thus he gave proof that his virtue was enduring, because such a blow could not overthrow it. There was one poor Indian slave woman whom a Spaniard, who had communicated a few days before in that village, tried to violate. She resisted him with spirit; and, as if horrified at the lack of respect which by his actions he showed to the Lord, whom he had received, she said to him: "How is it that, being a communicant, you dare to commit such a sin?" In this way may be seen how some of the new Christians surpass others who are old in the faith, going beyond them in virtue, devotion, and the fear of God. [In the village of Masi, which is near to that of which we have been speaking, there was an Indian, a communicant, the fiscal of the church, who was of blameless life. His name was Sebastian Calelao. His sown rice had not sprouted on account of the drought; but, in response to his prayers, God sent rain so that his crop was saved. In Pilitan there was an Indian woman, named Ysabel Pato, a faithful Christian. When she was about to receive the viaticum, the priest found that the Lord had anticipated him. Other marvels and instances of virtue have been exhibited among these Indians.] Some Indian women accused themselves of having eaten *buyos* on fast-days, but not on Fridays. When the confessor asked them if they had fasted on other days than Friday— for the Indians are not obliged to fast on the other days in Lent—they answered that they fasted the whole of Lent, performing these fasts as works of devotion; for the holy Apostolic See has excused them from this fast, because of their weakness and the scantiness of their food. When the religious thought that this was excessive, and told them that they could not do so much, they answered that by the favor of God they could do so, as they had already fasted during the whole of Lent on previous occasions. The buyo is an aromatic leaf, shaped like an ivy-leaf, which the Indians are accustomed to chew with a sort of wild acorn and a little bit of lime. Even some of the Spaniards in this country very commonly use it, though they do not swallow it, so that only the juice reaches the stomach; it invigorates the stomach, and preserves the teeth. To carry some buyos in their mouths, if there were not many of them, would not break their fast; but in spite of all this, these Indian women made a scruple of taking it in their fasts, out of pure devotion and in an entirely voluntary way. [Visions of demons are frequent among the Indians. One such happened in a part of this province called Ytabes, of which the order took charge in 1604. The Indian concerned had a vision of demons driven away by persons whom he did not know, but who were clothed with white underneath and with black cloaks. This was something which the Indian had never seen, because the religious rarely wear their cloaks in the Indian villages, assuming them only when they go into the pulpit to preach. At that time the Christians there were so few that the sermons were not delivered from the pulpit, but from a seat, the cloak not being put on for the purpose. Frightful visions of the anito drove the father of Don Francisco Tuliau to baptism. In Camalaniugan father Fray Gaspar Zarfate drove out several demons who were tormenting Indian women.]

Chapter XL

The great comfort which the religious commonly felt in their ministry both in life and in death

[In spite of the sufferings of the religious in this region—the heat, the strangeness, the homesickness, the poverty of their life—they had great joy in their work. The aniteras, or priestesses of the devil, who became Christians, often told them that as soon as they came to heathen villages the devil left the houses in which he was worshiped, which were wretched little hovels. They dreamed that they saw their anitos in the form of carabaos, or buffaloes, and of black men; and that they likewise suffered greatly at such times, because the devil was so much their owner that he used to enter them visibly—one of them, who was the mistress of the others, saying that he entered her in the form of a shadow, and in that way gave his oracles. The aniteras were, as the Indians said, beside themselves and out of their minds at such times. Many miracles were wrought by the fathers, and they had great joy in the marvels which the Lord showed them in permitting them to save by holy baptism children and others who were at the point of death, from eternal damnation. The bishop of Nueva Segovia, Don Fray Diego de Soria, writing to his great friend, father Fray Bernardo de Sancta Cathalina, or Navarro, on March 24, 1608, said that when they had come from the province of Ylocos, they had been detained in a port for two weeks by as heavy a storm as if they had been in Segovia itself, and that they had suffered much on the road; but that now they felt consoled by what they had found in the province, which was a perfect picture of Pangasinan. He reported that in the mountains of Fotol and Alamonag they had confirmed more than six hundred Indians; and that even the little boys and girls knew the definition of the sacrament of confirmation. He reports that the religious of the province are very harmonious, especially those who came from the college of Alcala, to which they purpose sending a golden cup worth a thousand pesos, hoping that the college may pay for it with missionaries, which will not be simony. He goes on to say that he had been three days in the village, and that they had already confirmed eight or nine thousand Indians. The cup of gold was sent, but never reached its destination. His remarks with reference to the college of Alcala are due to the fact that several of the religious who came over on various expeditions had been supplied by that college. Among them were some of the most devoted of the missionaries—for instance, the bishop himself, father Fray Bernardo de Sancta Cathalina, and father Fray Juan Cobo. The report of this father may well be followed by that of father Fray Francisco de San Joseph, or Blancas,[2] who wrote from this province of Nueva Segovia to the father provincial, father Fray Miguel de San Jacintho. His letter is given in full by Aduarte; the substance of it is as follows: "I have seen with my own eyes something of what I have read in the letters of your Reverence with regard to the great need of ministers here, and to the desire of the people for them. We found the inhabitants kindly and peaceful, and delighted to see us. When we disembarked at one of the heathen villages on the way, some of the children ran to kiss our scapulars. Some of the boys ran before us, reciting the prayers very well, not because they had been taught, but because they had picked them up from a couple of our boys whom they had seen several times. Yet in spite of all this they will be lost and damned, for lack of friars. The wife of the governor of this village was very ill; and desiring to die a Christian, she had herself carried to the village of Pia, which is a Christian village about a day's journey from hers. Father Fray Pedro was at Pipig, a village near there, at the time, so that he was in time to baptize her." In another letter to the same provincial, he said: "Your Reverence might see here this morning a company of old men learning the doctrines of Christianity; another of girls; another of married women; another of young boys—giving praises to God like so many choirs of angels, proclaiming His doctrine and learning it to prepare themselves for baptism." Father Fray Jacintho de San Geronimo,[3] who is still living, writes a letter to a friend of his in Nueva España, which is dated on the last day of the feast of the Resurrection, in 1607. It is substantially as follows: "I am at present in the province of Nueva Segovia, in great happiness to see the desire of the people to become Christians. Our poverty and disinterestedness have caused them to have great confidence in us. I would not change my lot for any other in the world, in spite of the hardness of our life here." The same father wrote another letter to a friend in Manila, to the following effect: "There are more than four thousand souls in this village, not the eighth part of whom are Christians, though all desire to become so. On Holy Saturday three of us baptized six hundred persons." The date of this letter was April 2, 1607. Although this father had been but a short time in the province, he had already learned enough of the language for such great results, and could rejoice in the fruit of his labors. From all this it is plain that the missionaries in this region who are busied with the ministry of souls have no need of España nor of anything Spanish for their comfort, except companions to help them in the work. As there is no rule without an exception, it must be so in this case; but if any missionary is unhappy here, it is generally because he has failed in his obligations and become lukewarm in his devotions. Those that can speak the language and thereby convert souls are happy in their work; and those who cannot learn the language should accordingly be unhappy. But the Lord is not so poor as that, as will be sufficiently shown by a letter from father Fray Garcia de Oroz, written from Nueva Segovia to a brother at Manila: "Though I have been told that I would be very unhappy and discouraged by the difficulty of learning the language, and though I find that it is very difficult to me because of my age and lack of memory, I am not disconsolate; because merely to be in company with a father who is a master of the language, and to act as his confessor, will greatly serve our Lord. This region is a pleasant one, and my health is good in it during the winter, which lasts from the beginning of October to March. It resembles the climate of Valencia during the same period, having cool and fresh nights. A great part of the country is very open, and the mountains are not high or rugged. Some of the convents are on the shore of the sea; others, on the bank of a copious river, which is navigated by canoes for a distance of sixty leguas up the river. No one has reached the head of it, or knows where the spring is." The happiness of the missionaries in their work will be plain from what has been said. As a result of having lived devoted lives they died happy deaths, rejoicing in their firm hope that they were going to enjoy the Lord whom they had served, and for whom they had abandoned their parents, kinsmen, native lands, and the ease which they might have enjoyed in España.]

Chapter XLI

The servant of God, Don Fray Domingo de Salaçar, first bishop of the Philippinas

By the ships which came to these islands from Nueva España in 1596, arrived the sad news of the death of their father and first bishop, Don Fray Domingo de Salaçar. This was one of the greatest losses which they could have met with at that time, for they lost in him a most loving father and a most faithful defender. In their defense he had not hesitated to set out on a long and perilous journey to España, and that in his very last years, when his great age would have excused him from such excessive labors. But the fervent love which he had for his sheep would not permit him to offer any excuses, when he saw them in so great need as they were in at that time. There was in these regions no place from which he could obtain relief for them, nor could he have obtained relief from España if he had not gone there in person to get it, for he had tried all other means. He had sent a procurator; and he had written most urgent letters, and had learned by experience that they did not bring about the results desired. In fine, these islands lost a shepherd and a holy bishop; and when this has been said, everything has been said. The Order of St. Dominic, which had been so recently established in these islands, suffered the greatest loss in this general affliction, for it had in him a father and a brother who loved it most affectionately; and a continual benefactor, who, though he was poor in the extreme, seemed rich and generous in the benefits which he conferred upon the order. Without them it would have suffered much, because the religious came as apostolic preachers, in the greatest poverty, and in the greatest need of the favor which they always received from this pious bishop. Don Fray Domingo de Salacar was born in La Rioja in Castilla, and had assumed the habit in the distinguished convent of San Estevan at Salamanca, where he was contemporary with some who afterward became famous professors of theology in this illustrious university—the father masters Fray Domingo Bañes and Fray Bartholome de Medina [Fray Domingo de Salacar was not inferior to them in scholarship, but his heart was set more on sanctity than on learning; and hence he desired to go to the province of Santiago de Mexico, which seemed to have renewed the primitive austerity of the time of our father St. Dominic. When he reached Mexico, though he wished to labor among the Indians, the orders of his superior kept him from doing so, and he became a teacher, and finally a master of theology, the highest degree of this kind which can be reached in the order. His virtue was such that during all the time while he was in Nueva España (namely, forty years), he never broke any of our sacred constitutions in any point. As one of the popes has said, a religious who thus follows the constitutions of our order, has done enough to be canonized. When the directions of his superiors at last permitted him to give the reins to his desire, he devoted himself to missionary work among the Indian tribes in the province of Vaxac. He suffered deeply from every wrong that the Spaniards did to the Indians; and his suffering was doubled because he could not remedy their wrongs. However, he did what he could for those that were under his charge by comforting them and encouraging them to patience; and it is no small consolation for the unfortunate to see that there is someone who pities them and sympathizes with their suffering. So desirous was father Fray Domingo of laboring for the Lord that he joined the expedition to Florida,4 accompanying the holy Fray Domingo de la Anunciacion in the hardships which he endured, which he felt the more because he could not make the conversions which he hoped for among those Indians. Before beginning his journey, he asked the superior to bless all the waters of the streams and rivers from which he should have to drink, that he might not break the constitution which directs us not to drink without permission and a blessing. The want of food from which they suffered was such that they were obliged to boil the leather straps of their helmets and of the other parts of their armor that they might have something to keep them alive, or to delay death a little. When they had exhausted this supply they ate roots and the bark of wild trees. On this journey our Lady of the Rosary showed her favor to father Fray Domingo by assisting him in a remarkable way on several occasions. Once she enabled him to save the life of a poor soldier who had been condemned to death, and once gave him grace to change the heart of a man who intended to commit suicide. Although he desired to give himself to work among the Indians, he was obliged by the orders of his superiors and by his vow of obedience to assume several honorable posts in the province of Mexico, becoming prior and vicar-provincial, and finally the chief consultor of the Holy Office; but he gave up these positions as soon as he could to devote himself to the work which he preferred among the natives. He spent thirty-eight years in laboring for those poor people, teaching them, and protecting them against wrong. He was at one time sent to España by his superiors on matters of important business connected with the missions to the Indians. Here he met many difficulties, as vested interests and great wealth were arrayed against him; and on one occasion the nuncio of his Holiness, to whom he had complained, commanded him not to visit the palace. But, though he did not attain the end for which he set out, he made a great impression upon his Majesty, who appointed him first bishop of the Philippinas.] His Majesty felt a particular affection for these islands, because their conversion had begun in his time and as a result of his initiative. As they had received their name from his, he desired also to give them a bishop with his own hand. He chose a man whose learning, virtue, and deep zeal for the good and the protection of the Indians qualified him to be the father and first shepherd of regions so new and so remote from the presence of their king. In such regions it is very easy for the wrongs which the powerful do to the weak to be more and greater than in others; hence they needed a valiant defender, and a strong pastor and master to contend with the great difficulties which are always met with in new conquests. At first father Fray Domingo did not venture to accept the bishopric, and consulted learned and able religious. They all advised him to accept it, as being a very heavy charge, but one in which he could do great service to God and be of great advantage to the Indians. They suggested that, if he were the bishop of the Indians, he could help them better in the great sufferings which it might be expected that they would have to endure, as all newly-conquered people have endured them. These sufferings he saw and deplored when he went to his bishopric; and he strove to remedy them as completely as he could. He accepted the dignity for the labor and the banishment which it offered him, knowing well that there was no honor and profit to be expected from it. At this time he strove to bring with him religious of his own order, feeling that they would be more closely allied to him and under greater obligations to him; and that thus they would help him to carry his burden. His Majesty granted them to him, and they reached Mexico;[5] but here there were so many who died or fell ill that he had left but one companion, father Fray Christobal de Salvatierra—who was a wonderfully helpful associate, and aided him greatly in the government of his bishopric, as well as in everything else which had to be done; and these additional duties were neither few nor pleasant. He went to the city of Manila and built in it his cathedral church, assigning prebends and arranging everything necessary for the service of the cathedral—although poorly, because he had no ecclesiastical income, and because the royal income in these islands was very small. He found his bishopric like sheep without a shepherd, and strove to gather them together and bring them to order; but, as they had learned to live without control, they took his efforts very ill. Some of them broke bounds entirely, one of them going so far that he dared to tell the bishop to his face that he would better moderate his enthusiasm; for that if he did not, the speaker could hit a mitre at fifty paces with his arquebus. But the good bishop in these and similar cases followed the commands of St. Paul to his disciple St. Timothy: *Argue, obsecra, increpa, in omni patientia et doctrina.*[6] The good prelate put his shoulder and his breast to the wheel against all these difficulties, and with all his heart strove to reform the morals of the colony. By his example he animated the preachers and confessors to tell the truth with greater clearness and courage than before; and, that this might be the better and more effectively done, he called a conference, or quasi-synod, composed of the superiors from all the religious orders and of the learned men who were in the land, both theologians and jurists. This conference sat for a long time. In it there were also six captains who had had experience in that country, and in the conquests which had been made there. These officers were added to the conference that they might give information with regard to many matters of fact upon which the determination of justice and conscience in the case depended; and that the truth and righteousness of the proceedings of the conference might be more apparent. It was hoped that in this way the decisions of the conference would be better received. In this assembly the holy bishop showed his great capacity, his great knowledge and the clearness of his mind; and skilfully directed and disposed of a great variety of matters which were there very effectively decided. Many questions were there propounded and settled; and from the decrees of the conference there resulted a sort of general list or set of rules by which the confessors were to govern themselves in assigning penance to all sorts of people in that country. These rules affected the governor, the auditors, the royal officials, the alcaldes, the corregidors, those who had taken part in the conquest, the encomenderos, the collectors of tributes, and people of all ranks—in a word, all the inhabitants of the country. It had validity for what had been done as well as for what was to come. This was a very helpful matter, because it dealt with affairs which offered no precedents, did not regularly happen, and could not be understood by everyone because of their great difficulty. On this account those who understood them best, and desired to deal with them as truth and reason required, were not respected by those who were most concerned. The latter, in order that they might avoid their obligations, ordinarily tried to find confessors who would show leniency, to their own harm and to that of their penitents. But as soon as these decrees appeared, having been voted by so many learned and holy men, they were such that neither confessors nor penitents dared oppose them. This conference was accordingly a very important one; and in a few days it was possible to see the new light which had come to these islands and to perceive how thoughtful and careful, and how full of knowledge, was the new shepherd and spouse of this church. The holy bishop afforded much edification with his teaching, his addresses, and his sermons, for he was a learned theologian and an excellent preacher; but he did very much more by the example of his admirable life. The sermons which he preached in this way had great power over the souls of those who looked upon this noble example, and even hardened hearts could not resist them. He did not alter his habit, his bed, or his diet. His habit was of serge, as was customary in Nueva España. He wore a woolen shirt, and slept upon a bed which was even poorer than that of the poorest religious. His food was eggs and fish; his dwelling had no paintings or adornments in it. He rose at midnight to recite matins, and after this he offered his mental prayer. That he might not trouble anyone to give him a light, he always kept a tinder and flint, and struck and kindled his own light without having any servant to attend upon him when he went to bed or when he rose. He was especially devoted to our Lady of the Rosary, whose grace and favor he had many times experienced; and he desired to see this same devotion well established in all. When he spoke upon this matter, he seemed to surpass himself; and some believed that our Lady spoke in him, because of the grandeur of the heavenly ideas which he uttered on this subject. When our religious reached this country, he entertained them in his dwelling, as has been said; and he kept and cherished them there for many days, gave them extraordinary alms, and bought a site for their convent. He helped very much in the building of the convent, without ever feeling poor for this or for similar objects—though he was really in extreme poverty on account of the smallness of the salary which he received, without having any other source of income. Although the salary was small, it never failed him when the poor required it, to whom belonged everything that he acquired. Thus he was always consuming his income, without ever lacking something to give.

Chapter XLII

A more detailed account of the virtues of the servant of God, Don Fray Domingo de Salaçar

The conformity of the good bishop with the divine will, and his desire to be approved before the pure eyes of that heavenly Lord with whom he always desired most intimately to unite himself, and the knowledge that he could not attain this approval without striving with all his heart to imitate His virtues, and by means of them to acquire something of His likeness, made the bishop endeavor constantly with great solicitude to attain these virtues—although to attain them it was necessary for him to strive manfully to conquer his own nature; in so far as it was opposed to them; and to multiply, in order to attain this victory over himself, penances and austerities, to the end that his nature might surrender and be subjected. The virtue of patience, which is in all circumstances very desirable, and no less difficult to acquire and maintain, was that which the bishop most needed, for at every step occasions offered themselves for the exercise of this virtue. Since he was by nature wrathful and hot-tempered, and was always engaged in defending the right, it cost him much to control himself and to be patient. However, he had so restrained himself and so become lord of his nature, that he did not permit it to display itself. This was not only in cases where he had time for consideration and for preparation, but in those sudden and unexpected accidents in which those who are wronged are accustomed to lose control of themselves, if the virtue of patience is not well rooted within their souls or has not reached perfection. He was often obliged to hear many insulting words from soldiers who were angry because he had interfered with their excesses; but he kept silent, and walked on as if he had not heard them, attending to his business without taking any account of things which did not belong to it. Since the Indians suffered from the abuses which were inflicted upon them, he went in one day to speak on their behalf to the governor who was then in office. He was not permitted to proceed with his business without hearing many insulting words from the governor, who even put his hands upon his breast and gave him a push. The bishop did not change countenance; and, following the counsel of St. Paul, who bids us give place to wrath, he left the hall that he might not more inflame the wrath of this man. After a while, when he thought it was time, he went in again, and with great serenity of countenance and with gentleness of heart and words, he said to him: "Bend your knees, because my heart does not permit me to leave you under so heavy a condemnation;" and he added: "By virtue of a brief of the Supreme Pontiff which I have for this purpose, I absolve you from the most dreadful excommunication which you have incurred." When he had done this, he went out again; and even commanded the cleric who accompanied him not to reveal to anyone what had happened, under penalty of excommunication. On another occasion another ecclesiastic whom he rebuked said to him, very angrily: "How badly you treat me, though you know that I am better than you are." The bishop answered, with great calmness, that he was delighted to have in his bishopric so honorable a person. With this gentleness he suffered the blows of those who exercised his patience, leaving his cause to God, as God commands us. The Lord assumed the care of his cause, and rigorously chastised those who spoke evil of him. Some people wrote letters against him to España; and, before the answer came back, they were called upon to give their answer before the tribunal of God, ending their lives in sudden and dreadful death. He took great pains to preserve his chastity and the purity with which he was born, esteeming it highly like a precious jewel, and performing many penances to defend it from the assaults of the enemies who hated its beauty and ever strove to destroy it. Two priests have borne witness that he was a virgin: father Fray Diego de Soria, late bishop of Nueva Segovia, to whom he made a general confession in his old age, at the time when he was about to embark on the last voyage which he made to España. The other priest was a clergyman to whom he had confessed more than two hundred times, and who was well acquainted with the state of his conscience. This priest confirmed his testimony with an oath. In spite of this, the world is such that the chaste bishop found it necessary to defend himself against accusations in regard to this matter, and to bear testimony to the purity of his own conscience. At a public celebration of the holy sacrifice of the mass, with the divine sacrament in his hands, he affirmed, because necessity required it, that he hoped this celestial food might be his eternal damnation if he was conscious of any fault of such a kind. If those who spoke against him in this matter had been only laymen, angry because they had been corrected and forcibly drawn from such vices, and mad with passion—for such persons will not forgive those who are most holy—if this accusation had proceeded from such as these, it would have been matter for sorrow, but would not have been intolerable; but there were even some ecclesiastics who saw that the bishop took great pains to seclude abandoned women, and who ventured to make themselves defenders of these persons of disorderly life. They declared that a man who gathered in so many of these women of evil life (some of them handsome), shut them up, and heard them at their trials, would be sure to put out his hand and select those who pleased him. This reached the ears of the bishop; and the vengeance which he took was to commend them to the Lord in prayer with all his heart—pitying them as being persons who were really worthy of compassion; since, without comparison, the harm that one who speaks evil does to himself is greater than the harm done to him who is wronged. The Lord heard these pious prayers, and touched their hearts. They acknowledged the evil that they had spoken, and very repentantly came to beg his pardon, at the episcopal residence, in the presence of those who lived there. The bishop received them with open arms and with abundance of tears, and had them that day as companions at his table. The vengeance which the saints desire to take upon their enemies is, to have them repent for their faults when they become conscious of their errors.

He was very compassionate, and felt the utmost pity for the sufferings of his neighbor. Of this a marked example was given on the voyage from Nueva España to Manila. There were in the same ship more than twenty Augustinian religious, and, while they were at sea, their water gave out. This is one of the greatest hardships which may be suffered on a voyage. The bishop took pity upon them; and, although he had not enough to supply the necessity of so many, he preferred suffering with the others to seeing them suffer while he was comfortable. Accordingly he offered them the opportunity to drink from what he carried in his *martabana*, which is a large jar holding twenty cantaros[7] of water. Their need would not permit them to refuse what was thus offered them voluntarily; and, though they all drank of it, the Lord was pleased that it should last until they landed on the islands, as the servant of God had prayed. It is no new or rare thing for the Lord to multiply food and drink, that it may not be lacking to those who bring themselves to need out of pity. This same virtue caused the bishop to watch over this municipality of Manila, by taking care that in the houses of the fathers of the Society [of Jesus] there should be religious to give instruction in profitable learning to those who desired to study it. That this might be made permanent, and that there might not be any failure in it, he brought it about that his Majesty gave command that the religious should receive an allowance to be spent upon the teachers. The answer of his Majesty is contained in the royal decree given at Barcelona the eighth [*sic*] of fifteen eighty-three. The document runs as follows: "To the reverend father in Christ, Fray Domingo de Salacar, bishop of the Philippinas Islands. Three letters from you have been received from my Council, etc. Considering the good report which you give of the great results which have followed and which are likely to follow from the maintenance of the Order of the Society of Jesus, and considering that to this end it is necessary that the Society should receive from me what is needed for the support of the religious who desire to teach and instruct in Latinity, sciences and good morals, those who come to them, I have, until some one shall come forward to undertake this business, granted the decree enclosed. In pursuance of this decree, the president of the Audiencia and you will together determine how this object may be carried out," etc. From this same spirit of compassion arose the benevolence which he displayed toward all the natives by building a hospital in Manila in which sick Indians might be cared for. He gave so much energy to this that he not only was the chief person who concerned himself with it, but he gave the first and the chief contribution to establish and endow it. At the very beginning of the hospital he did something worthy of his virtue and prudence. The sick in this hospital were cared for by religious of the order of the seraphic father St. Francis, and particularly by a brother named Fray Juan Clemente. The infirmity for which they were ordinarily treated was buboes, which are very frequent on these poor Indians because they ordinarily have to walk in the water in their grain-fields.[8] The brother had much to suffer with the Indian men, and still more with the Indian women, the care of whom was in general not very consonant with decency. On this account, the religious determined to give up this duty, and actually asked the bishop for permission to leave the hospital. The bishop, who was well acquainted with the conscience of Fray Juan, and who saw the reason for his unhappiness, encouraged and consoled him; and exhorted him not to give up, on account of these temptations, the good work and the service which he had begun there. He gave the brother holy and devout reasons for this, and finally said: "My son Fray Juan, fast for three days in the week; give yourself a discipline, and keep your hour of prayer. As for the rest, I will charge myself with it, and will take the responsibility upon myself." The result was marvelous, for, because of the good advice which had been given him and the prayer which the bishop made for him, Fray Juan found himself so much consoled and changed that he no longer felt the least difficulty or disquiet in the world; and, as if he had cast all these difficulties upon another person, he no longer perceived them in himself. Yet before this he had found himself so much oppressed by them that, in order not to fall, he had desired to flee. In a case of this kind, to take flight is to conquer—but not so nobly as when the Lord puts forth His hand that His servants may handle such serpents as these without being harmed by them, which happened in this case as the result of the prayer of His servant the bishop.

The many virtues which this servant of God possessed were higher in degree as a result of the fire of charity which dwelt in his breast, which, as a queen of all the rest, held the highest place in his soul and governed all. He could not eat or drink in comfort without dividing with the poor; and therefore every day he set aside a part of his food, and, placing it on the corner of the table, said: "You know for whom this is"—namely, the poor, as his servants understood. This was given to them, and not only this, but other alms. That the matter might be the better attended to, they kept, by order of the bishop, a memorandum of the poor and needy of the city. He directed his servants that whenever the poor women who asked alms were Spaniards, they should indicate the fact by saying, "Here is a lady that asks alms;" if they were Indians or mestizas, they should say, "Here is a woman." In this way, without seeing them, he would be able to tell their station, and to aid them conformably thereto. Still, when he was told about some such matter, he often went down with the servant; and, if it was the first time that she came, he used to say to her: "Come, good friend, what is the matter now? Beware not to offend God, nor to be tricked by the devil into doing any base act for need or for selfish interest. Trust in God, who will aid you; and I for my part will assist with all my heart." In order that she might see that these were not merely good words, he used to give her some assistance and to write her name with the rest, so that he might aid her with the care required by her need, and by that of her children, if she had any. Every week he visited the prisons and the hospitals, generally assigning Fridays for that purpose. He encouraged and consoled the prisoners and the sick with kindly words and with alms, according to the need of each one. The money which he could get together from restitutions and confirmations he kept with the greatest care, that not a real might be lost; and, as if he were the most miserly man in the world, he took care of it for the poor alone, without permitting the members of his household or anyone else to take anything from the confirmations, as is customary. He used to say that this belonged to the poor, and that it was not proper that one who was not poor should share with them. From some of these alms, and from what he could add from his own poor income, he bought some lots near the Franciscan convent, and some cattle, with which he established a stock-farm, and gave it for the establishment of a hospital for the care of the natives. The hospital was built and still exists, having been very greatly increased by the care of the Franciscan fathers, who attend to it with the greatest charity. To exalt the hospital still more, the bishop obtained for it a liberal concession of plenary indulgence for the Sunday of Lazarus,[9] as he did for the hospital of the Spaniards on Palm Sunday. So great was his charity and his desire to do good to the poor that once, when he was without money to give them, he sold his pectoral cross, which was worth one thousand eight hundred pesos, and gave it to them in alms. In the same way went his table silver; and his silver pontifical ornaments were almost always in pawn. His steward used to try to excuse himself when he was told to give alms, saying that he had not the means. The bishop, calling him to one side, would say to him, "Tell me the truth; how much money have you?" He commonly said that there was not in the house more than eight reals for the daily expense, and sometimes only four. The bishop then made him give half of what he had, saying that it was sufficient good-fortune to have some money in the house all the time, so long as the Lord would provide more; and the Lord to whom he gave took care that he should never lack, sending him what he needed for himself and for his poor from some source from which he had never expected it. When he got it, he would show it to the steward, or give it to him, and say: "Trust in God, father, and know that even if you had given me all that you had, the Lord would have sent us more." It was a common saying among the people of his household that the Father of the poor provided money miraculously, in order that the bishop might give them alms. A person of rank was once obliged by necessity to ask alms from him. The bishop was much grieved, as this person seemed to be an honorable one; and he directed the steward to give him all the money there was in the house. As he found no more than eight reals, the bishop gave this to him, and asked the man to pardon him, saying that there was no more at that time, but that, as soon as he had any, he would be sure to come to his aid. The Lord did not delay assisting him who had not only given alms from his superfluity, but had given all that he had for the maintenance of himself and his household. For on that very night He touched the heart of a man who had laid upon him for ten years the duty of the restitution of four hundred pesos, and caused him, without waiting till morning, to embark at night and to come from Cavite to Manila; and in the morning he gave the money to the bishop without the bishop's ever having spoken to him. The bishop had desired that his penniless condition should be cared for wholly by the Lord, who was called upon to relieve the urgent need of him who was in such need as a result of aiding the poor. When the bishop saw himself suddenly enriched with four hundred pesos, he gave thanks to the Lord, from whose hand he had received them rather than from the hand of him who had brought them hither. He instantly summoned the person to whom he had given only one peso the day before, because he had no more, and said to him: "For the little which I have given you and the much which you desired, the Lord has sent me some money. Take these fifty pesos and give me that one which I gave you yesterday; for it is that which attracted all this. Be sure that you spend well that which I give you; and, when you shall see yourself in prosperity, take care to be liberal to the poor." The good man promised this; and in a short time God, in fulfilment of what the bishop had said to him, gave him so much money that he brought four hundred pesos, and gave them to the bishop to be distributed among the poor. The rest of what the bishop had received he did not spend on his household, though it was so poor; but published in the church that he had some money to distribute, and summoned the poor to his residence. Among them he distributed it (as he wished to) very quickly; and, showing them the eight-real piece which he had given in the first place, he said to them with much happiness and joy: "Just this peso is for me, because it is that which attracted so many." When the bishop was at his meal, having with him at the table the first founders of this province, who had recently come to the city, a man came to beg alms. The bishop gave him a peso; and, as it seemed to the beggar too little, he showed it to the bishop, and said that he had not given him as much as he needed. This conduct appeared to those who were present bold, and even insolent; so they told the bishop that he ought to send the man away, because he had received sufficient alms, and that it was impossible at one time to succor every necessity. The bishop agreed; but before long his heart was moved to compassion at the thought that the poor man had gone away dissatisfied; and, with his eyes moist with tears, he said: "Call that poor fellow back again. His need must be very great, because it has forced him to be importunate." The beggar came back; and the bishop, augmenting the alms so that the beggar should be contented, was contented himself, and sent him away with his blessing. Once it happened that he went to bed with fifteen pesos, which, though for persons of his dignity it was a mere nothing, for him who gave everything to the poor it was great riches; and in the morning before nine o'clock he had not a penny, because the poor had taken it all. He used to say: "The riches of bishops are in caring for the poor, who are their proper purses; and, so long as my money is not in them, they will suppose that I have appropriated it." This did not appear only in his words, but he was so certain of the truth of it that he carried it out in practice; and it often resulted that he did not have money for the ordinary expenses of his household. He was obliged to set sail from Manila to España on important business; and one of the chief supplies which he ordered to be laid in was a provision of chickens and of conserves—things which he never tasted, and which were so foreign to his way of living that he ate nothing but fish, as if he had been in the refectory of an extremely austere convent. They got together three hundred chickens for him; but before he had left port two hundred of them were gone; while with the conserves and other things that he took he was all the time feasting and making presents to the poor and needy, so that nobody could even induce him to taste a chicken. [On the road from Mexico to San Juan de Ulua, though very ill, he charitably undertook the ordination of some candidates for the priesthood, who had been caught in a flood on their way to be ordained at Jalapa.]

Chapter XLIII

The marvels wrought by our Lord for His servants while in this life, and the happy death of the bishop.

[It is not strange that the Lord should have honored the virtues of the bishop by working many marvels through him. Many of these have fallen into oblivion because he strove to keep them concealed, and also because there has been no one to keep a record of them. Several times his prayers have saved men in imminent danger of death; among these was father Fray Miguel de Venavides, who fell overboard on the voyage from Manila to Nueva España.]

When he reached España it is said that his Majesty at first was vexed on account of his return, because his bishopric would need him during his absence. But afterward, when he saw him, his Majesty was greatly pleased with him, and carried out the wishes of the bishop in regard to the principal matters which had brought him there. The income of the church was greatly augmented, his Majesty bestowing upon him a large gift, and greatly increasing the small income assigned for the prebendaries. He succeeded in augmenting the number of prebends so that the church might be better served. A single bishop was not sufficient to attend to the confirmations and other episcopal acts in all the islands, still less to watch over the conversion of so many provinces as are contained in them, practically all of them being at that time heathen. Hence the bishop succeeded in having his bishopric divided among four prelates—an archbishop and three suffragan bishops—and he marked out the limits of each bishopric. He succeeded in gaining in Roma what he desired, and was himself appointed archbishop. This promotion did not suffice to alter the ordinary mode of life of this servant of God, and made no more change in him than if he had never been promoted. It is even said that he did not care to be informed or assured with regard to it; that as his soul had other purposes and more elevated desires, he cared little for these things. He was right in doing so, since he was soon to see how little substance there is in them; for he was attacked by a severe infirmity which, before the bulls for his archbishopric were despatched from Roma, despatched him to heaven, ending his labors and commencing his eternal rest. He had no need to make a will, for he distributed all that he could get among the poor. In the hour of his death, he had no more than six reals; and though he had a poor sister, he never gave her a real, because of his helping those who were in greater need. This came to the knowledge of his Majesty, and it pleased him so much that he displayed his royal generosity toward her, as indeed our Lord does command, who takes upon His own shoulders the obligations which His disciples fail to fulfil because of their love for Him. [These facts attracted great attention in the court, and the small estate of the bishop of the Indias became famous. He was buried in his convent of San Thomas at Madrid. The day before, the archbishop of Toledo had died, Don Gaspar de Quiroga; he was cardinal, and the richest prelate in Christendom. As he was to be buried on that same day, the counselors of the king did not know which funeral to attend; and his Majesty directed that they should go to that of the poorest. His epitaph states that he died December 4, 1594.]

Chapter XLIV

Father Fray Christobal de Salvatierra, associate of the first bishop of the Philippinas and governor of his bishopric.

There was but a short space of time between the death of the first bishop of this region of which we have just spoken, and that of his associate and vicar-general, father Fray Christobal de Salvatierra. The bishop, when he went to España, had selected him as governor of his bishopric—having by many years' acquaintance come to know that he was worthy, not only of this charge, but of much greater ones, because of his great and well-established virtue, his marked ability, singular prudence, watchful zeal for the honor of God, indomitable spirit, and the other noble qualities which he had found in father Fray Christobal. All these were necessary for the duties of vicar-general and governor of this bishopric at such times as these, which were so near to the first conquest of these islands. Even though the conquest had continued for some time, the very great difficulties encountered in their spiritual government will be evident. It will be even better understood by any one who has any knowledge of the conquests of the Indias; for though it did not involve so many cruelties as others, it was still impossible to avoid many evil deeds which wars always bring with them, however well justified they may be. This is still more the case against poor Indians, who cannot defend themselves, and sometimes who cannot even complain of the wrongs that have been done to them, since these are committed by those from whom their redress should proceed. Since there had not been in the islands, before the coming of the first bishop and his vicar-general, any bishop to govern them as their own prelate, the two ecclesiastics found them abounding in vices which by inveterate custom had put out such roots and obtained such strength that it was not possible to destroy them without great difficulty and labor, much vigilance, and a courageous spirit, in order to meet the thousand peril which these duties brought with them at this time. God, who never fails the government of His church, provided for these offices persons with such endowments as were possessed by father Fray Christobal. He was a son of the distinguished convent of San Esteban at Salamanca; and showed that he was so, not only by words, which often perish on the wind, but by works—and by noble works, which he had learned in that so prominent school of virtue and letters. He left his convent, intending to become one of the pioneers assembled by the bishop for this province. The number of these, as has been stated, was thirty. When they reached Nueva España, many died and others fell sick. The rest of them, daunted by the voyage which they had already taken, and attracted by the agreeable climate of Mexico, remained there. The good bishop was unable to persuade any of them to come to these regions except father Fray Christobal, who, like an immovable column, was always firm in his opposition to these temptations, never abandoned the company of the bishop, and remained constantly at his side—not only in this tempest, in which all the others fell away, but in all the other and greater tempests which afterwards fell upon them. He was greatly aided in this by the conformity that there was in the natures of the two men. They were both grave and prudent, intrepid of soul in the performance of the right, and fearful of everything that not only might be evil, but might even seem so. Above all, they were of one mind in their efforts to attain virtue—devout, chaste, charitable, religious; zealous for the honor of God, in themselves and in others; and ready for this cause to undergo hardships or dangers of any kind. Hence, though the dangers through which they had gone had conquered all the others and discouraged them, father Fray Christobal was always firm and faithful to his promise; and he accomplished it by persevering with constancy in that which he had begun, even until death. This he did to his own great good and to that of his neighbors, serving the Lord not only as one good religious, but as if he had been many. He was like another Aod [*i.e.*, Ehud], working with both hands, and having spirit, courage, and industry for every undertaking of importance that offered itself. He carried on together the offices of vicar-general and of missionary to Bataan, at a day's journey from Manila, where he was obliged to reside. Withal, he filled the functions of these two positions, which seemed incompatible, with such perfection and vigilance, that he has left for each one of them eternal fame behind him. As if this was but little in itself, whenever any military expedition was undertaken he accompanied the soldiers, in the capacity of chaplain, as if he had been the most unoccupied person in the province. He gave his greatest energies to the office of vicar-general, which he filled with the greatest justice and watchfulness, and in which he offered a very edifying example. He was greatly loved by the good and feared by the bad; for his only purposes were to do good to all, to adjust their disputes, and to make friendships, or to unmake them when they were bad. He defended and protected the Indians, as being a race in the greatest need of defense and protection. When it was necessary, he chastised them, but like a loving father. Hence he was much loved by them, and was feared both by them and the Spaniards—even by the Spaniards in official positions, because, when there was a question as to making restitution for the honor of God, he pardoned no one. The zeal which he displayed in rooting out vices and scandalous sins was extraordinary. He never hesitated at any labor in this cause, however great it might be; he never feared any danger which appeared in the prosecution of his holy purpose, not even the danger of death. He was at one time threatened with death itself; for a desperate man entered his very room with the purpose of taking his life, at a time when he was careless and not expecting any such evil intention. But the Lord, to whom he left his defense, protected him; and the malevolent man was unable to carry out his purpose and to conquer the constancy of Fray Christobal. The latter knew that whatsoever hardship or death befell him in this way would surely be for his own greater glory; and hence, certain that no evil could happen to him that was really an evil, he did his duty with courage in opposing all the wicked, fearing no one, but feared by all. This was the case not only when he was present in the city or village where people were living scandalously, but even when he was at a distance from them; because without any warning he would appear, like a ray of light, in any place where he was needed. He would be at night in the city, and in the morning ten or twelve leguas away, following the track of those who were living in concubinage. When they seemed to themselves to be most safe, he caught them *in flagranti delicto*. He used to take out wicked women from any house, no matter how prominent it was, and no matter to what insults he might be exposed. Nothing of this kind daunted him, or held him back, or harmed him; nay, it did him much good, for, armed with patience for any wrong to himself, he was able to overcome any opposition to his holy zeal, and came out always victorious and with the upper hand. He knew the women of evil life so well that they were not able to escape him, or to conceal themselves from him. The punishment which he gave them was very appropriate, because he shut them up in a secure place and forced them to work to earn their living; and this, on account of their licentiousness and idleness, was the worst punishment that could be inflicted upon them, while for the holy purposes of Fray Christoval, it was the most efficacious remedy which could be applied. By being shut up they were kept from the sins which were caused by their being at large; while by their bodily labor they paid for something of what they wasted in their idleness. Hence in the time of this father this wretched class of people fled to the mountains, without daring to appear in the city. The Spaniards feared and hesitated to do many things which after his days began to be very common. All of these actions of the father were accompanied by such prudence, purity of life and manners, and by such love and such good works for the people, that although at the time those who were blinded and carried away by their passions suffered greatly, and were very angry with the man who interfered with their vices, still afterwards, when their minds became calmed, they could not fail to recognize the goodness of father Fray Christobal. He even gained the hearts of these people, and forced them to love and esteem them. Wherever he went, he received information from the most honorable people of what needed a remedy; and being sure that they were persons who would not deceive him, he immediately applied the remedy, with the least possible cost to the delinquents. He knew them all very well, and knew how to treat them. Hence with some he used no more rigorous means than looking at them, and letting them know that he was acquainted with their faults; and this was enough to bring about their improvement, which was what he purposed and desired. But when more severe measures were requisite, he was not slow or hesitating in employing them. Accordingly he was very useful to God in his office by attacking many sins and scandals, and by preventing others (which is an act of higher prudence). For the juridical acts which he performed as an ecclesiastical judge he accepted no fees, and he moderated as much as possible the fees of the officials of his jurisdiction. Since he understood the language of the Indians, he had no need of an interpreter, a matter of great importance and the means of avoiding much injury, deceit, and expense in the suits of the Indians. Since their means are very small, it is very easy to distort justice by bribing them, unless the activity of the judges prevents this evil. Even when this does not happen, the expenses of suitors are always very large. The vicar-general was desirous of avoiding these expenses, and therefore employed no interpreter, as in everything he took care that all might plead and gain their rights at small expense. This is an evidence that the great fear which he caused was not due to the fact that he was quarrelsome or litigious, but because he was zealous for the honor of God and the good of the souls that were in his care. So long as the bishop was in the islands, he had some comfort and defense; but as soon as the bishop had gone to España the father, being the sole governor of the bishopric (which at that time included all the islands), could not fail to suffer from the great increase of his labors, and greatly feel the want of the bishop's support. The thing to which he gave the greatest amount of attention and in which he found the greatest difficulty, was the prohibition to the Chinese heathen of the comedies that they performed, and to Spanish men and women attendance on those comedies, on account of the manner in which they were performed, which was full of superstition and idolatry. Up to the time when our religious had come, there was no one who understood their language and customs, so no one paid any attention to this point. The Chinese felt sure that no one but themselves could understand their comedies, and performed them as in China, full of superstitions and idolatries. This was found out by Father Juan Cobo when he had learned their language, letters, and customs. He gave notice thereof to the vicar-general, who ordered the comedies to cease, as being superstitious. The

Chinese were greatly grieved, and so were the Spaniards—the latter because, although they did not understand the comedies, they enjoyed seeing them for the sake of the actions and representations which the Chinese make in a very realistic way; and the Chinese, because they are devoted to this kind of entertainment. So every one, including the governor, was opposed to the vicar-general. He, because he did not understand the evil in the thing, took the side of the Chinese; but the vicar-general was certain that these comedies were an offense to the Lord, as well for the reason stated as because they were performed by night, and many other evil results used to follow. They were attended at night by Spanish men and Spanish women and their female servants, and by other Indian women—who, covered by the dark cloak of night, did many things which ought not to be done in Christian lands. But the vicar-general put his shoulder to the difficulty, and commanded that no one, on pain of excommunication, should go to see the comedies. Since the governor was of the opposite opinion, there was no one who dared to publish the excommunications; so the vicar-general himself went and fastened them on the church-doors, accompanied only by his friars, since there was no one else who ventured to accompany him. At last, although it cost him much and much evil was said against him, he brought this evil practice to an end. Since that time Spanish men, and many more Spanish women, do not go to see these comedies; and no permission is given for their performance until they are first looked over and approved by a religious who understands the language, and who sees that they are not superstitious but are historical, or have plots which are not idolatrous. This is what ought to be done in the realms of a Catholic prince, although the comedies are performed by heathens and idolaters; for as the latter are not permitted to perform their idolatries, they ought not to be permitted to play superstitious comedies made in honor of false gods, for such comedies are part of the idolatry, which is forbidden to them. It would be supposed that father Fray Christobal, being so busy and so usefully occupied, would have no time to attend to anything else except to his position as governor and vicar-general of this diocese. Yet this was not the case, but whenever the opportunity was offered—as was not often, there being then so few whom he could employ—he took advantage of it to leave his duties for the time. Hence when the first Spaniards went to the pacification or conquest of Nueva Segovia, he went as chaplain of the soldiers, and was with them in all the conflicts which they had with the Japanese, which conflicts have already been described. He was the first priest that entered that country—as it were, to take possession of it for the friars of his order, who afterward converted it to the law of God and to His gospel. In the same way, when another expedition was made to Maluco, he embarked as chaplain, purposing in both expeditions to do the greater service to his king and lord by restraining the soldiers, by his authority and by the respect which they had for him, from the disorders which the inconsiderate are likely to be guilty of under such circumstances as these. This same desire of being useful in all things caused him to take charge of the district of Bataan, which, although it contained many Christians, had no minister and no one to take pity upon them or to assume the charge of them. This aroused great compassion in him; and though these Indians were a day's journey by sea from Manila, where he was obliged to reside, he assumed the ministry to them and cared for them with great solicitude and love and with no less labor. [The situation of that district made the labor of the ministry very great. Father Fray Christobal went on foot through all the lakes and swamps, attending to the needs of all the Indians, for whom the four religious who succeeded him were scarcely able to do the work. He did all this labor in spite of a painful ailment from which he suffered. Among the things which afflicted him was the necessity of sleeping in his clothes for the little time when he could repose. This is no small discomfort in so hot a country. His love for the Indians was such that, although his labors caused him this painful infirmity, he devoted himself to them up to the time of the coming of the other missionaries; and even after they came he used to take his holidays by visiting these Indians as his beloved sons. He greatly assisted the first religious to learn who were and who were not Christians, for the absence or loss of records had brought everything into confusion. He was very charitable, especially to the Indians. To the Spaniards he was a father and a master, assisting them in all their necessities in peace and in war. He showed his zeal for the honor of God and for the rooting out of vice in the very last hours of his life, by writing to the governor, Don Luis Perez das Mariñas, the request that he would have a bad woman taken from a captain's house which he indicated; and that he would send three soldiers to arrest a cleric of whom the report was spread that he was leading an evil life. The asthma from which he had so long suffered finally brought his life to an end. He died in the hospital of the Sangleys, in the midst of the brethren of his order.] He was mourned by the whole country, and especially by the religious of all the orders who were in it. All declared that there would never again come to this region such a friar, such a governor of the diocese, such a father of the poor, such a zealot for the honor of God, a man of such gifts for everything. When he died, the need of him was exhibited by the public way in which those vices which, so long as he lived, dared not appear or lift up their heads, began to prevail in the country. He received a solemn interment, attended by the ecclesiastical chapter and by all the religious orders, to all of whom he had done many friendly acts, and by all of whom he was therefore heartily beloved. At this very day his fame is as much alive as if he had died but yesterday. He appointed to be governors of the diocese, by the authority which he had received therefor from the bishop (whose death was not yet known), father Fray Alonso Ximenez, provincial of this province, and father Fray Juan de San Pedro Martyr, or Maldonado. The ecclesiastical chapter resisted; and although the nominees plainly had right on their side, and the governor, Don Luis Perez das Mariñas, offered to put them in possession, they were unwilling to obtain the control of the bishopric by lawsuits. They renounced or did not accept the appointment, and left the government to the chapter, as something which should not be sought or even received except as the result of compulsion or sheer necessity, not for one's own advantage, but for the common weal—which very seldom is attained when the entry upon such offices is obtained by lawsuits.

Chapter XLV

Father Fray Juan de Castro, one of the first founders of this province

[When father Fray Juan de Chrisostomo went to Rome to get the documents necessary for founding the new province, he carefully looked in every one of the convents that he visited for men of the devotion, prudence, and holiness which he regarded as necessary for a firm establishment of the new province. In it the rule and the constitutions were to be punctually observed, and the religious were not to be contented with observing them as others do, for we all profess to observe them as they were written. He purposed to make this province one of such virtue that it should be not only holy in itself, but should have power by the aid of the Lord to fix holiness and virtue in the souls of persons so alienated from them as were these Indians, who had always been in the service of the devil. Among those upon whom father Fray Juan Chrisostomo turned his eyes was father Juan de Castro, of the convent of Sancta Cathalina in Barcelona. He was from the city of Burgos, and was the nephew of the other father, Fray Juan de Castro, the provincial of this province. God always shows His power in His saints; but to be superior among many saints, to shine with special glory among shining stars, is a much more marvelous effect of the divine grace. Such was father Fray Juan de Castro in this convent, which of itself has the name of being a very religious one; and father Fray Juan Chrisostomo selected him for the high end which he designed. Christ our Lord did not need to seek for holy men. His divine power was such that He could make apostles of great sinners, like St. Matthew or St. Paul; but Father Juan Chrisostomo, being a man, was obliged to choose, for the foundation of the province upon which he had begun, persons whose holiness was already formed. In order to obtain father Fray Juan de Castro, he caused the general of the order to assign him by name to the new enterprise. In this way the convent of Barcelona, much as they regretted losing Father Juan de Castro, were obliged to let him go to the Philippinas. His uncle, having been appointed to the leadership of this company, sent his nephew to the most laborious, but most meritorious part of the work—namely, to the province of Pangasinan. Father Fray Juan, to save the other fathers from hardship, carried water from the river, brought and split the wood, kindled and stirred the fire, and was, in a word, the servant of the rest; he anticipated all the others in these works and labors, so that the rest of the religious might not be wearied out, and that the Indians might not be annoyed, or feel ill-will toward the preachers of the gospel, by being forced, against their declared intention, to bring what was necessary for the services of the church and of the poor convent. He suffered the lack of food with special content and joy. He took great care of the neatness and cleanliness of the church and the altar. In spiritual things he distinguished himself as he did in these material labors; yet his uncle did not appoint him to any place as superior, but gave him that which he most delighted in, the position of the greatest labor and the lowest honor. When the heaviest part of the duty in Pangasinan was over, the Lord ordained that he should seek labor somewhere else. It was decided to send an embassy to China after the death of the governor, Gomez Perez das Mariñas. He had been killed by some Chinese traitors, who had afterwards made their escape with the galley, in which was the royal standard, much good artillery, and other things of value. The purpose of the embassy was to demand justice upon these traitors. On account of father Fray Juan Cobo's success in the embassy to Japan, it was decided to select religious of the same order for the present embassy. Father Fray Luis Gandullo was accordingly chosen, and named as his associate father Fray Juan de Castro. As secular ambassador went Don Fernando de Castro, cousin of the governor who sent the embassy, and nephew of the dead governor. A storm blew them out of their course toward the province of Chincheo, to which they had intended to go, and drove them to the province of Canton, one of the thirteen into which the Chinese realm is divided. As the Chinese there had had no dealings with the people of Manila, they did not receive the ambassadors with the respect due their office, or with the kindness which ought to be shown to men who had suffered so from the storms of the sea. They were arrested on the charge of piracy, but, by giving two hostages, they obtained somewhat better treatment. They were finally permitted to go to Macan, and afterward proceeded to Chincheo, but could not find a trace of the galley which they were looking for. The traitors had not gone back to their own country, but to a neighboring kingdom which was less civilized and had less justice. Some of them, not expecting to be recognized, afterward ventured to go to Malaca, and paid for their crime with death. At last the ambassadors returned, without having obtained any of the results which were desired from the embassy. The fathers, however, had at least carried the sweet savor of the Christian religion to those regions. On the return journey, they met with such a storm that the vessel was lost, and the people aboard her had to save themselves by swimming. Father Fray Juan de Castro was carried by a plank to the coast of Pangasinan, a day's journey from the coast of Bolinao, where the wreck occurred. The exposure brought on a severe illness. Father Fray Juan was taken to Manila and died in the hospital of the Chinese, passing away serenely and devoutly.]

Chapter XLVI

The journey made by the father provincial Fray Alonso Ximenez to Camboxa

[After father Fray Alonso Ximenez had completed his provincialate, he went to Camboxa to preach the gospel there. Circumstances seemed to make this absolutely necessary. In 1595 there came to the city of Manila as ambassadors from the king of Camboxa two soldiers—a Portuguese, named Diego Velloso; and a Castilian, a native of La Mancha, named Blas Ruiz de Fernan Goncales. The kingdom of Camboxa is on the mainland, like China and like Spain. The king asked the governor of Manila for soldiers to assist in the defense of his kingdom against the king of Siam, his neighbor; and also for Dominican friars, to preach the law of God in his kingdom. The people of Camboja have special knowledge of our order because of some religious, from the India of Portugal, who lived there a long time.[10] One of them, named Fray Silvestre, was so highly esteemed by the king that he had him about his person continually. The Portuguese, however, were unwilling to attempt the conversion of this region, because they thought, and quite properly, that they could not carry it on to advantage from India. The governor, in spite of the small force of soldiers which he had, and the religious order, although likewise they had but few laborers, decided to do what they could to fulfil the wishes of the king. The order accordingly appointed the father provincial, who was within a few months of the end of his term. The governor gave him the title of ambassador, associating with him in the embassy the commander of the forces, Captain Juan Xuarez Gallinato. Great difficulty was found in providing an ecclesiastical companion for the father provincial, as those who were at first suggested could not be spared from their duties. Finally I was appointed, accepting this duty in accordance with my vow of obedience. Three vessels were prepared for the expedition, one of them of Spanish build, the other two of the sort used in this country which are known as juncos. These are large boats, and carry a great deal of freight; but they are weakly built to meet the storms, and have very little rigging on their masts, and accordingly are easily lost in bad weather. A hundred and thirty soldiers were collected, most of them without permission of the governor, who had given his license for only forty. There were also some Japanese, who are too much given to rashness in war; and some Indians of this country, who on occasions of honor are very good auxiliaries. The leader of the expedition [*i.e.*, Gallinato] commanded the frigate; Diego Velloso, the smaller junk, in which

50

we religious went; and Blas Ruiz de Fernan Gonçalez, the larger, which contained most of the forces.[11] January 18, 1596, we set sail from the harbor of Manila, badly equipped and worse accommodated, as usually happens on such occasions. We went to the island of Luban,[12] fourteen leguas from the fort, to finish our preparations for the voyage, which, though it is but a short one (only two hundred leguas in length), is across a treacherous sea; for the best-fitted vessels often suffer severely upon it, much more so those which are poorly equipped, as were ours. The frigate and the smaller junk made port that night; but the larger junk was unable to enter, and was not to be seen in the morning. We assumed, as was true, that it had taken advantage of the favorable wind and proceeded with its journey. We were, however, anxious; because it was not well supplied with food or water, though it was better supplied than the other vessels. Two days afterward, we set sail; but on a calm sea, and with the wind fair, our mainmast snapped as if it had been made of candy. It was all rotten; and we were left like a cart on the water, with nothing but our foresail, and that very small. The flagship took us in tow and we towed a small boat with four Chinese sailors, which was the cause of no little trouble. We sailed in this way for eight days, the sea being calm. One night at the end of this time, the boat cable broke. The sailors that were in the boat called out for us to wait for them; and the flagship hove to, and began to sound while we were waiting for the boat. Finding bottom in forty brazas, they perceived that we were near the country of Camboja. In order to reach port early on the following day, they left us, thinking that in spite of the smallness of our sail we could reach there on the same day. The result, however, was not as was expected; for by bad navigation we had gone many leguas to leeward of the port. To make our way back there we had to sail against the wind. A storm arose soon after, and the flagship was obliged to run before the wind; it made port in Malaca, more than two hundred leguas to leeward of its destination, and was unable to return for three months. Our vessel could not make sail against the sea, being entirely unequipped, and good for nothing but to ask for the mercy of God. Under these circumstances fell the night between the eighth and ninth of February. We all supposed that this was the last of our days, and no man expected to see the next morning. The force of the wind drove us aground more than two leguas from shore; we had to cut away the stump of the mainmast, which was still standing, and to throw into the sea the rudder and everything there was in the ship. The boat, which might have saved us, was swamped; and the sailors who were in it got aboard the ship. The waves broke over the vessel, but could not sink it because it was already fast aground.] I sat all that night in the waist (for it was impossible to stand), confessing the Christians and catechizing the heathen. I baptized twenty-two of them, feeling that the great danger in which we were, authorized the act. When they had all received the sacraments, I encouraged them to the work which was necessary to keep us from perishing. Several times I went into the poop to confess myself, and to receive the confession of the holy old man, my provincial, who was there waiting for death—at the point of which we now were, with the rope, as they say, about our necks. We could do nothing but put up supplications and appeal from the justice to the mercy of God, by whom sentence of death seemed to have been issued upon us. It was, however, only a sentence of warning; and He accepted our prayer for the time, giving us hope that with His aid we might atone for our transgressions. The efficacy of God's mercy we almost felt with our hands on this occasion; for death appeared to be actually upon us, making execution upon the lives of those who were there. We were somewhat encouraged by the hope of reaching the land which was so near to us; but we did not know what it was, and what we were to expect from it. If we had known, we would have preferred to die in the sea; for our sufferings in this way would have been less than those which we underwent by reaching the land. We were like those of whom Jeremiah speaks in his *Lamentations*, for whom it would have been better to have the lot of those who died with the sword at one stroke than of those whose lives were brought to an end by hunger; for the latter died a prolonged and painful death, being destroyed by the barrenness of the land. The barrenness of this coast was such that it greatly exceeded that of which Jeremiah speaks. It was such that no one would go to it, even to escape death, unless, like us, he was not acquainted with it. Finally those waves which were on their way to burst upon the shore pushed on the ship, which was practically empty, and went along as if it had been a dry stick. This was a result of the coming in of the tide, and when the tide ebbed afterwards, we were left aground, a cannon-shot from the sea; and we saw in the mud (of which all this coast is composed) the track of the ship like a trench, for the force of the sea as it rose had pushed it along, breaking a road in the very ground. On this same day the tide came in again with such fury, because it was a spring-tide, that it carried the ship up to the trees and even buffeted it about there with such violence that we were obliged to disembark for fear of perishing in it. When we were on shore, exploring parties went off in various directions. After they had made an arduous march, they brought back the news that it was a wilderness inhabited only by wild beasts, without any trace of a river or a spring, at least near the coast; and that the country within proved to be inaccessible because it was overflowed and very thickly overgrown. This news made us feel that the sea was less evil for us than such a land, and that the tortures which we had endured were slight compared with those to which we were exposed by this desired but unhappy landing. Since eating and drinking are a necessary and a daily obligation, and as our supply of food and drink was very small, while we were more than a hundred persons, we put forth all our energies to search for some remedy. As thirst was that from which we suffered most, we dug wells in the dryest parts we found, and when we met water, it was more salty than that of the sea. I declare, as one who has found out by experience, that the very dew which appeared in the morning on the leaves of the wild trees there, was salt. Hence since the land denied us the sustenance which we required, we determined to return to the sea, which had at least granted us our lives, and which now gave us greater hopes than the land of being able to preserve them. For this it was necessary to help ourselves by means of the unlucky ship which was stranded on the shore, for it had remained there after the spring tide was over. It had no masts, or sails, or rudder, or anything that could be used, because between losing them and perishing there had been no choice. To supply these, it was necessary to put our hands to the work, until it was finished. The most necessary thing to be done to the ship was to cut it down and fit it so that it would draw but little water, and might be rowed along the coast. Our relief was to be sought on land, but he who should find it had to seek for it by sea. We were not now planning for conquests or embassies, but for getting water—for which we would have given all that has been yielded by the hill of Potosi, if it had been ours. We spent ten days in getting the ship ready. We cast overboard all the upper works and a good part of the under works. We fitted to it twelve oars. In this way it was like a badly made galliot; rudder, masts, and sails we replaced by rowing. While some of us were at this work, others went to explore the country, doing their utmost in the search for water. Some of these came back very joyful, with good news, saying that about four leguas up the coast from there a great river ran up into the land; that where it flowed into the sea the water was salt, but that it must be fresh above. They also said that they had seen the footprints of men on the shore. The work was hurried on in the hope of satisfying our thirst, which was increased by it, and still more by the heat of that region; for we were in the most torrid part of the torrid zone, and had practically no defense or covering against the heat. The vessel, being of so light a draught, was easily launched; and embarking in it all that we had left of provisions and clothes, which was very little, we put forth one evening and entered the bight of the river of which we have spoken, reaching its mouth in the morning by hard rowing. We entered it with great delight, which was increased by the sight of a hut on the bank not far from the ocean. Though there was no one in it, we promised ourselves large towns when we saw it, and even assured ourselves of certain news of our companions, of whom as yet we knew nothing, nor they of us. But within a few days we found out the deceit and lost our joy in it. After going for three days up the river, we constantly found the water salt like that of the sea, whose arm it was, and not a river. Upon its banks on either side there was nothing but impassable undergrowth. At last we reached a point from which we could not go further up, because the seeming river divided into so many little creeks that the ship had not room in any of them. The change from the false hope of water and of towns, which had possessed our minds, served to redouble our misery; since now, as it seemed to us, we had lost the hope of relief by land or by sea. Our necessity had now reached such an extreme that the food was distributed by ounces, and the drink almost by drops—though the labor of rowing, each man in his turn (from which no one was excused), was such as to require much food; and the heat was so excessive that even if we had been in idleness we should have needed much to drink. But at last, having confidence in the Father of mercies—who, though He distresses, does not overwhelm; and, though He chastises, does not slay—we returned to the sea by which we had come. At sight of it we left the vessel, in order to rest a little from the labor which we had endured to attain that for which we were hoping; and I went on land with my four Chinese (with whom I was very intimate), and had them build a little boat of four planks—fastened together by some twigs, so to speak, for we had no nails; and calked with clay, for we had no tow, or any other thing better than the clay. This made a sort of canoe. If awkwardly handled, it filled with water. But, such as it was, I had two of the soldiers get into it—for if they kept close to shore they would run no risk—and told them to go up to the hut that we had seen to discover whether there were any people there; because perhaps they had hidden themselves, from fear of our vessel, when they saw it on the way up the river. They did so, and at nightfall they discovered two grown Indians and a boy. They made their way up to them, little by little; and when they got near them they found that they were asleep on the shore, not expecting anything to happen to them. They caught the Indians, and bound them. When the rest of us came by soon after in our ship, they called out from the land, telling us what they had done. Our joy was so great that to render thanks the holy old man and I sang a *Te Deum laudamus*; and at this hour, which was midnight, half a cuartillo [*i.e.*, pint] of water was served out to the troops in token of joy. The soldiers came on board with their captives, treating them gently and showing them all sorts of kindness. It seemed to us that God had sent them to us as angels to guide us, as He sent St. Raphael to Tobias. We began to put questions to them by an interpreter, asking what country this was, what population it had; and where they had come from, and where they ate and drank. They answered that they were from Camboxa, and that the country along this coast, and inland for many leguas, was uninhabited; and that to go to the towns we should have to enter a large river and to sail up for eighty leguas. They said that large vessels went up the river, and that it was many leguas to windward of this place. They declared that they were natives of that country, slaves of one of its chief lords; and that, because of the ill treatment which they had received, they had fled from him, and had come hither where no man had ever landed. They said that they ate nothing except shell-fish, which they caught with their hands, and wild cocoanuts, that grew there; and that they had no other water except what fell from heaven. When it rained they caught what they could and kept it in some large reeds to drink afterward. They said that two years had passed since they had come there. The effect of such sad news upon the hearts of men who had suffered as we had may easily be imagined. They also told us that some days' journey further there was a port; but that, if we meant to go inland, where the king was, it would be necessary to leave the vessel at the port, because there was no river that entered inland. Since our desire was only not to die of thirst, any means by which we could get water seemed easy and light to us. We accordingly set out by sea in search of this port, taking these Indians with us, not with the purpose of increasing consumers when we had so little to consume, but to have guides. We went along the coast, running up to it very often wherever we thought we saw any signs of water, and sometimes digging wells, but always in vain, for the land could not give what it did not have. On the day of St. Matthew the Apostle, we discovered a high island in the sea, named Pulonubi.[13] It was about six leguas from land. We laid our course toward it in search of water, thinking that doubtless it would have some, being high and mountainous, and having a sandy shore; but as the equipment of the ship was fastened on with pins, as the saying is, our rudder broke, when we had gone out a legua to sea. Being buffeted by the slight sea which was running, we had to return to land, and even to run aground, in order to mend the rudder. The Lord seemed to have declared that He intended to bring death upon us, because the sustenance necessary for our life was entirely consumed; for since we had no water, we were not only without drink, but also without food, our provision being rice, which cannot be eaten unless it is boiled in water. For lack of water, some ate it parched, which dried their entrails. Others ate it imperfectly boiled in the steam of salt water, putting it in a little basket over a pot of this water on the fire, so that by the steam thus sent out it might be softened. The water was so salt that it made the rice like itself, and left it uneatable. There were some who, even after this fine example of cookery, drank sea-water, which increased the thirst they were so impatiently desiring to remedy. Others distilled it over the fire and got some fresh water, but very little, at the expense of much wood and with the necessity of keeping up fire day and night, which dried them more than the water that they got moistened them. All this taught us the great need in which we live, with our life on a thread, and the Lord many times threatening to cut it short. When we had mended the rudder as well as we could at the time, we went on up the coast, being disillusioned, so that we would not have thought of going out to sea even if the ocean had been as smooth as milk. Three days later, the twenty-seventh of February, which was Shrove Tuesday, we took our hands from the oars and placed ourselves in those of God, despairing of life. The remedy came to us as from God's own hand without our expecting it, when we were overcome by labor, and dying of hunger and thirst, and had given up ourselves to death. Thus it is most certain that the Lord comes to the aid of him who calls upon Him when all things created fail him—blessed be God's holy name. We had reached such an extremity that of that sorry ration of water which we had now had about a month, and which was less than half a cuartillo daily for each person, there was only enough for two days. We were not now thinking of making any effort to find any, but had our minds wholly turned to preparing ourselves for death, when the Lord of life ordained that the waves of the sea should drive us into a little inlet which the land formed there, where we went on shore with the intention of never leaving the place, but of ending in it our voyage and our lives. It happened that one of the Indians in the ship went to bathe in the water, to relieve the great heat from which he suffered, and somewhat to moderate the thirst which was destroying us. He swam to land, and there right on the shore (which was muddy, like all of that along which we had coasted), his feet sank in at the foot of a wild palm-tree. Feeling that they had gone into water, he drew them out, applied his lips to the hole which he had made, and found that the water was fresh. The thirst from which he suffered not permitting him to wait until it settled, he drank mud and water until he was satisfied. He shouted to us to tell us what he had discovered, but no one believed him. At last, the Indian persisting in his affirmation, all hurried to the water to look upon this marvel, which might be compared to that which God performed in drawing water from a rock that His people might drink in the desert; for no less miraculous appeared to us this fresh water in a marsh so near the ocean. We gave God a thousand thanks, and rejoicing in the feast, we forgot the labor and the fasting which we had undergone in the long vigil. We easily dug a well, for the whole soil was muddy, and on the next morning we filled all our casks with the water, which had now settled. We set sail to look for food, and even aspired to greater things. [In a few days we reached the port, where there was a garrison of Indians against their neighbors, the Siamese. All the news which we obtained about our comrades, and about the country to which we had come, was bad. The flagship had not been heard of, and the other ship was at Churdumuco, which is a large town eight leguas from the port and eighty from the sea.[14] We were told that the king who had sent for us from Manila, and whose name was Langara, was not in the country; but that his place in the kingdom had been taken by his chief vassal, because of the following circumstances. The king of Sian had made war against the king of Camboja, with eight hundred thousand men. This number should not astonish anyone, because the kings could make war almost at no expense, their vassals providing their own arms and food. The king of Camboja did not dare to wait for so great a multitude of enemies, and retreated up the river to another kingdom known as that of the Laos. The king of Siam made himself master of the country, and after burning it all returned to his own country, being harassed by hunger, which made more war upon him than did the king his enemy. The army being in disorder, one of the chiefs of Camboja, with those who had retreated to the mountains (about thirty thousand men), attacked his rearguard, thus obliging him to hasten his retreat. This chief, having conquered him who had conquered his king, took possession of the kingdom. The new king regarded those who had come at the request of the previous king as allies of his enemy, and therefore as his own enemies. This news alarmed us greatly, as we were without our comrades, our commander-in-chief, and our ships. However, being obliged to disembark, and to put ourselves into the hands of the rulers of the country, we made an honest man of the thief, as the proverb goes, and decided to send a soldier to him as an ambassador—offering to him our aid and service, on the ground that we had come to help the king of this country, and found no other king in it but him. The king received him kindly, saying that he only held the kingdom as a regent, and that he was ready to restore it to the lawful king when he should return. He sent an order to the mandarin of the coast where we were, to provide us with boats and carts. The soldier on his return met the Spaniards of the other ship, and learned from them that all that the king had said was false and that his purpose was to kill us at his ease. They advised us to join them in their ship, dissimulating in regard to our affairs, and keeping on our guard. The father provincial sent me ahead to confess those in the ship, because it was Lent, and they had sent to him to ask for a confessor. I was on foot and suffered much, although some things that I saw on the journey afforded me some alleviation of these hardships. I one day reached a village where there was a monastery of religious of their sort, of whom there are many in this kingdom. I went to it and talked to a venerable old man, who was as it were the superior of it. He was seated on a little platform about a palm's breadth in

57

height, with a small mat on it, and the others sat on the ground. Without saying anything, I sat down next to the old man—at which they smiled, thinking that I had done so because I did not understand the custom of the country, which did not permit that. We both showed each other much courtesy by signs, and I by using some words of their language which I knew, although, because I did not put them together properly, they laughed much. They gave me a collation of some fruits; and the sacristan immediately took me to his temple, which was at some distance from the house. It had a sort of cemetery about it, surrounded by some slightly raised stones which divided it from the rest. The door to the temple was small, and the temple itself was arched, round, and small. (Here follows a full account of the appearance of the temple. Some description of their prayers and of their religious customs is also given. Aduarte states, upon the authority of the Portuguese religious, that these native monks are vicious and licentious in the extreme.) I finally reached the ship of our people, and on both sides we told each other what had happened.]

Chapter XLVII

The wars which followed in the prosecution of this embassy

[By the sufferings and danger which we had passed through, the Lord had prepared us to endure those which were to follow. To protect the ship, some of the men had encamped on a little sand island in the middle of the river. On one bank was the town (*i.e.*, Chordamuco) of the natives, near which there were about two thousand Chinese, some settled here, others who had recently come from China as traders, with their merchandise, in five large vessels, which they kept in the river near the town. They had controlled the natives, and resented the coming of the Spaniards, thinking that the latter had come to disturb or take away the superiority which they had. So they sought for an opportunity to quarrel with them, seeing that the Spaniards were few and that they were many. Whenever the men on the ship went to buy food on land, the Chinese tried their patience by annoying them without any reason. By orders of the captain, Blas Ruyz de Fernan Goncalez, they endured this annoyance, though sorely against their will. The captain sent a message to the king asking him to bring the Chinese to order. The king spoke fair words, but did nothing. Finally, the anger of our men got beyond their control. On the Sunday after Easter, when all had received communion, three or four were in the town with the captain's permission. One of them came back with his sword drawn, saying that the Chinese had chased and abused them, and that they had not dared to violate the captain's orders. The troops armed themselves, and, breaking away from all restraints, went to take vengeance on the Chinese. I went along to calm the Chinese, if I could, by speaking to them in their language, which I understood. They were all armed with their *catanas* (a sort of hanger), and *languinatas*, or long knives drawn to a point. I dared not put myself in their hands, because I was told that they would be better pleased to get me than anyone else. Soon after, sixty of our men in two companies, with some of our Japanese and Indians, came ashore and instantly attacked the Chinese. As our bullets took effect at such a distance that the latter could not attack our troops hand to hand, the Chinese were routed; and our men followed, killing them, until they had driven them out of the town. The natives of the country took no part in the conflict on either side. I saved as many lives as I could. The soldiers, seeing themselves masters of the field, pursued the Chinese to their ships, into which the Spaniards were able to shoot from the high banks. In this way they soon got control of the ships, which was necessary, because with these large ships they would easily have overcome our smaller vessel, and thus all hope to escape from the anger of the king would have been taken away from us. The king[15] was in great wrath. To send a message to him, and to carry a statement of the case, the father provincial, Fray Alonso Ximenez, was chosen. He went accompanied by half of the forces, the rest of us remaining in the ships. Several days were passed in sending messages backwards and forwards, but the king would not receive the ambassadors in person. It was plain that the king was planning to take all our lives. The demands which he made would have put us entirely in his power; and, when the father provincial asked permission to return and discuss them with the rest of the forces, the king refused permission for anyone to return except the father provincial alone. The intention of the king was to wait for a rainy day, so that our powder should be moistened and we be unable to use our arquebuses. When the father provincial came back, he asked me if I would venture to go to the camp, confess the soldiers and encourage them, and carry to the king our response declining to follow his wishes. When I reached the forces near the palace of the king, we did not consider the question of taking any answer to him, but discussed two plans of escape. One was to withdraw in good order, defending ourselves on the way; the other to attack the palace of the king by night and strive to capture him, his son, or his wife, whom we might use as hostages. Captain Diego Velloso declared that if we should attack these Indians boldly they would retreat to the mountains, and leave the field to us; but that if we should retreat they would all attack us. He had had experience in this part of the world, and what he said was confirmed by others, so that his plan was accepted. That night I confessed the men and told them what under the circumstances it was lawful for them to do, enjoining them to commit no unnecessary violence, and to take no lives except in self-defense. The attack was planned carefully, the troops being divided into a front and a rear guard, and some of the soldiers being left with a barge in the river near where we were encamped, with orders to capture two Indian boats as soon as they should hear the noise of conflict, so that we could make use of them in our retreat. I should have been glad to remain with the barge in order to avoid being present at the conflict, which promised to be sanguinary.] However, it seemed necessary for me to accompany the rest, and, armed as they were, and wearing no part of my habit except my scapular, I accompanied the troops who advanced against the palace. We were immediately detected, but succeeded in reaching the royal dwelling—which was built of wood, like the other houses in the town, but was very large. We broke in the doors, but the people all escaped through other doors; and thus, though we gained control of the palace, it was empty and we had failed in our purpose. I restrained the troops from burning the palace; but we lighted some bonfires, so that we might see each other. One of these saved my life, for as an Indian on an elephant was charging upon me and was already very close to me, so that I looked around at hearing the noise, the beast fled in alarm, being scared away by the fire. The Indians were not frightened by our daring, as we had falsely imagined that they would be, but gathered in a large square near the palace to face us. Everything, however, was noise and confusion among them, surprised as they were, and there was no less among us; for the number of our opponents was so much greater than theirs that, if darkness had not protected us, they could have buried us in handfuls of sand. [Like Joshua, I would have held back the dawn if I could. At daylight we were all in disorder. When the Indians could distinguish us from themselves and saw how few we were, they began to rain arrows upon us, several being wounded, Captain Diego Velloso having one leg pinned to another, so that he could not walk. Our troops were in entire confusion, some calling out that we ought to come to an understanding with the Indians, others finding fault with the plan that we had followed, until God was pleased to give me courage that I might give courage to the others, and I took upon myself the office of captain. Our last day, as we expected it to be, was bright and clear. A body of courageous Indians charged down the street at us, and their captain almost reached our line. I confess that I wished to leap out upon him, not that I might kill him, but that I might be the first to die, and not see the carnage which I feared—or the worse than carnage, if we were taken alive. But wisdom ruled me, and I ordered Captain Blas Ruiz to attack him with his halberd; with one blow he thrust the Indian through, shield and body. The death of their captain somewhat abated the courage of the rest. God was pleased that one of our bullets should strike the king, who was in the rear, unseen by us, animating his troops. We did not learn of this for some days afterward, but we could see that the Indians attacked us with less ardor. The Indians cut off our retreat to the barge, and we were obliged to leave the soldiers who were with it and to make our way, back by the road. As we marched along, we were obliged to defend ourselves on all sides, and especially against the crowd of Indians which followed in our rear. We could go but slowly, burdened as we were with our arms, and being obliged to carry our wounded.] Two arrows struck but did not wound me, one being caught by a coat of mail which I wore, and the other by my shield. We suffered greatly from hunger and thirst. When we came to some puddles with rain-water in them (which was more mud than water), all drank of them, and when I came there, though I was one of the last, I did the same; and though the best had already been drunk, and the rest was mixed with mud, it tasted better to me than any water that I ever drank in my life. Under all these circumstances, we marched on this day, which was the twelfth of May, four leguas by four o'clock in the afternoon, [when we were obliged to halt because we had reached the bank of a river. The Indians and we ourselves supposed that we should never be able to cross. Here some of our men urged that we ought to give ourselves up to the Indians as slaves for life; others declared that we ought to attack them, and force them to kill us. At nightfall, rain began; and the Indians, supposing that our powder would be moistened, prepared to attack us. I passed along the line, confessing some and encouraging all, though I must admit I was in great fear myself lest before midnight we should be cut into bits, that each one of our enemy might have his piece, as is the custom of Indians when they are victorious. The storm ceased before they dared to attack, but the river was still before us. There were two fords, one narrow and deep; the other, wide and shallow, and at about ten o'clock at night I decided that we ought to make the venture, and learn whether we were to live or die. We chose the longer and shallower ford, marching as quietly as we could, and leaving behind us a number of burning bits of the matches that we used for firing our guns, tied on the bushes, in order to make the Indians suppose that there was a large number of troops there. Our retreat was covered by six courageous men with two arquebuses each. When we entered the river, our vanguard, which was already in the middle, began to retreat upon us, fearing the people who were on the other bank, and their elephants, which they said they were driving into the water. I succeeded in reanimating them, and they fired a volley from the middle of the stream, where the water reached the beards of many of them. The enemy fled, and our passage was impeded only by the difficulty of dragging ourselves through the mud. We marched on for the rest of the night very slowly, with our clothes sticking to our bodies. On the morrow we found some fruit-trees and broke our fast of two nights and one day. We had great difficulty in carrying our wounded. One of the men being left behind by all, I had to carry him myself with his arms over my shoulders, for he was taller than I, until, after his wound began to grow feverish, he was able to walk a little himself. Not long before sunrise we reached the great river in which the ships were, but at a distance of two leguas from us. We put three of the wounded who were the hardest to carry into a little boat there, and ordered them to row down the river and carry the news of what had happened, and to direct the others to bring the ship near the bank where we were. In the meantime we cut some trees and made a breastwork; and when the Indians (who are not accustomed to attack by night) prepared to make their last rush and overwhelm us, our ship came up and, approaching the bank as closely as possible, played on the Indians with some artillery, and fired at them with arquebuses. Under this protection we succeeded in getting to the ship, being carried in two boat-loads.]

Chapter XLVIII

Our departure from the kingdom and the events which happened during our return to Manila

[On the same day on which we reached the ships, Captain Juan Xuarez Gallinato arrived. He was told of our experience with the Chinese and with the Cambodians, and of the good-will displayed in this kingdom for its conversion, and also for the temporal ends proposed in the service of his Majesty. Captain Gallinato showed that he disbelieved much of what was told him, and that what he did believe impressed him badly. In spite of all that was done to persuade him to wait a few days, he was resolved to depart immediately; so we sailed to Cochinchina for provisions. Here we were at first very well received. Then Gallinato sent Captain Gregorio de Vargas as ambassador to visit the king, and to ask him for the royal standard, the galley, and the artillery, and the other things which had been carried to that kingdom by the traitors who murdered Governor Gomez Perez das Mariñas. The king took this demand so ill that he tried to kill the ambassador, who barely escaped with his life. The king, partly because of his rage, and partly from fear that the news of his treatment of the ambassador would be carried back by the Spaniards, sent two fleets and a large land force to destroy us. We here got news of the death of the tyrant who had ruled over the kingdom of Camboja and of the plan of a number of loyal chiefs to reinstate the lawful king with the assistance of the Spaniards, to whom they meant to offer great rewards. The Spanish ships were just putting out to sea when the Indians reached the shore with the purpose of giving them this invitation. It was known that the kingdom of the Laos (to which the king of Camboja had withdrawn) was very near that of Cochinchina; and Captains Blas Ruyz and Diego Velloso asked permission to go by land and find the king. Gallinato permitted them to do so, and I accompanied them to the city of Sinoa, where a son of the king acted as viceroy. Some Augustinian friars who were in that country begged father Fray Alonso Ximenez to go with them and celebrate the feast of St. Augustine. During his absence, the rumor that the Indians intended to murder us treacherously kept increasing; so that we all went aboard, in order to be able to defend ourselves better. The time for sailing to Manila had come, of which we had to take advantage without waiting for either father Fray Alonso or the captain, because we should otherwise have been obliged to winter there. On the third of September, a multitude of people suddenly appeared on the hills, and a fleet came sailing up into the cove where we were. There were many galleys and small boats, and among them there were fifteen larger two-masted vessels, fastened together three by three, with no one on them but a steersman. These were loaded with wood and fagots, to set fire to us; while, if we took refuge in the water, the people in the small boats were ready to receive us. The men on the hills began to shoot at us with their arquebuses, which they used skilfully, aiming well, though they were slow in taking aim. The bullets, however, fell short. Our two smaller vessels set sail, and by the aid of a light breeze moved out into the middle of the bay. The ship in which I was was larger; and, though we tried to do as the other boats did, the wind was too light for us, and the fire-boats came upon us and gave us a great deal of trouble. They came so near that from the top of our poop we could see the steersmen, some of whom our men shot, while others took refuge in some little boats which they towed. When the fire-boats were left without anyone to steer them, they followed the current of the water, and left us in peace. At this point father Fray Alonso Ximenez reached the shore. They took off his habit and dragged him, with nothing on but his breeches, before the viceroy, who had come as general of this enterprise. He told him to put on his habit again, and talked of his ransom; but our captain was so angry at their treachery that he sent back a very wrathful answer. Thus father Fray Alonso Ximenez was left a prisoner, but was not ill treated. He received permission to live with the Augustinian fathers, and at last was permitted to go to Macan without being obliged to pay a ransom. From there he came back to this country at the end of a year and a half. On the next day we set sail for Manila. There are shoals in the midst of this gulf running for eighty leguas directly across the straight course for Manila; and to pass these shoals it was necessary to round one of the two ends of the chain—one in latitude nine, the other in latitude seventeen. The latter being nearer the direct line, we governed our course by it; and the flagship, sailing well against the wind, rounded it. The vessel in which I was, being a poor sailer, went by the other end, but got out of its course. We were becalmed one night, so near the coast of the Philippinas that the people were already beginning to prepare their clothes for going on shore. In the morning we found ourselves in the midst of reefs which were not on the charts. To make our way out from them, we were obliged to sail back on our course; and after we had made our way out the wind was against us, and we were obliged to sail toward the country which we had left. We decided to land at Malaca, that we might at least escape with our persons, for we cared little for anything else.] We reached an island named Pulotimon,[16] which is forty leguas from Malaca. The Indians here told us that there were some pirates in that sea; that they were anchored about five leguas off, and that we should have to pass them. This news greatly disquieted us, because our vessel did not sail well or answer the helm well, which is the worst thing that can be in a sea-fight. But it was not possible to escape this danger, because there was greater danger in every other direction where we wished to go. So we continued our voyage and met with the pirates, as they had told us. They had five ships, four of them small, and one of them large, strong, and well equipped, and provided with nettings. On these boats there were many little flags, which, we were told, were tokens of the prizes that they had taken. They were of a tribe called China-patan, descendants of Chinese who have colonized the kingdom of Patan. They had learned this business [of piracy], because it is easier than others; and they had now sailed out to practice it. That we might not show fear, but might excite fear in them, we passed close to their ships, with our flag flying and our drum beating. They failed to see that our invitation was feigned, accepted it, and, weighing their anchors, followed us all night, giving us chase till morning. The small vessels surrounded us, and with the large one attacked us. Their arms at close quarters were pikes and javelins with points hardened in the fire [*tostadas*]. The arms which they used at a distance were culverins and arquebuses. In using our arquebuses we did not waste a bullet, for there were many on whom to employ them. [We were alarmed by the explosion of a keg of powder, but fortunately only one man was killed. I was standing alone on the poop, watching for the result of the fight; and at first the enemy did not notice me, since the waist was full of their pikemen. At last, one of them perceived me and flung a pike at me, giving me a wound of three dedos in depth. I descended from the poop; but, before I reached the deck, one of the fire-hardened lances struck me in the right jaw, leaving its point and innumerable splinters in the flesh. With my two hands upon my two wounds I went to confess some wounded men who were in danger. At last when the enemies saw that their prize cost them much, they left us and went away without our being able to follow them, because our vessel was so unfit. We afterward learned in Malaca that out of two hundred pirates (which was their total number) more than half had been killed. Most of us were wounded, and two or three died—besides two others, who were shot by accident by their own friends. After we had escaped this danger we came, two days later, upon a surprise which was equally great. In the strait of Sincapura, by which we were obliged to pass, we found a fleet of eighty large galleys, with heavy artillery amidships and along the sides. This was the fleet of the king of Achen, who was going to do what injury he could to the king of Jor [*i.e.*, Johor] to whom belongs the country of that strait. The latter had sixteen galleys for its defense, which were in the mouths of the rivers to prevent his enemy from entering them. Malaca is between these two kingdoms. There was at that time an agreement that neither of these kings should be assisted with men, but only with provisions and ammunition, one side receiving the one and the other the other, but neither receiving both. We passed ourselves off to them as Portuguese; and when they called upon us to enter their galleys we excused ourselves, because of the aforesaid agreement, and went on in peace to Malaca. I went to our convent, where the religious were surprised at my coming, partly because it was the middle of November, when they did not expect a vessel from any direction, and partly because they saw me in so coarse a habit, very different from that which they wore. Besides that, I was very dirty and very lean, and had my body and face all bound up because of my wounds. Although my appearance was so strange, they were so discreet (or I had better say so charitable) that, without asking any questions they arranged to take care of me, called in the surgeon, and brought me underwear and a habit after their fashion. After I was cared for and clothed, they asked me whence I came and how I had been brought there. I was charmed with the kindness which they had shown me, and told of my wanderings and of the sufferings which I had endured, by which they were greatly astonished. I remained there for six months. My cure took three months, and from the wound in my face every day two or three splinters were discharged, some larger and others smaller, until at least a hundred had come out. Though the wound closed, two remained within, which came out two years later, two dedos below the wound. I was much inconvenienced during those three months, because I could only open my mouth a little way; and hence it was very painful for me to eat until, by exercise, my jaw came back to its former usefulness. Of the soldiers who came with me, some went to India and twelve to Camboxa, supposing that the rightful king was now probably there. They found on the throne his son, who with a great army given him by the king of the Laos, and with the captains of whom I have spoken, had returned to his kingdom of Camboxa and pacified it. Here they remained for a considerable time, though they were disappointed in everything. I and the others returned to Manila. The voyage is one of five hundred leguas, and it took us fifty days because of the many calms.] One calm night, when there was no one at the helm, the binnacle, or three-wicked candle which lights up the compass, fell down from the quarterdeck; and the flame instantly burst out through a hatchway which was over it, frightening all of us—for there is nothing more dreadful at sea than fire, for everything in a ship is like tinder. In this ship, although it was small, there were more than three hundred slaves, men and women. All of them raised their cries to heaven. The captain, whose duty it was to encourage them, immediately fell on his knees to make his confession, as if things had already gone beyond remedy, but I pushed him away a pace and a half, saying that it was not time for that yet, and that he ought to look out for the fire first. I am almost certain that if he had been permitted to confess to me we should all have burned to death, because, however little our safety might have been delayed by confessions, there would have been no remedy afterwards. We put all the clothes there were there into the water, to soak them, and then threw them down the hatchway, one on top of another. In this way God was pleased that the fire should be put out; and we were left as much amazed by this sudden and dangerous accident as people are who are waked out of their sleep by a beam of light falling on them. We at last reached Manila by St. John's day at the end of a year and a half of this tedious and painful journeying. Soon after, father Fray Alonso Ximenez arrived by way of Macan from Cochinchina, where he had remained a prisoner. After all our hardships, afflictions, dangers, and wounds, we brought back no other fruit but that of having suffered for the gospel. Our only intention was to go to preach in that kingdom, having been invited by its king, and influenced by his promises to that end. These were great, though he was unable to fulfil them, since he had been despoiled of his kingdom when we reached it, as has been said.

Chapter XLIX

The election as provincial of father Fray Bernardo de Sancta Catharina or Navarro, and the churches which were incorporated in the province

On the fifteenth of June, 1596, the fathers assembled in the convent of Manila to elect a provincial, because father Fray Alonso Ximenez had finished his term. The definitors (who, as they afterward were to confirm the provincial, were elected first) were: father Fray Diego de Soria, second time prior of the said convent; father Fray Bartholome de Nieva, a religious of very superior virtue, as will be narrated in due time; father Fray Juan de Sancto Thomas, or Ormaca; and father Fray Juan Garcia—all persons of conspicuous devotion to their religious duties, and of noble example. Several times they cast votes for the provincial without result. Because there were many who deserved the office, and because the votes were divided among them, no one had the number necessary for election. Those who had the largest number of votes were father Fray Diego de Soria and father Fray Juan de Sancto Thomas. These same persons endeavored to persuade everyone to vote for father Fray Bernardo de Sancta Catharina, who was accordingly elected. The election was a very satisfactory one, for, in addition to being a very holy man, he was very wise and learned, and most devoted to the ministry and preaching of the holy gospel—in which, and in patience, and in the endurance of the most severe hardships which befell him for this cause, no one ever surpassed him, and he surpassed many. During his time he had seen the province greatly favored by the Lord, by a very great spread of the Christian faith among the Indians who were under his care. Many of them in the villages where there were religious were baptized; and, where there were no religious, they were desirous and eager to receive baptism. Accordingly, at this chapter not only were new churches admitted which had been built in the towns where there were already religious—as, among the Chinese, the church of San Gabriel at Minondoc; and, in Bataan, the church in the village of Samal, besides others—but it also seemed good to admit heathen villages, although they had no religious, and there were none in the province so that teachers could be provided for them. Yet in this way they strove to comfort those who asked and desired them, and raised in them the hope that in this way they would receive religious when they came from España. Thus were received the church of San Vicente of the village of Buguey, afterward called Sancta Anna; Sancta Catarina of Nasiping, afterward called San Miguel; and others like them—to which, in the course of time, religious were sent when they came to the islands.

Soon after this provincial chapter had come to an end, another shipload of religious arrived from España. They had been gathered with great care and diligence by the new bishop of Nueva Segovia, Don Fray Miguel de Venavides, whose new dignity had not sufficed to diminish the love which he felt for his associates. He gave to this matter more than ordinary attention, because he knew how greatly needed were good workmen to aid in the great harvest which the Lord had placed in their hands, ready to be gathered by the means of baptism into this church militant, that the faithful might pass from it to the church triumphant. The Indians themselves asked to have preachers sent to their villages, and were grieved that these could not be given to them. This not a little afflicted the religious, who desired to satisfy them by the fulfilment of their just desires, but were unable to do so on account of their own small number—too small even for that which they had undertaken, and much more to go to the aid of new regions. Besides this, the careful bishop was influenced by the need of his own sheep; for nearly everything to which we ministered fell within the bishopric of Nueva Segovia, which was under his direction. Accordingly, taking advantage of his authority as a bishop, and of the reputation which he had as a learned and holy religious, he gathered the second shipload, and afterward the third (with which he came). Father Fray Pedro de Ledesma[17] happened to be in Castilla when the shipload which the good bishop sent was about to sail. His presence was very convenient for his superior, because he was an old and venerable father who had been many years in the Indias in the very religious province of Guatimala, and who therefore knew what was needed for the voyage. He was also of a very gentle disposition, which is of great importance for such purposes as his. The bishop laid upon this father the charge of conducting the religious who had been gathered for this province; and he, being inclined to all good, readily accepted the office, although he knew that it was a very troublesome one. It not only required him to go on business to the office of accounts—and, to him who knows what that is, it is not necessary to say anything more—but he had also to keep in contentment many religious who, as it was the first time when they were at sea, were seasick, miserable, and very much in need of someone to comfort them, bear with them, and encourage them. For all this father Fray Pedro was very well suited, and conducted them as comfortably as possible through the two long voyages which have to be made on the way from España here. He did not shrink from the great labor which this duty brought with it, that he might serve the Lord, and aid in the preaching of His gospel and in the conversion of these heathen. They arrived in the month of July in this year of

1596, and were received with great joy; and with them those missions which were in need of religious were strengthened.

Captains Blas Ruiz de Fernan Goncalez and Diego Velloso, who (as has been stated in the preceding chapter) went from Cochinchina to the kingdom of the Laos to look for the king of Camboja, met with success. They found his son (for the king was already dead), and told him all that the Spaniards had already done to help him, and how they had slain the tyrant who had undertaken to establish himself in the kingdom and had usurped it. They told him that they had come to seek him that they might put him in quiet possession of his kingdom, and other things of this kind, and roused his courage so that he put himself in their hands. Depending upon them, he returned to Camboja with a tolerably large army, which the king of the Laos gave him; and the Spaniards fulfilled their word and established him in his royal throne and palace, causing the largest and best part of the kingdom to be obedient to him. The king in reward of services so faithful and useful gave them lands and vassals in his kingdom. To Blas Ruiz he gave the province of Tran; to Diego Velloso that of Bapano, with titles very honorable in this kingdom. The two captains in their new favor did not forget God, to whom they had so especial reasons to be thankful; or their natural king and lord, from whom also they had received rewards. They informed the king of Camboja of the great good that it would be to his kingdom to know and reverence God by entering into His service through holy baptism, and to have the king of España for his friend. For the first purpose, father Fray Alonso Ximenez and myself were proposed. They urged the great devotion, virtue, and prudence of the holy old man, and the many sufferings which we had both undergone from favoring the king's own cause; and they said that, if he sent to call us back, we would very readily come to preach the holy gospel. As for the second purpose they said that he ought to send an embassy to the governor of Manila; and, as a sign of the beginning of this friendship, that he ought to ask for some soldiers, by whose aid he might easily complete the pacification of his country. The king assented to all this, and sent his embassy with letters to the governor, telling him that his principal reason for asking for soldiers was that his vassals might be baptized with greater certainty and less difficulty. To father Fray Alonso Ximenez he wrote another letter, in the language and characters which those people use, and sealed with his royal seal, of a red color. In the Castilian language its tenor was as follows: ["Prauncar, king of Camboja, to father Fray Alonso Ximenez of the Order of St. Dominic: Greeting. From what I have heard from the captain Chofa Don Blas Ruiz of Castilla, and from the captain Chofa Don Diego of Portugal, with regard to the conduct of father Fray Alonso Ximenez when the Spaniards slew Anacaparan, I have conceived a great affection for father Fray Alonso Ximenez. Now that I am in my kingdom I beg father Fray Alonso Ximenez to come to it, and to bring with him father Fray Diego. I promise to build them churches and convents, and to give permission to all in my kingdom to become Christians. Though I have shown the two chofas[18] great favor and wish to keep them in my kingdom, they are unwilling to stay, because there are no religious here." The two captains wrote in the same strain to the fathers, begging them to come and reunite this kingdom with the Church.

The governor of Manila saw how much could be done for the service of the king by sending the soldiers for whom the king of Camboja asked; but they were in such need of men and money that they could not well meet his desires. For this reason, a knight of the Habit of Calatraba who had been governor of these islands, by name Don Luis Perez das Mariñas, promised to pay the expenses of the expedition from his own fortune. The enterprise thus being made possible, we two religious of the order for whom the king of Camboja asked were obliged to go; and with us some religious of the Order of St. Francis, who were much beloved by Don Luis. There were equipped for the expedition two vessels of Spanish build, of moderate tonnage, and a galleot. The preparations were made (as preparations usually are made by the hand of servants of the king) slowly and faultily, as was seen by the results. We did not set out for some months, and our ships were so badly equipped and so weak that they began to leak as soon as the voyage began—a forewarning of the evils that we afterwards suffered, in which the poor knight Don Luis was disappointed, while all of us who accompanied him paid for the inadequacy of the preparation.[19] Since we were so late, the pilots decided to follow the course by the gulf of Haynau to go round the shoals by the end in latitude seventeen, because in that way the wind would be favorable; while if they rounded the end in latitude nine, which was the regular course, the wind would be adverse. They left Manila September 17 [1598], with one hundred and fifty soldiers and sailors. In the flagship Don Luis, who went as commander, took with him father Fray Alonso Ximenez and the two Franciscan fathers. He directed me to go in the ship of the second in command,[20] giving that officer orders to govern himself by my advice. Within six days the vessels were scattered in the storm and were all lost, no one knowing anything of the rest, and each one supposing that the others were continuing their voyage in safety. The galleot met with the best fortune, for, although damaged, it reached a friendly port, was repaired, and continued its journey. The flagship was obliged to cut away the mainmast, and sailing under its foresail, ran aground in China on the eve of St. Francis. All who were on board had to save themselves by swimming, and lost even their clothes. In the ship of the second in command, in which I was, the mainmast broke close to the deck, fortunately falling over the side so as not to injure the vessel or to kill any of the men. The mizzenmast, being badly wedged, began to topple, and had to be cut away. We sailed on under the foresail, hoping to reach a port. But the fury of the tempest and the force of the waves were such as to break the gudgeons of the rudder. Some of our men flung themselves into the sea after it and brought it back, but it was lost again; and we steered the vessel with two long spars fastened to the side of the boat with a cable. The ship was so strained that the boards on the sides began to play up and down like organ-keys; but we threw cables about her, and drew them taut with arquebuses. Then the bow began to work loose, from the weight of the foremast and bowsprit, and we were forced to bind it firmly with cables to the poop. All that we could do against the storm and the wind was like the strength of a child exerted to restrain the fury of a mad bull. In fear of another storm, we took refuge upon an island which we encountered, one of the group called the Babuyanes. We found a harbor, ran the bow ashore, and dropped two anchors from the poop. We put the ammunition and the provisions that we had on shore; and had hardly begun to dry our clothes, on the eve of St. Francis, when the storm broke upon us with such violence that it seemed to me to try to swallow us. The ship was broken in pieces; but the keel, and the artillery which was carried as ballast, being too heavy for the deck, were buried in the sand. We protected ourselves from the storm—which lasted two days, and was one of both wind and rain—in some huts, which we built on the beach of branches.] After the storm was over we dug up the artillery, which consisted of four medium-sized cannon, mounted, and set them up in a little fort which we made of logs, because there were many Indians on the islands, and we did not know whether they were friends or enemies. In a short time many of them appeared in a troop on the shore, with their weapons. These consisted of two lances, one for hurling, and the other large like a pike, with iron points; both were made of ebony, of which there is much here. For defensive armor they had sheets of the bark of trees, resembling cork. We sent to them a man as a hostage and mark of peace, and they made signs to him from a distance to put down his arms. He laid them at one side and went to the Indians; and then they sent to us one of their own number, whom we treated kindly, and after giving him some trinkets, sent him back to his comrades; agreeing with him that they should bring us provisions at a just price. They did this for two days, although very scantily; and on the third day they broke the peace by killing one of our Japanese, and badly wounding another who had come in our company. He came back with his arm pierced, and with a wound a span long above the pit of his stomach, but not entering it; but he was very well satisfied because, by throwing himself forward by the pike, he had killed the Indian who had wounded him—so proud is that race. Now that our supplies were cut off, we were obliged, since food is necessary, to take it by force, where we could find it, since they would not sell it willingly; so for several mornings a troop of our Indians went out under escort of our soldiers, gathered what they could from the fields, and brought it back as food for all. At one time when they were engaged in this, they thought that they had discovered a great treasure; for they found some jars of moderate size covered by others of similar size. Inside they found some dead bodies dried, and nothing else. In that shipwreck we had had the good luck to bring the boat ashore, and thus to save it. This we intended to make use of by sending it to ask for aid from Nueva Segovia, which was only twenty leguas distant. In order to do this, it was necessary to lengthen the keel a braza, and to raise the sides about half a vara. Both these things were done, though there was no one among us who understood more carpentry than that best teacher, Necessity, had taught them. We all thought that it was best that the pilot and two men and I should go in it, because they believed that, if I went, more effectual aid would be sent. We did so, and then, when we sailed around the island we gave thanks to the Lord for His kindness in having brought us to this little bay; for on any of the other sides of the island we should certainly have been drowned in the ocean, or, if any of us had escaped, should have perished at the hands of the Indians. The Lord gave us a favorable wind, which was needed by our tiny boat in that rough ocean, and we reached the river of Nueva Segovia, which is very large; the distance from the mouth to the city is three leguas. The alcalde-mayor immediately set about the rescue, appropriated two fragatas, and had them prepared to go to our people who were in the islands. At the same time I wrote to Manila to the agents of Don Luys to send a ship, ship-stores, and everything else required for continuing the voyage. I also wrote to my superior, giving him an account of what had happened. The answer to my letters was made plain, both on the island and in Manila. The governor commanded that the voyage should be continued, all of the expenditure being made anew, while my superior directed me to return to Manila; and so I did, although my companions were greatly grieved. In truth, by failing to go with them I caused their destruction; because, as they were sailing toward the coast of China, they saw a Chinese ship, and, against the will of the pilot and some few others, the rest determined to pursue and plunder it. The ship fled, turning toward the coast of its own country, which was all sown with shallows, well known to them but not to our men. So eagerly did the Spaniards chase after them in their greed for the prize, which they now regarded as certain, that our ship ran aground and broke into two parts. The men were all thrown into the sea, where some of them were drowned immediately, and others, who took refuge on shoals, were drowned when the tide came in. Some few only escaped, with the pilot, in a raft which they made of planks from the ship. Even of those few some died of the cold, which was very great, and was still more severe for them because they were all wet. At last those who escaped reached the coast, with difficulty enough. They were seized by the Chinese, and carried about for many leguas from one judge to another. In this way they learned that Don Luis was on the same coast, and that he had been wrecked on the same day of St. Francis, and at the same time with us. They learned that he was twenty leguas from there, on an island called Lampacao. They received permission to join him; and in spite of their miseries they forgot their ills in their pity for the poor knight and his men, who kept themselves alive with shellfish, which they found there and ate in small quantities. They all suffered patiently, because of the example of their commander—who, that he might not offend [the people of] the land, never allowed his men to ask for anything, even what necessity almost compelled them to request.

Chapter L

I am commanded to go to China; events there, and the death of father Fray Alonso Ximenez

[In spite of the wretched state of the noble knight Don Luis, the Portuguese of Macan, who were only seven leguas away, were so far from pitying him that they rather made bloody war against him. He accordingly decided to send the pilot of the second in command, with eight other men, to Manila in a small boat, to ask for what was needed to escape from that labyrinth. They arrived after great peril, and delivered their letters which were filled with the innumerable complaints of those who remained there. They moved all the city to great compassion, but our religious more than the others, who always had a very tender regard for the good knight, Don Luis, both for his virtue, and for his great love toward us. He never forsook us or our churches, where he received all the sacraments, and went to hear all the masses that were said, to the great edification of the village of Minondoc—where he lived, near to our house. Consequently, I was charged with the immediate care of procuring what was needed for the relief of the present trouble, since the past troubles had none. My superior notified me that I should go to take the relief to Don Luis, and ordered me to attend to that matter with the greatest possible despatch, since delay meant manifest danger. With all that care he was unable to get the help out within four months, and notwithstanding that I exercised very great earnestness in it, and attended to the equipment of the ship that was assigned, which I had fitted up so that it would stand any storm—having taken warning from the previous ships, which had proved deficient in the first storm that came upon us. By such diligence, we set sail, with suitable relief, on September six. Arriving with it in less than twenty days, we were as well received, as we were so heartily desired. We also found bad news from Camboja, which had been brought by some ships that had returned from that country. That news was that all the Spaniards there—both those of our galliot, and all the others—had perished at the hands of the Indians themselves, because of quarrelsome persons among them, who were intolerable to the natives. Since it was impossible to go thither as friends, and since our forces were very few to go in any other manner, consequently, a general council having been held, it resulted that we should return to Manila. To carry that into effect, it was necessary to go to the court of the viceroy at Canton to get permission, for we could not leave his port without it. It was determined that I should go to get the permission. I was accompanied by two soldiers and an

Indian up a large river with most beautiful and refreshing banks, which contained some very densely populated villages. Arrived at Canton, we were lodged in a house in the suburbs, as foreigners were not allowed to live in the city, nor even to enter it without express permission from the judge who is in charge. Guards are stationed for that reason at all the gates, so that they may refuse admittance without such permission. It happened that there was a eunuch of the king there at that time, as inspector of that province. Within his palace the king of China is served only by eunuchs, and many are castrated, in order to be eligible to serve the king; and as they alone have access to his person and ear, they persuade him of whatever they wish, and derive immense bribes from the judges throughout the kingdom. The latter give them the bribes, so that the inspectors may hand in a good report of them. That year the eunuchs got for themselves the inspection of the provinces of that kingdom, as a great harvest was offered therefrom, not only to the king but also to the others who remained at his side in order to perpetuate their acts of injustice with security, the gates to the complaints that could have been uttered against them having been closed. Then was it my unhappy lot that I should fall into the hands of one of them, called Liculifu, who had charge of the visit to Canton, and who, under pretext of the visit, was making haste to impoverish the country and the inhabitants; for his charge there also comprehended the inspection of a pearl-fishery for the king in the gulf of Haynao, which was situated about one hundred leguas farther along the coast. It was said that he had borrowed one thousand ships for that purpose, and that he was in haste; but that he wanted first what fish he could get on land—for which he had innumerable parasites at his side who were wont to seek out means by which, rightly or wrongly, he could employ them, by which they were always the gainers; and who, in addition, always flattered him by showing him such means of gain, by which he considered himself as well served, and rewarded those most who were most advantaged by it. Certain of those creatures, ferreting us out, immediately went to denounce us, not as evildoers, but as men absolutely rolling in silver; for that is their opinion of the Spaniards, even though they see them going naked. Therefore, it suited him to employ his greed on us, although asking silver from us was equivalent to asking pears from the elm tree. The inspector, believing that we had maliciously concealed the silver, tried to get it by force; but instead of silver he drew blood. Acting upon that information he had us summoned before him, a day or two after our arrival. We entered the gate used by foreigners, and there is only one such gate. The guards registered us there, so carefully do they watch and guard their city, although so rare are the foreigners who enter it. We approached the inspector's court, but before we entered it I had the inspector notified, by an interpreter whom I had with me, that I would not kneel before him, as such was not the custom of Castilians—whether religious or captains—even were it before the kings of that land. He had me told that I should do so, but I answered to the contrary twice more. However, finally paying greater heed to the advantage that he expected [to derive], than to his honor and courtesy which he claimed, he had me told that the soldiers should kneel and that I should make him the bow and reverence that I was wont to make to my king. Thereupon we entered, and found him seated in great state at his desk, on which were the instruments used in writing, according to their usage. Many servants stood near him, in a chapel-like place that faced a large open court, whence those having business entered as he summoned them. Placed on their knees between two rows of executioners with frightful visages—twelve to the side, who stood there—their cases were disposed of, and they were punished there immediately, as soon as he ordered it, without further appeal or recourse. The soldiers and the interpreter knelt before them, while I remained upright, after having made him a very deep bow. He received us well, and addressed some pleasant words to us. I thanked him heartily, and made him a present of a piece of scarlet cloth and a large and excellent mirror, with its silver chain by which to hang it up, which had been given me for that purpose by General Don Luis. The latter already was aware that no business was transacted without a present. The inspector received the present very gladly, as it consisted of articles that were scarce in that country. He expressed many scruples in regard to it, so that it might not appear that he was receiving it as a bribe, and said that it would be taken as part payment of the duties due and to be paid by the ships; and that he had a conscience and kept his gaze on the heavens, so that he might not commit any unjust act. But in truth, although I thought that he would be satisfied with that present, he regarded it as the beginning of what we had to give and waited for the rest. I asked him to send someone to measure the ships and receive the duties, for it was now time for us to leave. He did so immediately, and sent officials like himself. Those officials declared, because they were not bribed at the beginning, that the duties amounted to one thousand eight hundred ducados. Don Luis, having been advised of what ought to be done, asked that the measurements be made a second time; and after he had given them their bribe, they took off the thousand ducados, and the duties remained at only eight hundred. Believing that the inspector's greed was satisfied, I delayed two or three days in going to see him; but he, as his appetite had been whetted for the desire of more with the taste that he had received, took my delay very ill, and had only the two soldiers and the interpreter summoned, but ordered me not to go to him. On seeing them, he broke out into great anger because they had not treated him according to his dignity. He ordered the interpreter to be beaten as the most guilty, since, knowing the custom of the country, he had not advised us thereof. They actually administered five blows to him, and the blows that they give are always few, but very severe. Those blows accordingly formed great wounds on the upper part of his legs, that being where they are administered. He ordered the soldiers to be all but lashed. They were thrown to the ground, and their legs bared, while the executioner stood near them with his lash raised. That instrument is made from a very large bamboo (such as grow there), split in two and weighted somewhat with lead, and having many slits, whose edges cut like knives. And as the executioner stood thus, waiting for the order to strike the blow, he ordered him to stay his hand, being satisfied to see them thus fearful. Then he ordered all three to be taken prisoners to a public prison, which was located at a considerable distance from his house. While on the way thither they had me summoned, and bribed the officials to stop in an idol temple. I went there alone, although with great difficulty. They implored me again and again not to leave them in custody, for they would die in prison. I promised them not to leave that place until they were liberated, or else I would share the same fortune with them. I well understood that those blows were directed at me, rather than at them; and that, although given to others, were a threat to me so that I should tremble and give the inspector what he desired, or he would cause me also to suffer such things, or even greater. I knew already that his parasites had informed him of the esteem in which the Spanish hold their priests and religious, and that they would redeem by weight of silver whatever insult he might try to inflict on me; and that if he wished to fill his hand well, he should make what extortions from me his tyrannous and greedy taste dictated. I had no silver to satisfy his desire, nor, even had I desired to supply that lack by any efforts, did I have any method or means to do so. It even cost me very dearly to enter the city, and I could not go on that account. I was persecuted by children, who accosted me as did the children of Bethel the holy prophet Elisha; while not one of the men had compassion on me, for they do not know what compassion means toward their own countrymen, however afflicted they see them to be. And further, if they behold them persecuted by the more influential men, then in such case they flee from the sight of them, in fear lest they receive a portion of the punishment, as being accomplices in the guilt. The soldiers, as they were afflicted, attributed the slowness of the relief to my neglect, and the inspector to obstinacy. Finally he endeavored to satisfy his greed by making open proof of my patience. Therefore, he summoned me on All Saints' day. I heard of his resolve some days beforehand, and prepared for it by saying mass—for which I had the opportunity, as the Portuguese from Macan happened to be there at that time, by virtue of their ordinary permission to go to Canton twice each year, to purchase the articles that they need in certain fairs which are held there at that time. However, they are not permitted to live in the city, but must remain in their own boats in the river. As that purchasing (which lasts many days) is a matter of consequence, the Portuguese bring a priest, who says mass to them, in a little house near the river. At that time there were three fathers of the Society there, one of whom was acting in the capacity of chaplain for the traders, while the other two were about to enter the interior with Father Matheo Riccio, who had lived there for years. One of those two fathers, one Lacaro Catanio, had lived with the above father for some years; and, having gone to Macan on business, was then returning with another Spaniard named Diego Pantoja. Both of them dressed themselves, on the afternoon of the eve of All Saints, in Chinese habits, in order to make their journey with some guides that they had with them. Father Lacaro Catanio, as he had been a long time in China, had long hair and beard, but the other father, having only recently arrived, did not; and consequently he was in some danger, as he did not follow the customs of the country in everything. By way, then, of those fathers I was enabled to say mass. Scarcely had I concluded it, when I was accosted by an official of the inspector, with his *chapa* (or summons) to take me before the inspector. I went thither, and found him in his courtroom, as at the first time. Although I intended to show him the same courtesy as the first time, he made me kneel down, besides going between those two files of executioners, who appeared to me like demons. The inspector began then to shout at me, in his treble voice, and poured forth a torrent of words, which were explained to me by a Chinese who understood some Portuguese. He charged me in his speech with being a spy, as I had not observed my duty. At the end of the speech came his deeds. At the inspector's order one of those executioners threw me to the ground, and, baring my legs, raised himself in a position to lash me. While in that position, the inspector repeated many times his assertion that I must be a spy. Thereupon I drew a report from my bosom that I brought from the Chinese who were living in Manila, both Christians and heathens, which told of the great good that the members of my order had done there to all of their nation—how we cared for their sick, supported the poor, and defended them all from injuries which were attempted against them. It was written in their own characters, on a sheet of paper one braza long, and was folded within a covering, also made of paper, after their manner and custom. I had come prepared with that for whatever might happen, and accordingly I presented it at that so pressing moment. The inspector read it, while I was kept stretched out and bared ready for the lash, and the executioner awaiting only the sign to chastise me. As the letter was not to the inspector's liking, he paid no heed to it. However, he did not carry out the execution [of the punishment], but ordered me to rise and adjust my clothing and come to his desk. I thought that it was to make peace, but it was only to vary the mode of affliction by changing the torture, which he ordered to be given me between the fingers, while placed on my knees before him with folded hands. For that purpose some little rounded sticks were brought, in which there were some small grooves at each end and in the middle. Those sticks were placed between the fingers of both hands and were then pressed together by some cords, tighter and tighter as the inspector ordered—until, when I fell as if in a faint, he ordered the torment to cease. He ordered me to be gone, and said that, if I did not give him a thousand taes of silver on the morrow (each tae being equivalent to ten reals, thus all amounting to about one thousand ducados), he would kill me. I left his presence, with the bad treatment that I have described, and went to my lodgings as best as I could, where I found an order from the inspector not to receive me. I knew not where to go, for all fled from me, being fearful lest some blow should come upon them by reason of me. I determined to go to the ship where the fathers were. Then the merchants returned, much earlier than was their custom, saying that all the city had risen against them, because I had gone to their ship. They besought me not to do so evil an act, for they feared a serious danger from that. As they refused to receive me, I returned to the shore, where a Chinese trader who had been in Manila on various occasions received me into his house. He got me the loan of one hundred taes of silver, payable with interest; and that night I went clad as a Chinese, so that I might not be recognized, to the Portuguese ships. On my word—which I pledged on that of General Don Luis, in whose cause I was acting—they lent me two hundred more. I sent that whole sum to the inspector next day by my host, who was a man of esteem in the city; I also had him ask that the inspector would be satisfied with that amount, as I had borrowed it as an alms, and could find no more, and that he would be pleased to liberate the prisoners, and grant us permission to go to our ship. That was a just petition, but it was ill received and worse despatched; for although I thought that that gift would soften that heart of stone, I discovered that it had been like throwing a little water on the forge which blazes all the fiercer. The inspector sent a constable with his chapa to summon me that afternoon. It was necessary to go; and, thanks to my host, who accompanied me, they took me to the entrance by another gate of the city, as it was nearer his house. But when the guards saw me they refused to allow me to enter, and although the constable showed them the chapa of the inspector, they declared that that concerned me, and not them; accordingly, they refused me entrance. It was necessary for the constable to go to his master, and report the matter to him. The latter gave another chapa for the gatekeepers, and they, taking it, copied it and allowed me to enter. I did not find the inspector in his court, but in a lodging nearer the center of the city. He was the only one seated, while all his officials were standing. The money which I had had sent to him was on a desk. I knelt down, at a considerable distance from him, whereupon he began to chide me, and to say many things to me that I did not understand. It seemed to me that he was asking questions of me, and I only answered *Purhiautet*—that is to say, "I do not understand." He rose from his chair, and came toward me, in order to address me from a shorter distance. It seemed from his actions that he meant to scratch out my eyes with his fingers (they are great men for such deeds, the more when they are angry). He finally satisfied his wrath by ordering me to be taken straight to the prison where the soldiers were. An iron chain was therefore quickly put about my neck, and fastened with a padlock; and one of the executioners, holding the end of it, walked before me, obliging me thus to follow him as a captive. The prison was at a considerable distance, and was under the orders of another mandarin, to whom he sent me, so that the latter might incarcerate me. In such guise, I crossed all those streets, which swarmed with people, at four o'clock in the afternoon, and appeared before this mandarin—who was in his tribunal, into which the door of the prison opened. When the soldiers saw me through the door, they began to weep. [I fell on my knees before him, and he asked me through my interpreter the cause of my imprisonment. I replied, and the cause seemed to him bad: but he told me that no one could undo what the inspector did. He said that he would try to satisfy the inspector, because the latter was obliged to go off very quickly on his inspection, and, if he left me a prisoner here, no one else had the authority to release me. With this he ordered the chains to be taken off, and sent me into the prison. When I saw myself in prison with the soldiers I was without anxiety, because for their sake I had made all these stations,[21] and after all without succeeding in rescuing the prisoners—though I could have taken refuge in our ships if I had chosen, as I afterwards did; while now, by adventuring the same fortune with them, I left God to watch over all. There were in this prison some three hundred prisoners, many condemned to death, but permitted to work during the daytime in order to earn their food. I suffered in the prison, because I had little protection and the weather was very cold. God delivered me within only three days; my host became my security for a thousand taes. As I was about to leave the prison, all the servants crowded about me asking for *plata* (silver), for they already knew its name in our Castilian. There were so many that, even if I had had much to give, there would have been little for each one. As I had nothing to give, I gave them nothing, and they paid me with hard words

82

and blows. It was very late; and we were obliged to go to the house of the inspector, and from it to that of the guarantor outside of the city, in which we were not permitted to sleep. All this was to be done before they closed the gates. We were kept waiting in the courtyard of the inspector for some time. In addition to falling on our knees before him, he made us bow our heads and then turned us over to our bondsman. When we reached the latter's house, we had to enter by leaping over a lighted fire which they said was the ceremony of security. The poor guarantor immediately began to suffer persecution, for all the servants and attendants of the inspector, though they had in no way intervened in our business, came to beg money from him from that which they said he must have received from me, to persuade him to become my security. The man brought all these demands to me; but I answered him that nothing more was to be paid than the thousand taes, and these we should get from Don Luis. He was unwilling to go to Don Luis, and took great care to prevent us from escaping. We, fearing that Don Luis and his soldiers might be forced by our delay to leave us in this embarrassment, determined to save ourselves. We agreed with a Chinaman, for ten taes to help us escape, letting us out through a secret door opening upon a creek that flowed into the large river, and taking us down in a boat. We sailed down stream that night and the next day, no one appearing on the boat in the daytime except the Chinese sailors. We succeeded in eluding all the vessels that might have wished to inspect us, and reached our ships. As soon as our sailors received their pay they ran away. A few hours later, my guarantor appeared with an armed vessel. He was unable to find out who had helped us, and was satisfied with receiving the amount of money for which he had been pledged. We then set sail, Don Luis and the rest to Manila, and I to Macan, for I was in such a condition of ill health as a result of hardship and exposure that I did not dare to undertake the voyage to Manila. At this time father Fray Alonso Ximenez died in Macan. His death was caused by the hardships and exposure which he had undergone in endeavoring to evangelize the kingdom of Camboja. Though he was almost seventy years of age when he set out on the expedition, he endured everything that befell him with patience and courage, consoling the others, though he had always himself the most to suffer. He was very devout, never omitting his daily hours of prayer on his journeys or voyages. When in Cochinchina, his captivity was comforted by the opportunity given him to convert two condemned criminals. The failures of his attempts to reach the kingdom of Camboja and to convert the people there did not discourage him or diminish his enthusiasm. When Don Luis and his men were cruelly attacked by the Portuguese of Macan, father Fray Alonso went to Macan to interpose his authority, and to act as mediator between the Portuguese and the

Castilians. Father Fray Alonso had great difficulty in pacifying the Portuguese, and was obliged to encounter much vituperation; but he received more joy in the baptism of two sick persons at the point of death than he had lost in all the sufferings which have been narrated. He died in our convent at Macan, to the great sorrow of the religious about him at the loss of so holy an associate. General Don Luis and all of the troops that he had brought with him attributed to the loss of father Fray Alonso all the sufferings which they were obliged to undergo afterward; while they ascribed to his presence and his prayers the rescue of their ship in the dreadful storm which they had experienced on the day of St. Francis. On that day they had been in the midst of shoals, and had seen many Chinese vessels wrecked about them; and the wind had been so violent that it had thrown down many strongly-rooted trees on land. Father Fray Alonso was a son of the convent of S. Esteban at Salamanca. Desirous for the conversion of the Indians, he passed his youth in the devout province of Guatemala. Having retired to his convent, to take up the works of Mary after he had done those of Martha, he heard of the foundation of the province of the Philippinas. When many were turned back by the difficulties in Mexico, father Fray Alonso was always firm and constant. When he reached Manila, the ministry of Batan fell to his lot. In spite of his age, and the great difficulty which he had in learning the Indian language, he at length succeeded. In this ministry he suffered the hardships which have been described already. He was especially kind and serviceable to sick Indians, preparing dishes of meat or eggs for them, and even putting the food in their mouths, with his own hands. Being taken severely ill as a result of all the hardships to which he was exposed, he was carried to the convent of Manila. Scarcely did he feel better, when he left his bed and began to work at the building of the church, turning his hand to this manual labor with the greatest skill. When he was elected prior, he had no assistance in the convent except one priest and one lay brother; but, few as they were, they performed all the offices of a community. As he had a sonorous voice and understood music well, he would sing the whole mass alone; then leave the choir to go to the pulpit and preach, and then return to the choir, though he had been hearing confessions all the morning. This he did without failing to make his regular daily prayer. Even when alone he used to say matins aloud, and on some feast-days would sing a great part of them. He was elected provincial from this office of prior; and in his provincialate he made many excellent ordinances for the ministry to the Indians, which are still observed and esteemed as if they had been ordained yesterday. During his time the province was greatly extended, the whole of the province of Nueva Segovia being admitted, and many new churches and missions being established in that of

Pangasinan. It was his desire also that the kingdom of Camboxa should be added to it; and in the glorious enterprise of extending the gospel to that kingdom he ended his life.]

Chapter LI

The coming of some religious to the province, and the transactions of the intermediate chapter

Though the procurator whom this province had in España [*i.e.*, Benavides] had become bishop of Nueva Segovia, he gave his main attention to the augmentation of the province, having seen with his own eyes the service done by the religious here to the Lord, and their service to their neighbors. So, though he had sent off two shipments [of missionaries], he prepared to send a third, whom he should accompany when he went to his bishopric. So greatly had the hearts of the religious of all the provinces in España been moved that sixty were found gathered and assembled together, having been designated by Father Juan Volante. They were all far advanced in religion and letters, which are the excellences that the order desires and strives for in its sons, that they may fulfil the command of its institutes, by laboring not only for their own salvation, but for that of others. It happened at this time that the English found the city of Cadiz unguarded and unprepared, and sacked it.[22] This aroused a great excitement in all the ports of Andalucia; and the announcement was made that in that year there would be no fleet for Nueva España. Though all these religious were at that time in or near Andalucia, they returned to their provinces of España and Aragon whence they had set out, with the exception of some few who waited to see the end of this matter. Although it was true that there was no fleet, a rumor spread that some ships were being fitted out for the voyage. Hereupon the bishop—who had come on foot from Madrid, but had been several days on the return journey because of the misfortune which had happened—took courage and went to the port a second time, reassembling the religious as well as he could. With these, and with some others who offered themselves, he made up a reasonable number. When they reached the port they found that the ships which were about to sail were only some galizabras, with troops who were going to guard the silver which came from Peru and Nueva España. It seemed that for a second time the purpose of the bishop and the religious had been frustrated and their labor wasted; but God sent them a patache or fragata, with only one deck, which was to carry the baggage and the ship's stores; but it had no accommodations for passengers, and was not designed to carry them, because of its small size. In spite of this, their willingness to suffer even greater evils for God made them despise the hardships which they might suffer by making so long a voyage on so uncomfortable a vessel, and they determined to sail in it. They spread the

86

only tarpaulin which there was, that they might have some defense from the sun and the rain. They could not place it high enough for them to stand under it, and whenever the sea was rough the waves dashed over it; but, as there was no better ship, the bishop and the religious had to take advantage of this one. The Lord felt such compassion for their discomfort as to give them fair weather, so that during the sixty days of their voyage it only rained twice: thus they were able to sleep on deck, and at least to enjoy the coolness of night if they could not avoid the heat of the day. During the voyage, they acted as if they were in a very well-organized convent. The bishop filled the place of reader; and upon what he read they held daily conferences, and very frequent sermons and spiritual discourses. On the great feasts they had, as it were, literary contests, composing verses in praise of God and of His saints. Being thus very well occupied, they felt the discomfort of the ship less; and as a result of the fair weather they were all cheerful. The bishop alone was silent —so much so that his religious became anxious, and felt obliged to ask him the reason. He answered: "I am afraid, fathers, that the Lord does not look upon us as His own, so much happiness does He grant us in so cramped a ship. Such fair weather, and not more than one religious sick; we are not what we ought to be, for the Lord has sent us no hardships. My coming was sufficient to prevent you from receiving that blessing." When they reached Mexico, he planned to buy a house where the religious who came to this province from that of España might be cared for. He wished to avoid scattering them among the towns, the evil results of which had already been learned by experience. He found someone to make a gift of a piece of land suited for the purpose, with the obligation of building a church upon it named for St. Just and Pastor. The writings were already made out; but afterward, because of difficulties which arose, the agreement went no further and had to be given up.

The voyage which they made from Acapulco to Manila was very prosperous. The religious having been divided between the two ships, those who embarked in the flagship, called "Rosario," were unable to get their ship-stores on board because of the great hurry of the commander, Don Fernando de Castro. But God provided for them from the ocean; for every day without exception they fished from that ship, and thus the food of the religious was supplied. This is something which never happened before or since that voyage to any ship. Being so extraordinary, it caused astonishment, and gave reason for reflecting upon and praising the divine Providence, which with so free a hand comes to the aid of those who depend upon it in their need. The intermediate provincial chapter was in session when the bishop and the religious reached Manila; and thus they were received joyfully and gladly, and the meeting was enriched by their presence. Religious were assigned to the conversion of villages which, though they had been admitted for their own comfort and for the sake of somewhat encouraging the holy desires with which they so eagerly begged for missionaries, could not hitherto obtain them, because of the lack of missionaries to send. In the convent of Manila a regular school of theology and arts was established. The chapter appointed as preacher-general father Fray Diego de Soria in place of father Fray Miguel de Venavides, who had hitherto held this place and had now become bishop. Because of the small number of religious and of convents up to this time, it had been customary that some should be designated from the distant provinces to come and vote in the provincial chapters, although they were not superiors. Now, however, as there was a sufficient number of convents and of superiors, vicariates were designated, the vicars of which were to be in the place of priors. These and no others were now to have a vote in the provincial chapter, in conformity with the constitutions and privileges of the provinces of the Indias. It was also ordained that the confirmation of the newly-elected provincial should belong to the eldest definitor, according to the privilege of Nueva España, which is likewise that of this province. At this chapter there were received: in Nueva Segovia the village of Dumon, the church of which at that time was called San Antonino; the villages of Gatarang and Talapa, with the church of Sancta Catalina; and the village on the estuary of Lobo, the church of which was San Raymundo. The title of vicariate was given to San Pablo of Pilitan in Yrraya.23 In this place it seemed that another climate had been found, different from that of the rest of this province, other fields and spacious meadows, another temperature, and another race of people. The country is very fertile, and abounds in game. It is very well watered, very pleasant and very healthful, although at first it did not seem so for the religious. The first vicar straightway died, and those whom he took as associates were afflicted with severe illness. For this reason and because of the distance from the other convents, it seemed to many that it would be best to abandon it; but the desire prevailed to go to the aid of those souls, though at the cost of health and life, since on no occasion could these be better offered. [The devil greatly resented their coming, and complained and uttered frightful howlings through the mouths of his priestesses or aniteras. The coming of the missionaries and the building of churches forced him to show himself in his true light to his deluded followers. He often appeared to them in dreams, bidding them resist and not become Christians. When they reminded him that he did not resist, he answered that he could not endure the sight of "those barbarians with white teeth." He called the religious "barbarians," because of their little knowledge of the language at the beginning; and he spoke of their white teeth because the Indians regard this as a blemish, and make their own teeth black.] In this mission of Pilitan the fathers found a madman with a child, whom they desired to baptize as other children generally were baptized; the father feared that they wished to take it away, and never left it. He ate with it, slept with it, and went to the bath with it. He did all he could to give it pleasure, but as a madman would. Hence, often, in bathing it, he plunged it down so far under the water that he drew it out half dead. The religious was in great anxiety, fearing some disaster, and finally baptized it. Soon after, the father caught a venomous serpent, ate it, and caused his child to share in the meal. They both died, but the child to live forever, thanks to the care of the missionary in baptizing it so as to give it grace and glory. [From the last village which at that time had been discovered, which was named Balisi, an Indian came with his family to that of Pilitan to spend a few days. He brought with him his little daughter, who was only six years old. She was so bright and charming that all who saw her loved her. She grew so fond of the church that, though she was a heathen, she wept bitterly when she was obliged by her father to return to their own village. Soon after, falling sick to death, she was baptized by a Spaniard named Alonso Vazquez, who happened to be there. The Lord showed His kindness in several other striking or marvelous instances of baptism. In one case a little girl was very ill and the father had given his permission for baptism, but the relatives and all the rest of the village resisted. Father Antonio de Soria went there and asked him that they would let him look at her to cure her. Spreading over her a moist cloth which he had brought purposely, he cured her soul, which was soon to taste the joys of eternal salvation.

To the province of Pangasinan there was added by this chapter a church and village, that of San Jacinto, which was formed here of people from different regions, on a very pleasant river named Magaldan,24 the inhabitants gathering to it from several villages and some from the mountains of the region. The Lord showed His kindness to one woman by striking her with blindness when she purposed to run away from the baptism which she had promised to receive, and by thus bringing her back to the salvation of her soul.

At this time the Lord took to himself father Fray Antonio de Soria, one of the first missionaries of Nueva Segovia. He did not enter upon the religious life, as generally happens, when he was in boyhood or youth, but in mature manhood. He had been left a widower; and though he had sons to care for, he provided for them in such a way that he was no longer needed to attend to them. Being thus left free for the service of God alone, he determined to become a religious, and was accepted in the convent of our order at Puebla de

Los Angeles, in Nueva España. Most persons of this age and condition, especially when they have lived in the luxuries which are common in Nueva España, find it difficult to accommodate themselves to the severities of religious life, both in little and in great things. Father Antonio was not such. He began with the greatest humility to study Latin, and became a master of the tongue. He entered upon greater studies, following them with such success that he was made lecturer in arts and a director of students. And as he was so superior not only in his learning, but also in virtue, he was also appointed master of novices, which is the same thing as being a teacher of the religious life. He joined the fathers who came to these islands in 1595, and became one of the first missionaries to the province of Nueva Segovia, there suffering all the want, discomfort, and hunger which have been described. The first results of his mission were at Camalaniugan, where he drove a demon out of a woman who was possessed. In the following provincial chapter, he was appointed superior of Nueva Segovia, to preach to and teach and guide the Spanish, who in these new conquests need the best of teachers. For his consolation they gave him the care of the villages of Camalaniugan and Buguey. Not satisfied with all this, he also took charge of the village of Daludu.] There lived in that city Captain Alonso de Carvajal, encomendero of Pilitan, which is distant from the city five or more days' journey. He collected his tribute from the natives, and desired to give them a minister, as he was obliged; but he was unable to find anyone who was willing to undertake the mission. He accordingly urged father Fray Antonio to go to visit these Indians and their country, called Yrraya, to see if he could attract them to the law of God and the belief in His holy gospel. The journey was long and hard, not only because it was up the river, but because there were enemies on the road; and, besides, there was no religious to leave in his place. Yet the desire of converting heathen was so strong in father Fray Antonio that he overcame all these obstacles and went to this new spiritual conquest, in which all of the rest of the religious soon aided him. He preached the holy gospel, and the Lord gave him such favor with that tribe, that he led them by his command like tame sheep. The credit which they gave to his teaching was such that long after, when Christianity was more settled in Yrraya, and there was some difficulty in rooting out some superstition which had remained among them, the old people said: "If father Fray Antonio had commanded us that, there would not now be a trace of it, or anyone to contradict him." To build the church in the village of Pilitan, he threw down the hut of an old woman, a noted anitera, by whom the devil gave answers to the questions which were asked him. As this was done in this hut, the devil regarded it as his own, and therefore greatly resented the overthrow of it. This he said on many occasions, and he even sometimes said that he had killed the father for tearing down his hut. But in this the Father of Lies should not be credited; for, as he often confessed, he was not able to appear before the religious; how much less, then, to kill them. The manner of living followed by this father among these Indians was exemplary, and such as to cause wonder among them. He suffered and endured many hardships, and hunger and want, that he might not inconvenience them. He was at once the master and the servant, at the house. In order that a boy who served him by preparing his food might not be offended at the work, the father went to the river and carried the water that he had to drink; he was the sacristan who cared for the church, the porter who closed and opened the doors of the house. He it was who attended to everything that was needed, that he might not trouble any persons by making them serve him. It was a journey of a day and a half from Pilitan to the village of Nalavangan. He went there and built a church, and baptized many; for the spirit of Fray Antonio was to undertake much, and he was never contented with that which would have seemed excessive to others. While he was engaged in these holy exercises, the time of the intermediate chapter arrived, and he was obliged to go to it to Manila. Here he was definitor, and gave an account of the good work which was being wrought by the Lord in the conversion of Yrraya. The chapter, feeling that the Lord had chosen him therefor, appointed him as first vicar of San Pablo at Pilitan. He returned in great contentment, because he was going where he would have more to do than in other places, much as there was to do everywhere, since all of these were new conversions, where the labor is great and the ease very little. When he was among his children he gave himself with such devotion to the labor of the ministry that within six months he was attacked by a mortal disease, which obliged him to return to the city to be cared for. Here, when he had received the holy sacrament, he gave up his soul to his Creator, to the great sorrow of all the religious, who were greatly afflicted to lose such a father and associate. He made some compositions in the language of the natives, which served as a guide to those who followed him; but the greatest guidance that he gave was that of his life spent and consumed in these so holy exercises.

Chapter LII

Fathers Fray Pedro de Soto, Fray Juan de San Pedro Martyr, and Fray Pedro de la Bastida who died at this time.

[Father Fray Pedro de Soto was a native of Burgos, and assumed the habit in the convent of San Andres at Medina del Campo, where he professed, and whence he went to study in the distinguished convent of San Pablo at Valladolid. Here he showed signs of his great ability and the subtlety of his mind, soaring above his fellow-students as does a royal eagle above all other birds of less flight. In him the fathers hoped that they were to have a third Soto, in addition to the other two famous ones whom that province has had. He exhibited as much virtue as learning. When the religious for this province began to be gathered, his superiors were planning that he should become a professor. The devotion and the severity of the discipline, and the opportunity to save souls, attracted father Fray Pedro; he was also influenced by the example of his two masters, Fray Miguel de Venavides and Fray Antonio Arcediano, who had left their chairs of theology to enter the new province, as had also two other fathers, lecturers in arts at the same convent. The father master Fray Hernando del Castillo, who was then prior, strove by all means to prevent him from going; but the calling and inspiration of God prevailed in the heart of father Fray Pedro. He arrived at Manila July 23, and on the day of our father St. Dominic, less than a fortnight later, they asked him to hold some public discussions of theology in the main church. Father Fray Pedro avoided display of his knowledge and ability; but, on occasions when necessity required him to speak, he made evident the great superiority of his mind and his great learning. In the first distribution of the religious, he was assigned to Pangasinan. The people of this region still lived in their ancient villages and rancherias in the hills and mountains, without civilization, order, or system, any more than if they had never known Spaniards. Father Fray Pedro lived among these tribes for three years, suffering the hardships and perils which have been already described. He was constantly in danger of death, being particularly hateful to the hostile natives because he was the first one who learned the language of the Indians. When some of them began to accept the faith, he offered money for information as to those who continued to sacrifice to the devil. Keeping secret the source of his information, he immediately went] in haste to the place, sometimes alone, and caught the sacrificers in the very act. Without waiting an instant, he upset everything, and broke the dishes and bowls and other vessels which they used in their rites; poured out their wine; burned the robes in which the aniteras or priestesses dress themselves on such occasions, and the curtains with which they covered up everything else; threw down the hut, and completely destroyed it. In this way he made them understand how little all those things availed, and how vain were the threats which the devil uttered against those who would not venerate him; and, in brief, that this was all falsehood and deceit. Many were thus aroused and undeceived; while others, and not a few, were angry, so that it was a wonder that he was not slain. [The rest of the fathers followed his plan; but father Fray Pedro led them all, following the track of this chase, in which his scent was so keen that nothing could escape him. At his death, father Fray Pedro was able to say that he was sure of the two aureoles of virgin and of doctor, and that he had almost succeeded in gaining that of martyr. The village of Magaldan was the most obstinate of all these villages in their errors. They had striven to kill a father of the Order of St. Francis, insomuch that the dagger was already lifted above him for that purpose, and he had fled. They had refused to admit the fathers of the Order of St. Augustine, and they would not listen to a secular priest who was assigned to them, although the alcalde-mayor fined and punished them. It was these Indians whom father Fray Pedro de Soto came to conquer with patience and Christian charity. The Indians said that he never employed a word of their language wrong. He was engaged for a whole year in translating the gospel into this language, and translated some lives of saints and instances of virtue —which though they were composed in the very beginning, are still esteemed and are greatly prized, because of the propriety of the words and the elevated style with which he treated these matters. He was devoted to the study of theology and sacred letters, and was continual in both mental and vocal prayer, to which he added fasting. Being taken to Manila to be treated for the fever from which he suffered, he died there.

In spite of the failure of the two previous expeditions to Camboja, the governor, Don Francisco Tello, judged it desirable to send another ship with troops, and asked the order to send some of their friars with it. The father provincial directed that father Fray Juan de S. Pedro Martyr (or Maldonado) and father Fray Pedro Jesus (or de la Bastida) should go. Father Fray Juan was then commissary of the Holy Office. He was a native of Alcala de Guadiana,25 and belonged to a rich and honorable family. He studied canon law at Salamanca, and assumed the habit in the illustrious convent of San Pablo at Valladolid. The influence of Father Juan Chrisostomo attracted him to the new province to be established in the Philippinas Islands. When he was about to set forth, a certain Doctor Bobadilla, a canon in the church in Valladolid, took him to one side and assured him that he was to die a martyr;

and this prophecy was corroborated by another devoted monk. It was on this account that he changed his name of Maldonado to that of S. Pedro Martyr. He spent his first year in the Philipinas in Manila; and in his second year was sent as vicar to a village in Pangasinan, which was at that time the most difficult in the province. From that place he was transferred to the vicariate of Bataan, the language of which he learned very well. When Father Juan Cobo went as ambassador to Japon, father Fray Juan was assigned to the mission to the Chinese, being thus required to learn a third language in addition to the two which he already knew. He learned more words of the Chinese language than any other member of the order, though he was not successful with the pronunciation. He assisted the Chinese so much that they named him as their protector; and he was, as it were, the advocate of their causes, so that they became very much attached to him, and listened with good-will to his preaching and his corrections. During the absence of the father provincial in Camboja, the province could find no one more suitable to govern it in his place, and accordingly father Fray Juan was nominated as vicar-general. In the following provincial chapter he was appointed lecturer in theology, for there was nothing which the province did not find him competent to do. He made no objection to carrying out any orders that were given him, although they dragged him about hither and thither, causing him to learn so many languages and immediately to drop them again. This is a great evidence of his obedience and subjection to his superior. His reputation outside of the order was very great.] The tribunal of the Holy Office of Mexico appointed him commissary-general of the Philippinas, which office he filled with the prudence and strength of mind which the Lord has given in these regions to the sons of the first inquisitor-general, our father St. Dominic. Don Luis Perez das Mariñas, a wise and holy knight, refused to accept the governorship of these islands until Fray Juan persuaded him to do so, stood security for him, and undertook the duty of confessing him and of aiding him with his good advice, that he might the better fulfil the office. This he did in spite of the fact that this was certain to be, as it was, to his own damage; for suitors who did not receive what they desired immediately threw the blame on Father Juan, whom they well knew that the governor consulted as to the appointments which he made. Father Fray Juan knew all this well, but accepted it very readily, in order that he might undertake the direction of so upright a man as Don Luis. In spite of the fact that the esteem which was felt for Father Juan within and without the order was very great, the counterweight of humility and the consciousness of his own inferiority which he had was much greater. He regarded himself as the most useless in all the province, and treated himself as such. Hence, when he was named for vicar-general of the province,

he managed that this title and office should be given to father Fray Juan de
Sancto Thomas. [In the same way, when he was nominated prior of the
convent of Manila at the time when father Fray Diego de Soria went as
procurator to España, he succeeded in bringing about the election of another
religious. He likewise strove to resign the office of commissary in favor of
father Fray Bernardo de Sancta Cathalina, or Navarro. Such was the character
of father Fray Juan de San Pedro Martyr, whom the province was willing to
spare for the mission to Camboja. They would have spared an even more
perfect religious if they could, well knowing that he who had to preach the
gospel in a heathen kingdom like this should be such as father Fray Juan was,
or even greater in all things. The companion of father Fray Juan, father Fray
Pedro de Jesus or de la Bastida, a religious of great virtue, had come to the
islands in the previous year, 1591, with the rest who were brought from
España by father Fray Francisco de Morales. He had displayed high qualities
in the mission to Bataan, to which he had been assigned. He had come from
the very devout province of Aragon, of which he was a son. When they
reached the great river of Camboja, father Fray Juan endeavored to carry out
his mission, both for the conversion of those tribes and as an ambassador of
the king our lord. He was contemptuously treated by the king,26 the son of
that king who had sent to ask for religious. The present king was wholly in
the hands of Mahometan Malays, who persuaded him that the embassy
involved some evil to him. When father Fray Juan asked his permission to
return to the ship which they had left in the port, the king refused to grant it,
and thus showed that he was plotting treachery. Father Fray Juan saw no
opportunity for preaching the gospel, as the country was disturbed and in
arms; and as the two captains, Diego Velloso and Blas Ruiz de Fernan
Goncalez, were in a difficult situation because their comrades were so few,
and the Malays, their enemies, were in such favor. The captain of the ship
[i.e., Mendoza] attempted to secure peace between these factions, but did not
disembark from his vessel. The same thing was done by the captain of a
fragata that had come from Sian. The Malays, seeing that they had the
advantage because their vessel was larger and stronger than ours, made an
attack and shot contrivances of fire and powder to burn the Spaniards and the
Japanese. The ship caught fire, and those on board had to leap into the water
to escape. Father Fray Pedro de Jesus was unable to swim, and took refuge
from the fire on the poop. Here the Moros came out in small boats and thrust
lances at him. He fell into the water and died of his wounds, or was drowned
by the hands of the Moros. This vessel had done no harm to the Moros, and
had not even tried to aid the Spanish captains in the kingdom. The only reason
for attacking it was the desire of the Moros to prevent the preaching of the

gospel; and hence father Fray Pedro died a glorious martyr. Father Fray Juan succeeded in reaching the fragata commanded by Juan de Mendoça. In it father Fray Juan made his escape to Sian, being wounded in the throat by a shot which had passed obliquely through it; and thus half of the prophecy had been fulfilled that he and his comrade were to die the death of martyrs. Father Fray Juan went to Sian that he might be near to the kingdom of Camboja. The king of that country was a cruel and barbarous tyrant; he took delight in causing men to be thrown to wild elephants, who tore them to pieces with their trunks. He caused others to be fried with a very small quantity of oil, and their flesh to be torn off from them with pincers while they were thus tortured, and to be thrust into their mouths, that by force of the pain which they suffered they might bite and eat their own flesh. When there were no criminals, he used to perpetrate these cruelties solely for his own recreation; and that not to one, or a few, but to a thousand at a time. Only a few days before, he had had four or five Portuguese fried alive for some trifling offense, for which they had already paid a fine to him. There were here at this time a Portuguese religious, Fray Jorje de la Mota,[27] and several other Portuguese who were now trying to escape from the country. The force of the tides is so great that, when the tide is coming in, it is impossible to make head against it; and as they were fifty leguas from the sea, it was easy to follow and catch them. Overjoyed with the possibility of escape offered by the coming of Father Juan, they prayed him for the love of God to rescue them in his boat without the knowledge of the king. The Spaniards planned to do so; but, because of the too great haste and anxiety of the Portuguese, the vessel was followed and found before it had made its escape into the sea. The king was mad with rage, and sent three separate expeditions after it. They surrounded the boat and fired at it with small cannon, arquebuses, arrows, and lances. There were about twenty persons, Castilians and Portuguese, on the ship, and they had about a dozen muskets and a few arquebuses to protect themselves with. So long as the tide was going out, they managed to defend themselves fairly well, because they could manage to engage a part of the enemy only at one time. When the tide came in they were obliged to anchor, and they were like a target for the Sianese. After three days of this torture, they managed to get to sea. The pilot had been slain by a shot; and the captain, Juan de Mendoca, and father Fray Jorje de la Mota were so badly wounded that they afterward died. The arm of father Fray Juan de San Pedro Martir was broken by a shot from a small culverin. As they had lost all their drinking-water in the combat, the sufferings of father Fray Juan were very great. He saw that his hour was come, and confessed to father Fray Jorje. He wrote to the fathers in this province an account of the fortunes of this voyage; and expressed his joy in dying on an expedition carried out by the command of his superior for the purpose of preaching the gospel, in which he had saved those poor Portuguese from dreadful danger to both their lives and their souls.] Almost at the end of the letter which he sent he wrote: "What we have in this province is good, and God is greatly served in the province. Let us strive to keep what we have, by observing those things which we have established; for I am sure that God will show us a thousand favors. The arms of Saul do not fit all men; nor is preaching in these regions suitable to any but a very holy man." [They buried him on land near the port of Cochinchina, on an island called Pulocatovan, at the root of a tree—not daring to set up a cross, for fear of the derision of those heathen. He had set out upon this voyage certain to meet his death in it; and at the beginning of the expedition he had shown the perfection of his obedience in several ways.]

Chapter LIII

The election as provincial of father Fray Juan de Sancto Thomas, and the death of father Fray Damian Valaguer.

[On the second of June, 1600, the electors assembled in the convent of Manila to elect a successor to father Fray Bernardo de Sancta Cathalina. The example of father Fray Bernardo was so grand that it was difficult for his successor to reach the same pitch of excellence. Although all felt that father Fray Juan de Sancto Thomas, or Ormaca, was fitted for the position by character and abilities, there was some doubt whether his ill-health would permit him to fill the office as it ought to be filled. He was constantly under the necessity of receiving dispensations from the severity of the rules; and though this did no harm in a private friar, it was most unfortunate in a superior. It was also feared that he would be physically unable to perform the duties of the situation. One of the best physicians of the city was called in, without the knowledge of father Fray Juan, to express his opinion as to the ability of father Fray Juan to fulfil the duties of the office. His judgment was favorable, and father Fray Juan was elected. The election was a most fortunate one, for father Fray Juan was able, learned, and holy; and his nature was so gentle that the vicar-general, Fray Juan de Castro, who had a gift from heaven of special insight into character, chose him as his usual associate, and appointed him to the first position as superior in a mission to Indians. He filled the office well, and not only lived out the four years of his provincialship, but has seen ten other elections of provincials since his own; and he is still alive while this is being written, in the year 1637. Since he is still living, let us content ourselves with what has been said—leaving the rest till the time when, after the end of his life, it may be discussed with greater freedom. During his term, the Lord opened the gates for the entrance of the order to Japan, as will be narrated later; this was a great reward for the hardships suffered by the religious of this province, and by him in particular, from the perils and miseries of travel by land and by sea. Many new convents were admitted at this chapter, both in Pangasinan and Nueva Segovia; for the duties of the ministry in these regions were constantly increasing, and the religious kept constantly reaching out to new places. Many excellent ordinances were passed for the exercise of the ministry to the Indians, and also for the better maintenance of the rules affecting us—especially in the matter of showing ourselves disinterested, and careful not to annoy the Indians.

In the province of Nueva Segovia the religious labored hard in the search throughout mountains and valleys, and other secret places, for the huts where the devil had been adored, to which those people used to make pilgrimages in search of health or other favors, giving offerings of bits of gold, or of stones regarded by them as precious. The natives dared not take anything from those places, or cut a reed or a tree from the natural growth of the earth in them, for fear of death, with which the devil had threatened them. In the villages on the coast many such little huts were found, with many little figures and idols in them. The religious burnt and broke the boxes with the offerings; took the gold and the stones, and all the other offerings; and burnt and ground to dust everything, and cast it into the sea, that it might not remain to be a stumbling-block to the Indians. When the heathen saw that the threats of the devil were not being carried out, their eyes were opened and they were very eager to be baptized. Great aid was received from an epidemic of smallpox which attacked a whole region. In this way the Lord took to himself many souls, especially of children; for there were many newly baptized in the province of Pangasinan and in that of Nueva Segovia.] Many of those who seemed to be near their end recovered after they received the water of baptism. All, therefore, came to be baptized, and the Lord, by means of those who recovered, gave authority to the baptism; while of the vast number who died baptized He peopled heaven with new angels. This brought great comfort to the missionaries, who, although worn out and greatly fatigued by going from house to house baptizing and confessing, and giving the sacraments to sick persons, saw their labors successful and rewarded by the sending to heaven of so many souls, and also by the strengthening of their hope that they should go to accompany those souls in glory; for it is not possible that these should not be grateful, and pray and strive to obtain salvation for those who labored, with such zeal, to give it to them by the means of baptism, without which it cannot be obtained.

[Soon after the provincial chapter, one of the definitors, father Fray Damian Balaguer, died. He had lived but a short time in the province, but had gained great reputation in it; and his early death was much mourned. He was a native of the kingdom of Valencia, and had two brothers in the same order—one, the present Fray Pedro Martyr de Balaguer; and the other master Fray Andres Balaguer, at one time bishop of Albarracin and afterward of Origuela. Father Fray Damian took the habit in the convent of the Preachers in Valencia, which has been happy in giving saints to the church. During all his novitiate, the master of the novices never had occasion to discipline him, even for the merest trifle—although by the advice of another father he assigned him some discipline, without any fault on the part of Fray Damian, but not without a cause; for it is necessary for the novices to be initiated in these punishments of the order, that they may not afterward be new and strange to them. He was constant in prayer and fasting, given to speaking of the things of God, and to mortification. For many years he was accustomed to repeat the whole of the Psalter of David daily, in imitation of St. Vincent of Ferrara. He studied at Origuela, becoming a lecturer in arts in the same college, and afterward in theology—having a singular grace given him to declare with clearness the gravest and most profound difficulties of this holy science. He was an excellent and a moving preacher, having the power to change the hearts of many of his hearers, who selected him as their spiritual guide. Whenever he left the convent, which he did only on important occasions, he was followed by a troop of his disciples, who gathered not only to honor him, but to profit by what they heard him say. He showed all his life the greatest humility, and from day to day did not change, except by the augmentation and advance of his virtue. Being eager for the conversion of souls, he went to Mexico with master Fray Alonso Bayllo, who was going out to Mexico with authority to divide the province of Vaxac from that of Santiago.[28] For the space of two years he directed the schools in the city of Vaxac; but, as that was not the end which he had intended, he was dissatisfied. When he heard that many ministers of the holy gospel were needed in the Philippinas, he took advantage of the arrival in Mexico of father Fray Francisco de Morales to ask that he would take him to the islands with the rest of the company whom he was bringing over. Arriving in 1598, he was assigned to Nueva Segovia, where in a short time he learned enough of the language to be able to hear confessions. Father Fray Damian was first vicar and superior of the mission of Abulug. As such, he was a definitor in the provincial chapter, and returned to Nueva Segovia as vicar of the village of Pata. He died greatly mourned.

At this time there died in the same province of Nueva Segovia brother Fray Domingo de San Blas, a lay religious of much virtue and known sanctity, a son of the convent of San Pablo at Sevilla, who came to these islands in the year 1594. He was of much use to the Indians, of whose language he learned enough to be understood by them and to teach them to pray, to attract the Christians to the church, and to teach the heathen the knowledge of the doctrine of Christianity. He was fervent in prayer, being often moved to sighs and tears during his devotions. He strove to hide them from his companion, father Fray Ambrosio de la Madre de Dios, but was unable to do so. Father Fray Ambrosio said to him that, as they two lived alone and like brothers, there was no reason why one should try to conceal anything from the other. With this permission from his superior he broke out in sobs, and his heart melted away in tears, directed mainly to the conversion of these heathen and to the perfecting in Christianity of the already baptized. Two extraordinary things happened in this village of Pata while this brother lived there: One was the receiving of a fish on the day of St. Dominic, under such circumstances that there could be no doubt that the Lord had sent it to enable them properly to celebrate the feast of the holy founder of this order. The second event was the marvelous recovery or restoration to life, at the intercession of St. Dominic, of an Indian who had been given over for dead. It was the very man who had given them the fish. Father Fray Domingo died from exposure to the sun. He was sent back to the convent of Manila for care, and there grew worse; and, after having very devoutly received the holy sacraments, exchanged this wretched life for the eternal one.]

Chapter LIV

The intermediate chapter; an extraordinary event which took place in it, and the coming of religious to the province.

In the year of our Lord 1602, the voting fathers assembled in their intermediate provincial chapter, at which was accepted the house of San Juan del Monte, which is situated a legua from the city of Manila in a solitary place, a healthful and pleasant situation. There were two motives and ends with which this house was built. The first was the consideration that some aged fathers, after their many labors and years passed in the ministry, desired, having performed the duties of Martha, to give themselves up wholly to those of Mary by leading the life of contemplation. For this purpose the locality is very well suited, for there is nothing in it to disturb the calm of prayer and contemplation. But it did not serve much for this end, because it was soon found by experience that these servants of God, the aged ministers, were of much more usefulness in the ministries, since their example and authority were very efficacious for the spiritual increase of faith and devotion in the Indians. Teaching and doctrine were received much better from such venerable ministers, who were well known, loved, and regarded. It was also found that the example of these venerable fathers was of great use to those who had newly entered upon the ministry, since they could not fail to venerate and follow the acts and the teaching which they beheld in these ancient and venerable ministers. Even though there are some who on account of their great age and infirmity can not continue in the service, they are of more use in the convent of the city, where their infirmities may be better cared for, and where their good example and venerable age are more valuable. The second motive and object is one which is obviously of great advantage. It is found that in the city convalescence takes place slowly, or not at all; therefore those who are being treated for any sickness leave the city for their convalescence, by the advice of the physicians. If the order did not have this convent outside of the city, in a situation which is healthful and where the air is good—which is what convalescents most require—the religious would be obliged to ask for permission to go for their convalescence to the farms or fruit-gardens of laymen, which are never so appropriate as the convent. Now that they have this convent, no permission is granted to go for convalescence to any other place, which is to the great advantage of the province. Also when a religious is worn out and afflicted by the heats of the city, which are very great, he is permitted to go and obtain some refreshment and ease at San Juan del Monte, and soon returns to his labors in the city with new energy; and this, too, is of great value. While the fathers were assembled at this chapter an event occurred which caused special awe in the hearts of the religious, and created greater respect for the sacred constitutions which we promise to observe. Even when the obligation does not involve a matter of sin, even venial sin, still the Lord desires us to keep them with the greatest accuracy—not only in matters of importance, but even in the less significant ones. It was a very extraordinary incident, and one which seems to have happened like the blindness of the man who was born blind, as the gospel tells us, "not because of his own sins nor those of his fathers, but for the glory of God." Although there was a fault, it was such a fault as the Lord is accustomed to pass over (and even greater ones) in us. Therefore it was, as I said, that it seemed to be for the greater glory of God and of St. Cecilia, who, as we shall see, had a share in the remedy. There was a religious who came from the province of Andalucia, in which he had lived in a very devout convent. It happened one evening that this religious ate between meals a few capers without the permission and blessing of the superior. This is something which in the eyes of men did not appear a special fault; but it was so in the sight of God, who punished this excess. From that evening the religious suffered from a pain, which seemed to him to be in his heart. Although from evening to evening it sometimes was very severe, still it was not of such a nature that on account of it they hesitated to ordain him, or, after he was ordained, prohibited him from the use of the orders which he had received. He came into these regions, and went as minister to the Indians in Pangasinan. In the course of time his sufferings increased, and afflicted him to such an extent that he was prohibited from saying mass, as it was feared that the malady would attack him during the celebration. During this time when he did not celebrate mass, his malady continually increased and afflicted him more than before, so that the religious suffered great torture; and they gave him great care, and as much comfort as was consistent with our poverty. In spite of this he grew worse and worse, and suffered greater afflictions and torments. It attacked him one day, and they gave him some relics. Thereupon he began to be so furious that he lifted up and carried along the religious who came to hold him. It seemed to them that it was some evil spirit which received the holy thing so ill. The prior at that time, who was father Fray Francisco de Morales, afterward a holy martyr in Japon, asked permission of the father provincial to exorcise him. While he was saying the litany, the grimaces and gestures made by the afflicted man were many; but when the prior reached the glorious name of the martyr St. Cecilia, his fury became so great that with the torment of it he fell to the ground, deprived of strength as if in a faint. Now it happened that this religious was very devoted to this most illustrious saint, and had composed a special office which he used to recite out of devotion to her. He had even abandoned his own proper surname, and was called and called himself "de Sancta Cecilia." Although he did not perceive it himself, this was of great aid to him against the devil who tormented him; therefore it was that the evil spirit resented it so much when the religious invoked her. When the religious saw this, they called upon her many times, and all those present made a vow to fast for a day on bread and water, from reverence for this saint. The provincial vowed to celebrate a feast in her honor, and the church and an altar were prepared for saying a mass to her with great solemnity. All the religious were with the afflicted friar in the choir, singing the mass to the saint. At the first *Kyrie*, he began to be changed; and, when the priest said the first prayer, the noise which he made in the choir was so great that he disturbed the ministers who were at the altar. While they were singing in the creed the words *Ex Maria Virgine, et homo factus est* [of the Virgin Mary and was made man] the noise became very much greater; and at the lifting up of the Host his sobs and groans and cries were so loud that, to avoid exciting the people in the church, they kept sounding clarions to the end of the mass. They took him from the choir to the oratory. Here in the presence of all the religious gathered together, he performed an act of humility, saying that his faults had brought him to this wretched state, and begging them to pray to God to pardon him; and that, if it was best for him to suffer all the pains of hell, he was ready to receive them. He asked permission of the provincial to kiss the feet of those who were present. The provincial comforted him, and they went on with the exorcism, during which the devil became calmer. The friar answered all the questions which were put to him, and, when they gave him the holy cross, he kissed it with reverence. These were evidences of his recovery. The friar became so weary that it was necessary for him to repose. When he lay down to sleep it seemed to him, whether in dreams or not he could not tell, that the devil complained of being suffocated, that a religious was repeating exorcisms to him, and that the glorious St. Cecilia came to his assistance. On the following day the religious fasted, as they had promised, on bread and water, and repeated the exorcisms. During them it became evident that the evil guest had departed, and that he must be one of those of whom the Lord said that they are not to be cast out except by fasting and prayer. There was no more necessity of cure for that malady. As a result, the religious became very much devoted to this glorious saint, who has favored the order on many other occasions; and they became very fearful of violating the constitutions, when they saw that the Lord was zealous for them in such a manner. Among the babblings which the Father of Lies muttered through the mouth of the afflicted friar, it was noticed that when he was directed to read the epistle in the mass of the cross, where the apostle says, *Christus factus est pro nobis obediens usque ad mortem*,[29] he read *pro vobis* [*i.e.*, "for your sake"], excluding the devils from the benefit of the holy Passion. When one of those present said that Christ our Lord had not died for devils, the proud one answered immediately: "Then we have the less to be thankful for." When he reached the words of the apostle, that "at the name of Jesus every knee shall bow, of those who are in heaven, on earth, and in the hells," he refused to utter this last word, which affects the devils; and, when they forced him to utter it, he answered that it was enough to say that every tongue should confess that He was seated at the right hand of the Father. All this was to continue further the pride with which he was always tormented.

At the same time, at the end of April, those religious reached Manila whom father Fray Diego de Soria had collected in España during the previous year. He assembled them at the port, where he delivered them to father Fray Thomas Hernandez,[30] father Fray Diego remaining in España to collect and conduct another company, in which he succeeded. The body of friars which arrived at this time was one of the best which had come to this province.[31] It contained fourteen members from the colleges of the provinces of España, Aragon and Romana. These were all very superior in ability and advanced in knowledge, and still more so in religion and virtue. The provinces of España were not a little grieved to lose them. There, however, there was a very easy remedy because of the many who were left behind; while for this province these friars were of the greatest value, and have given it dignity and support in various ways, in the offices that belong to it. It appeared from the beginning that the Lord gave them His benediction, and such a spirit of constancy and firmness that, although they had the most urgent reasons for remaining behind, not one of those who were designated failed to come. This is something which probably never happened with any other shipload. There also came many besides [the fourteen above mentioned], taking the chance as to their being desired, which was an even greater marvel. This was in the year sixty-one, when Sevilla was afflicted with the plague. It was here that the religious were to assemble, and to wait for the sailing of the fleet. On the road, they met many who asked them where they were going. When they answered, "To Sevilla," those that heard them were amazed and answered: "You see, fathers, that we, who are inhabitants of Sevilla, have abandoned our houses and our fortunes almost to destruction, fleeing from the plague there. Are your Reverences going to place yourselves in the midst of it?" But nothing sufficed to prevent a single one of them from continuing his journey, for they regarded dying in such an enterprise as good fortune, and death on such a journey as happy. At the court father Fray Thomas Hernandez and three companions who were with him found the father provincial of España, who at that time was the father master Fray Andres de Caso, an intimate friend of him who at that time was president of the Indias. He said to them, "Where are you going? There is no fleet, for the president of the Indias has told me so." In spite of all this, the religious were all moved by a higher impulse; and although it was true that, on account of the plague, it had been ordered that there should be no fleet, one was afterward permitted to sail. The religious reached Sevilla after much hardship; because in many places they were unwilling to admit them to the towns, or to private houses, or even to our own convents, so great was the fear of the plague. They were even unwilling to be satisfied with the evidence that the religious brought with them that they were healthy. When they reached Sevilla they saw the plague-stricken taken almost dead to the hospitals and even this did not frighten them. They were in the Guerta del Corco [*i.e.*, "garden of the deer"]; and there one of them was taken with the plague, and was carried suddenly off in two more days. Even then, not one of them even thought of giving up the voyage, although they saw the plague and death within the house where they were dwelling. The Lord favored them so that no one else took the plague. When they saw the danger more clearly, they gave greater thanks to Him who had not only rescued them from it, but had taken from them the fear which they naturally had of it—especially as they had almost all come on foot, asking alms, all the way from the innermost parts of Castilla la Vieja; and though they were persons who were not inured to that sort of hardship, and therefore were the more likely to fall sick, especially in a season of plague. [The religious who died was Fray Juan de Solis, a son of the licentiate Jofre de Solis. He was a man of jovial disposition and fond of company, but corrected his weakness when he proposed to go to the Philippinas. His relatives and several of his fellow-friars tried to dissuade him, but he insisted upon going. In Sevilla, as there was no lay religious with them, he undertook the duty of cooking for the rest of the company; and it may be that the great heat and consequent exhaustion were the reasons for his being taken by the plague.] When the religious reached Sevilla, they were received with much joy and charity by father Fray Diego de Soria. Everything they had—their books, their clothes, their money, and everything, down to their very handkerchiefs—all became common property; if they had any debts unpaid, the community took charge of these, and the religious were left without any care, and even without the use of anything for themselves, except the habit which they wore. From that day they even said all their masses for the community, which provided for every one what he had need of, while no one possessed anything (not even by permission) except books. Everything else was in common for all of them; and hence they did not have to think of carrying anything with them for the voyage, except the very small outfit provided for the whole company. [On the voyage they strove to live as much as possible as if they were in a very strict convent. They encountered a frightful storm, so great that there was not a single vessel which did not lose at least one mast; and one of the largest and best of the vessels foundered, although without loss of life. Even the pilots confessed, which they avoid as much as possible for fear of disheartening the crew. The ship on which the religious were was very old, and was being sent on its last voyage, to be broken up and sold as old lumber in the port. In response to a vow of the religious, the Virgin of the Rosary showed them grace, and brought the storm to an end. In Mexico some were sick, but none died; and not one remained behind. This greatly astonished the fathers of the province of Mexico, because in every shipload some give up the distant mission—being wearied by the voyage which they have taken, fearful of the dangers to come, and pleased with the delightful climate of Mexico. This shipload was the first which occupied the hospice of St. Hyacinth, where they lived as if in a convent, following all the rules of the province. While in the hospice, they studied and had frequent theological conferences. They very rarely visited the city. On the journey from Mexico to Acapulco, which is very long and over a very bad road, many of them went on foot. As this was not customary at that time, it greatly edified those who saw them. There was only one ship in from the Philippines; and this and more were needed by the governor, Don Pedro de Acuña, for the accommodation of himself and his troops. But while the religious were praying and offering vows to the Virgin for her aid, they were rejoiced by the news that one ship had come in from the Philippines and two from Peru, which were all taken to make up the fleet. On the voyage they did much for the consciences of those who were in their ship, dividing among themselves all the people, from the admiral and his companions down to the lowest convict or ship-boy. They taught these men and heard their confessions, opening the way of peace and liberty to many a captive and unhappy soul. At the port of Acapulco died father Fray Vicente de Liaño, a religious of much devotion and patience under suffering, for he was a confirmed invalid. When they reached Manila they were immediately distributed by the provincial council, which was then sitting. The number of religious was the largest that has entered the province since its establishment. All of the houses in the province were filled, and enough were left to comply with the wishes of the king of Satzuma, who had sent to ask for religious.]

Chapter LV

The causes of the entry of our religious into Japon, and the circumstances under which they entered Satzuma.

[Christianity in the kingdoms of Japon took its origin from the Society of Jesus, the first preacher and apostle therein being St. Francis Xavier. The fathers of this Society had entered Japon according to the rule of the gospel, without weapons or soldiers, but with peace and mercy and in the strength of holy living. Christianity flourished so that the first missionaries were obliged to call in aid; and they sent for assistance to the Philippinas, where at that time there were discalced Franciscans and Augustinians, besides members of the Society. Father Gaspar Coello, vice-provincial of the fathers in Japon, wrote to the governor, Dr. Santiago de Vera, to the bishop, Don Fray Domingo de Salacar, and to the guardian of St. Francis, and the rector of the Society in Manila, urging the establishment of trade between the Philippinas and Japon. The bishop made a number of formal inquiries, which were verified before a notary. One is dated at Nangasaqui, September 11, 1584; and the other from the kingdom of Fixen, January 24, 1585. The witnesses when asked especially if it would be an advantage to have religious of various orders, and especially religious under the vow of poverty, replied unanimously that such would be very well received. They called to witness the case of the holy Fray Juan Pobre, a discalced friar who disembarked in Japon on his way to China, and whom the Japanese, both heathen and Christian, adored. It must be admitted that soon afterward the fathers of the Society in Japon changed their opinion, in spite of the fact that the extension of Christianity in Japon required more laborers in the field and that the empire was large enough for all the religious orders. God was pleased to put it into the heart of many of the kings, or *tonos*, of that realm to send to Manila to ask for religious of all the orders. The particular reason for the calling of our religious was as follows: In 1601 a number of Japanese vessels, with many Christians on them, touched at Manila. A number of these Christians became very fond of our convent, and often visited it. One of them, by name Juan Sandaya, brought the captain of his ship to the prior, Fray Francisco de Morales; and they discussed the possibility of sending religious of the Order of St. Dominic to Satzuma, whence the captain came. In the following year a letter was brought from the king of Satzuma, Tintionguen, inviting them to come to his kingdom. The letter was dated on the twenty-second day of the ninth month in the sixth year of Keycho.[32] In response to it religious were sent. Father Fray Francisco de Morales went as vicar and superior, accompanied by the fathers Fray Thomas Hernandez, Fray Alonso de Mena, and Fray Thomas del Spiritu Santo, or Zumarraga, and brother Fray Juan de la Abadia, a lay brother.[33] They set sail on the day of the most holy Trinity. They carried but little in the way of temporal things, expecting to live upon the alms which they should receive in Japon. They rested the first night in a heathen temple in the island of Coxiqui.[34] The priest of the idols removed the images, and left the temple unoccupied, and the fathers consecrated it and set up in it an altar. The Japanese were very curious about the new missionaries, and were greatly pleased with them. They were welcomed in a few days by some Japanese gentlemen, who made them a very ceremonious greeting and welcomed them in the name of their king. They were escorted to the court of the tono, where they were honorably received. The black and white colors of the habit pleased the Japanese, for these are customary in that country; while the eating of fish as an ordinary article of food is very common in Japon. They also greatly admired the devotion of the fathers to study, for they esteem their *boncos* [or "bonzes"] in proportion as they are learned; but what above all they admired was the contempt of these fathers for comforts and worldly advantages. The favor with which the religious were received enraged the priests of the idols, who insisted that the Japanese princes who had become Christians had been unfortunate. They mentioned the instance of Don Augustin Tzunotami,[35] a great and valiant lord who had been destroyed by the emperor; also that of Don Francisco, the king of Bungo,[36] who had been conquered and lost his life; while this kingdom of Satzuma had been protected by its devotion to its gods, and especially to Faquiman, who is their god of war. It was no wonder that two Christian princes should have been overwhelmed when thousands of heathen had suffered the same overthrow, but the idol priests passed that over. The emperor intervened, and enacted a decree that no king or tono, and not even any gentleman of distinction, should become a Christian. The king of Satzuma, however, would not banish the religious, but gave them permission to build a church and a house. Not infrequently, however, they were forgotten, and did not receive their customary supply of rice. The fathers converted the family of the man in whose house they lived, and made a chapel in the oratory of the house. The queen was desirous of seeing the image of the Virgin which was set up in the chapel; and it was carried to the palace, and there worshiped with the greatest respect by the chief personages of the court. The king, being unable to make up his mind how to treat the religious because of the opposition of the emperor, permitted them, at their request, to return to the island of Quoxiqui, where they had landed, and where they had something of an establishment.

Here they suffered from the rigors of the Japanese winter in a wretched hut. They had insufficient food, and received very small alms. In case of illness, it was impossible to give the sick man any treatment, or even proper food. The Lord, however, preserved them; and the tono at last, pitying them and being edified by their way of living, offered them a town, the income derived from which would suffice to maintain them. This they declined, as being against the rule of the province to which they belonged. The king was much amazed, and gave them some interpreters to speak for them when they preached. Being on an island seven leguas at sea, they could not preach to advantage, or learn the language; the king gave them permission to build a house and a church in the city of Quiodomari. They said their first mass here on the day of the Visitation of the Virgin Mary in 1606. Here the fathers made a number of conversions, although they were permitted to baptize only the common people, the conversion of persons of rank or of soldiers being forbidden. Some, however, came secretly and were baptized. One of them, a soldier by the name of Leon, received the crown of martyrdom in four months.]

Chapter LVI

Another mission of the religious to the kingdom of Camboja

In España many times the conquest of Camboja, Sian, and Champan, neighboring kingdoms, was much discussed. The theologians whom his Majesty consulted declared that this conquest was justified within certain limitations. As captain-general was appointed the Conde de Bailen. There came to Manila in 1603 an embassy from the new king [of Camboja] asking for the friendship of the governor, for a force of soldiers, and, most important of all, for religious to come and preach the gospel. The king disclaimed any part in the murders which had been committed a few years before by the king his predecessor (who was his nephew), and by the Malay Moros whom that king favored. By them all the Portuguese and Castilians who were there had been slain, except one who made his escape.[37] This new king had had nothing to do with that murder, because he was at the time a prisoner and captive in Sian, and had been taken from prison there to the kingdom at the death of his nephew, who had been slain by the Malay Moros whom he had favored. They had taken possession of the kingdom, thus rewarding the ungrateful treachery which he had shown to the Spaniards, although they had restored him to his kingdom. At this time the governor of these islands was Don Pedro de Acuña, a man of noble birth and a brave soldier, a devoted servant of his Majesty, and a true Christian. In this same year the Lord had given him a glorious victory over fifteen or sixteen thousand Chinese who attacked this city, of whom scarcely one was left alive, the Lord aiding this noble gentleman and the few Spaniards who were in Manila. Not long afterward He gave him the great victory by which Maluco was recovered and given into the possession of his Majesty, without the loss of a man, which greatly enhanced the victory. [The governor was delighted by this embassy from Camboja, and sent to ask preachers of the order which had spent so much and labored so hard to introduce the gospel among these tribes. The province immediately appointed father Fray Iñigo de Santa Maria as vicar, and, as associates and apostolic preachers, father Fray Geronimo de Belen[38] and father Fray Alonso Collar, or de Santa Cathalina—whom the governor despatched with six Spaniards, letters, and a present, in a good frigate. They had bad weather, and were obliged to touch at Cochinchina and to coast along the kingdom of Champan, where they were attacked by Indians when they went on shore to get fresh water. They reached the port of Camboja called Chordemuco, in April. The king received them with great marks of honor, showing particular favor to the religious. The kingdom was in constant disturbance, but the king was greatly encouraged even by the presence of these Spaniards. He was greatly desirous of receiving further assistance from the Philippinas; but the fathers were doubtful whether any ought to come, for fear that things would turn out as they had before. Some vessels came from Cochinchina, the captain of one of them being one of those Sangleys who had killed the governor of the Philippinas (Dasmariñas); he took possession of the Spanish galley, and became a pirate. He had at this time the title of ambassador from the king of Cochinchina. Some of the Japanese knew him, since he had stolen a ship from them; and they wished to kill him, but were restrained by the religious. Soon after, when some more Japanese vessels came into port, they plotted against the man, and took his life, before the fathers could hinder them. At this time the fathers and the Spaniards suffered great risks, because the Siamese, the Chinese, and the Cochin-chinese, and much more the Malay Moros, who were all assembled here, hate Christianity. There was promise of much disquiet and many factions; and, to pacify them, the king asked one of the fathers to go to Manila and to ask for reenforcements of soldiers and for more fathers, promising to pay the soldiers, who might defend and guard those who were converted. Father Fray Iñigo went back for that purpose. The priests, or bonços, frequented our church and approved our manner of life, giving hopes of their conversion if the religious should remain. Some conversions were made, and the manner of life of the fathers greatly impressed all the people of the city. On his way back to Manila, father Fray Yñigo lost his life. He was a son of San Estevan at Salamanca, and was almost one of the first who came to this province, having been sent as a result of the activity of the first bishop of these islands, and of his associate, Fray Miguel de Venavides. He was a great preacher and very devout in prayer. He was elected to the priory of Manila, and was most useful in enlightening the consciences of the inhabitants of that city. He was most devoted to St. Cecilia and to St. Ursula; and when he called upon their names, miracles were wrought for him by the supplying of a convent in Pangasinan with fish at his prayers, and on other occasions. He showed at some times the spirit of prophecy.

At the same time there died in Camboja father Fray Alonso Collar or de Sancta Cathalina. Father Fray Alonso was a native of Cangas de Tineo, and assumed the habit and professed in Oviedo. He had come to the province in the previous year (1602), and after beginning to learn the Chinese language, had been sent by the order of his superior on this expedition. His death caused great grief in Camboja, and his funeral was attended like that of one of the grandees of the nation. His bones were afterwards taken to Manila, that he might be buried with his brethren. Thus there remained in Camboja, in the midst of many and great perils, one single religious (Jerónimo de Belén), who dared not baptize the people, although he had the license of the king to do so, because of the confusion and disquiet of the time. Looking for no future success, and knowing the fickleness of the Indians of that region—who had asked to have missionaries and soldiers sent to them, and who then had received them so ill, and had finally killed them—he wrote back asking permission to return; this was granted him by the provincial, until such time as the affairs of this kingdom should promise greater stability and quiet.]

Chapter LVII

Some misfortunes which happened at this time, and the experience of the religious during them

The city of Manila is the finest and richest of its size known in all the world. It is of great strength, being almost surrounded by the sea and by a large river, which wash its walls. It is the capital and court city of these islands, where the governor and captain-general of them has his residence, as well as the royal Audiencia and Chancillería. Here is situated the largest garrison of soldiers, with its master-of-camp, sargento-mayor, and captains. From here are sent out the forces and garrisons subject to this government, which are very many and very wide-spread, for it includes Maluco and the island of Hermosa—one of them almost under the torrid zone, and the other almost within view of Great China and very near Japon. This city makes the name of España renowned and feared throughout all these neighboring kingdoms; for, although its inhabitants and its soldiers are few, yet by the aid of the Lord, whose faith they spread abroad, they have performed so many glorious exploits that even the barbarians of the smallest capacity have come to esteem above measure their greatness, when they see the Spaniards always victorious over enemies who so surpass them in number that experience only might make such victories credible. As a kind father with his son, whose good he desires, not only strives to give him honor and wealth, but in time provides him with punishment and discipline, therefore, after our Lord had made the city illustrious with glorious victories and had filled it with riches, then in the year 1604, at the end of April, He sent upon it a fire which, defying all efforts to control it, burned to the ground a third part of the city—with such swiftness that many had no opportunity to escape it (although the fire occurred about midday), and they perished in the flames; while the loss of wealth was so great that it can hardly be believed. Hearing the news of the fire, which was at some distance from our convent, the religious went to help extinguish it; for on such occasions as this they labor more and have more confidence than others. In a moment, as if it were flying, the fire reached our convent; and since there was no one to protect it, it was almost wholly burnt, the Lord leaving only so much as was necessary to supply a crowded shelter for the religious, without being obliged to go to the house of any other person. In this we were among the more fortunate who escaped; for the fire was so extensive that others had not even this small comfort. Many who on that morning were rich, and had great houses and great wealth, had that night no house where they might lodge or shelter themselves, such is at times the fury of this terrible element.

At the beginning of October in this same year, this city, and consequently all the islands, were in great danger of being lost, because of a revolt against it of the Chinese who lived near it. The event happened in the following way. In the previous year, in one of the merchant vessels which come to this city from China every year there arrived three persons of authority, who are called by the Spaniards "mandarins." These are their judges or leading officers in war. They entered the city, borne on men's shoulders, on gilded ivory seats, having the insignia of magistracy: and they were received with the display due to ambassadors of so powerful a king. They had come to search for a mountain which a Chinese, named Tiongong, had described to his king as being all gold. The name of this mountain was Cavite, and from it he promised to bring back to China ships laden with gold. The mandarins made their investigations, for which purpose they carried Tiongong with them; and when they reached the place which he described, they found no mountain of gold, nor any sign of one. When they accused him of fraud and deceit, he answered, "If you wish it to be gold, it is gold" (referring to the ornaments which the Indians wear, and much more to the wealth of the Spaniards); "if you wish it to be sand, it is sand." All this was done in the sight of the Spaniards, who came there with a good deal of interest to know the reason why these mandarins had come so far away from their regular duties—and especially their chief, who was, as it were, sargento-mayor of the province of Chincheo, one of the most prominent officers in their army. The whole thing aroused suspicion; and the archbishop, Don Fray Miguel de Venavides, a friar of our habit and a religious of this province, urged the governor to send them back immediately, that they might not perceive how small a force the Spaniards had, and might not make the other reconnoissances which are customary when foreign cities or kingdoms are to be attacked. They feared that China was intending an attack upon us. The religious of the order, as they knew the language, visited the mandarins and learned from them that this Tiongong meant to inform the king that the wealth of these islands in the hands of Spaniards and Indians was great; and that, if he would send ships and forces, he might easily make himself lord of it all. They accordingly urged the governor to hasten sending the mandarins away, and he did so. After this event the Spaniards did not rest secure, but were very fearful that the king of China, being a heathen, might be carried away by avarice, and might be greedy for the great wealth which this trickster offered him. Since he was a very powerful king, his resources would certainly be greater than this country could resist without great damage to itself. Even if the city were to be victorious, the result would be its destruction. It would lose a great many of its people, and the indignation of the king would be aroused because of his defeat. He would therefore take away their commerce from them, without which this country could not be sustained. All these reasonings and considerations made the Spaniards very anxious and suspicious. Their suspicions were very greatly increased when the heathen Chinese kept saying that they believed a fleet would come the next year. This was heard by some Chinese Christians who were so in truth; and they went immediately and told it to our religious who had the direction of them. There were some of them who put on false hair that they might look like heathen, and went with studied negligence to the alcaiceria [*i.e.*, "silk market"] where the heathen lived, and heard their conversations at night with reference to the coming of the fleet. They immediately reported these things to their religious, and they to the governor and the archbishop. The archbishop, in a sermon preached at the feast of the most holy Sacrament in our convent, informed the governor and the city that they ought to make preparations, because the Chinese were about to rebel. Although the governor knew all these things, because he had been told of them by our religious, on the aforesaid authority, he could never be persuaded that the Chinese were going to rebel, because of the great harm and the little or no advantage which they would receive from the revolt. Yet, to make ready for what might happen, he began to show special kindness to the Japanese who lived near Manila, and to prepare them so that in case of necessity they might be on the side of the Spaniards. He followed the same plan with the Indians, directing them to prepare themselves with arms and arrows, to be ready if they should be needed. None of this was conceded from the Chinese, for it could not be kept secret from so many; and they even heard with their own ears the most prominent people in Manila say: "We cannot go out against the Chinese, if they come with a fleet, and leave behind us such a multitude as there is around the city; so, if we have news that there is a fleet of the Chinese, we shall have to kill all there are here, and go out and meet those who are coming." This kind of talk greatly afflicted them; and besides this, the more ignorant class of people already began to look at them as enemies, and treated them very badly. The result was that they became very much disquieted and fearful. In addition, there were not lacking some to go and tell them lies, bidding them be on their guard, for on such and such a day the Spaniards were going to break out upon them. In proof of this lie they called their attention to some facts which the Sangleys could see—for instance, that all the Spaniards were getting ready their weapons, and the Indians were making new ones, though they had no other enemies, unless it were the Chinese. At last, more out of fear than from any purpose of their own, they rose in revolt, insomuch that some of them were seen to go where others had fortified themselves, weeping bitterly because they saw their destruction, but feeling that there was no other means to save their lives. The governor and the Audiencia made great efforts to undeceive them and to pacify them, but nothing that was done gave them any security. On the contrary, it seemed to them a trick to catch them unawares. It was a pity to see them leave their houses, which were many, and flee without knowing where, or considering how they were to obtain food for so great a multitude. Some of them in this affliction hanged themselves, to avoid the miseries which as they saw would befall them if they revolted, and the violent death which they feared if they did not rise. Finally, on the eve of the glorious St. Francis, they threw off the mask and came forward as declared rebels against the city. Sounding warlike music and waving banners, they began to burn houses and to kill people; and on that night they attacked in a body the town of Binondo, which is composed of Christians of their own nation. Their purpose was to force these to join them; but our religious, to whom the teaching of these Chinese was committed, caused the women and children to be brought for protection to the church, while the Chinese Christians took their arms and defended the town under the leadership of the good knight Don Luis Perez das Mariñas, who lived there next our church. With twenty arquebusiers, who were on guard in that town, they drove the enemy back without suffering any damage. The enemy, however, inflicted injury upon those who were at work in the fields, many of whom were taken by surprise and were compelled to join them or to suffer death. They also attacked the church and town of Tondo, which belongs to the religious of our father St. Augustine. As the latter had provided against them by a Spanish guard, they did no harm. After having defended the town all night, Don Luis das Mariñas sent one of our religious to the governor before daylight, asking for some troops to attack the Chinese rebels who had fortified themselves near the town of Tondo, not far from Manila. He was of the opinion that as these people had spent all the night, disturbed themselves and disturbing others, they would be tired and sleepy, so that it would be easy to inflict great losses on them. The governor took the matter before a council of war; all approved, and he sent his nephew, Don Thomas de Acuña, with more than a hundred men, the best in the camp, together with some of the men of highest rank in the city, who desired to accompany the nephews of the governor and the archbishop, who went with this party. This small force was regarded as sufficient to attack more than six thousand who were said to have banded together and to be in fortifications— so little did they regard the Chinese. The Spanish, marching in good order, met at least three hundred Chinese enemies, and, attacking them, put them immediately to flight. They were near some large plantations of sugar-cane, in which the Chinese concealed themselves; and the Spaniards followed them, being thus divided and brought into disorder. The rebels were posted not far from there, and, when they saw the Spaniards in disorder, they all sallied out against them, and, surrounding them, killed them almost to a man, although with great loss on their own side. As a result, they plucked up courage to advance against the city, and to try to make an entry into it. For this purpose they made some machines of wood, much higher than the wall. They came forward with these, with no small spirit, but soon lost their courage because, before the machines were brought into position, they were destroyed by the artillery, which inflicted much damage upon the enemy. So, after some slight encounters, they abandoned the siege and fled into the country. Against them was despatched the sargento-mayor, Christobal de Azcueta, with as many Spanish soldiers, Indians, and Japanese as could be got together. As a result of the good order which he maintained, the Chinese were killed off little by little, until there was not left a man of them. This was accomplished without any harm to our troops, for, no matter how much the Chinese strove to force them to give a general battle, they constantly refused it; but they kept the Chinese in sight while they were marching, and halted whenever they halted, surrounding themselves with a palisade of stakes which they carried for the purpose. These they arranged not in one line, but in two, so that in case of attack—and many attacks were made—before the Chinese could reach the palisades and pass them, the Spaniards with their arquebuses and arrows killed the greater number of them. The loss of life was especially great among the most courageous, who led the van; while the rest turned back in terror, without effecting anything. Hunger also fought with them powerfully, because, as our soldiers kept them constantly under surveillance, they could not go aside to forage. The little food which they had brought from Manila was quickly exhausted; and, after that was gone, their lives followed rapidly. Thus by the twentieth of October the war was at an end and everything was quiet. But the city was greatly in need of all sorts of things, for all the trades were in the hands of the Chinese, and, now that they were dead, there was no shoemaker, or tailor, or dealer in provisions, or any other necessary tradesman; and there was no hope that they would come again to this country for trade and commerce. On this account it was determined to send an embassy to China, to give information as to the facts of the case. There were appointed as ambassadors Captain Marcos de la Cueba and father Fray Luis Gandullo, one of our religious—a man of great virtue, sanctity, and prudence, who had gone to China on two other occasions. They suffered much hardship on the voyage, but finally succeeded in their negotiations with the viceroy of the province of Chincheo, which is the place from which the Chinese come to

Manila. After he had given them license to get a supply of ammunition for the city, he dismissed them, promising to continue the trade. This promise was carried into effect, for in the following year there came thirteen ships; and from that day forward everything has gone on as if nothing of what has been narrated had ever taken place.

Chapter LVIII

The election as provincial of father Fray Miguel de San Jacintho and the coming of religious

On May 9, 1604, father Fray Juan de Santo Thomas having completed his term as provincial, there was elected in his place father Fray Miguel de San Jacintho, a religious of much prudence, great virtue, and a mind greatly inclined to goodness, and one who loved and honored those who were good. He exhibited in the course of his office great talent in governing, watching over the order with great care, and filling his office with much affability and simplicity, which caused the religious to love him, and to feel particular satisfaction in him because they had shown so much wisdom in appointing him as superior of the province, out of all the many candidates who had been put forward at that election. His excellent and prudent manner of governing was not displayed on this occasion for the first time; for he had previously exhibited his high abilities in such offices when he was elected by his associates as their superior on the journey from España, that position having been vacated by the death in Mexico of father Fray Alonso Delgado, who had come as their vicar. In spite of the youth of father Fray Miguel, he filled this office so much to the satisfaction of all that they regarded themselves as fortunate in having found a superior who looked out so carefully for the advantage of every one without ever forgetting the general good of the order —which, as being more universal, takes precedence and commands higher esteem. In the affairs of the voyage, which are many and full of difficulty, he conducted himself so well and anticipated them with such accuracy that it seemed as if all of his life had been spent in the office of conducting religious. This is a function that calls for many diverse qualities, difficult to find united in a single person unless he is a man of so superior a nature as was father Fray Miguel. When he arrived in the province, they sent him to the district of Nueva Segovia. Here he was one of the first missionaries and founders of this conversion; and was one of the best and most careful, most beloved by the Indians, and most devoted to his duties as a religious, who had ever been in that province. He suffered all the hardships and necessities, the poverty and the lack of sustenance, which have been recounted. From them, although he was a man of strong constitution and fitted to endure much, the want and the lack of food resulted in causing severe pains of the stomach. This evidently resulted from hunger, for as soon as he had a moderate amount of food he was well; but this happened seldom, and most of the time they had nothing to eat but some wild herbs which they gathered in the fields, and which were more suited to purge their stomachs than to sustain their lives. Hence in jest father Fray Gaspar Zarfate, who was his associate, said to him that he was greatly in doubt whether they were properly keeping the fasts prescribed by the constitutions, because they ate the same thing for supper in the evening as for dinner at noon; for, as they had nothing else, they ate quilites at noon for dinner, and quilites at night for supper. There were received at this chapter the church and house of Nuestra Señora del Rosario [*i.e.*, "Our Lady of the Rosary"] in the kingdom of Satzuma in Japon; and, in the province of Nueva Segovia, those of San Vicente in Tocolano, San Miguel in Nasiping, San Pedro in Tuguegarao, San Raymundo in Lobo, Sancta Ynes de Monte Policiano in Pia, Santa Cathalina de Sena in Nabunanga (which is now in the village of Yguig), and Nuestra Señora de la Asuncion ["Our Lady of the Assumption"] in Talama. These were all villages which had been waiting for religious; and as the bishop of that region, Don Fray Diego de Soria, a religious of the order and of this province, had written that he was about to come back to it with a large following of religious, the new provincial was encouraged to take the charge of so many new churches and villages which were so much in need of teaching, for they had never had any, and were nearly all heathen. The good bishop did not fail of his promise. He had been one of the first and most prominent founders of this province, had seen and passed through the great sufferings which the establishment of it required, and had likewise had his share in the great harvest which the religious had reaped in these regions. He therefore loved it much, and strove with all his might to increase it; and hence, when he was about to come to his bishopric, he endeavored to bring with him a goodly number of excellent religious. The vicar in charge of them was father Fray Bernabe de Reliegos, a son of the distinguished convent of San Pablo at Valladolid, where in the course of time he went after some years to die, leaving the religious highly edified by his happy death, which was to be expected from his very devoted life. The example which they gave on the way from their convents to Sevilla was such that it highly edified the people of the towns through which they passed. The religious who set out from San Pablo at Valladolid were four in number, and they made their way to the port on foot, asking alms and sustaining themselves solely by what the Lord gave to them as to His poor. Although on some occasions they suffered from need because there was no one to give them sufficient alms, they never made use of the money which the superior had sent them for the journey—esteeming more highly that which was given them for the love of God, and putting aside the shame which begging alms at the doors brings with it. They came to a small hamlet in the Sierra Morena, and, though they went two by two to search for lodgings, they found none, and still less did they find any food. Hence in their need, which was great because they had gone on foot, they went to find the alcalde, to lay their necessities before him. After he had several times refused to see them, he at last admitted them at night, and sent them to a house with orders that they should receive the friars. A gentleman from Baeca was there, who, seeing that they were poor, had compassion upon them and sent a page to invite them to eat dinner, although he had already dined before the religious could reach the house. They thanked him for these alms, but declined them, saying that the alcalde of the town had provided for their dinner and lodging; and the gentleman sent them forty reals in charity, saying that he did not send them more because he was journeying on business to the court, where the expenses were so great that they left him no more with which he could help the friars, as he wished to do. That the Lord permits such needs is not due to His lack of power or of love, and He ordinarily makes up for them with similar or greater recompenses. In Baylen they went around the town two by two, and when they had all come together, without obtaining more than two or three cuartos in alms, night came upon them without any inn or lodging. A man was following their path who had noticed what happened to them, and he offered them his house. They thanked him, and accepted his charity; but the house was nothing but a poor peddler's shed, three brazas long and two wide, and, that he might take them in, he sent his wife that night to sleep elsewhere. But a house of charity could not fail to be large and spacious, and hence the religious rested in it with much satisfaction and joy. In the morning the Lord paid the charitable host for the lodging; for the conde, learning of what had happened, called him to appear in presence of the religious, thanked him for what he had done, and, promising him his favor for the future, forced a man who had done our host some wrong, some days before, to recompense him for it immediately. Thus he went away happier than if it had been a feast day, though this is not the principal pay for such works, for they earn glory in the sight of God. All the religious reached Sevilla, and set sail on St. John's day in a small vessel to go to Cadiz and take ship. At noon they were at a considerable distance from land, and the master of the ship was very inattentive. The religious saw three vessels with lateen sails following them, and were amused at these because they had never seen that kind of sail before. This called the attention of the master, and he went up and looked at them. Seeing that they were Moorish vessels, he trimmed his sails, and turning the helm, set out to run ashore. When he succeeded, he said: "Some saint is sailing in this boat, on whose account our Lord has delivered us today from falling into the hands of Moors; for it is they who were chasing us with their light sails and swift boats, from which it was impossible that this heavy bark with its heavy load should have escaped, if some superior power had not been watching over us by some saint who has been traveling with your Reverences." On the following day it was learned that at that very same place some people who had taken the same voyage had been captured, wherefore they saw themselves obliged anew to render most humble thanks to the Lord for His singular mercy and kindness. They went on board the ships; and when the fleet was sailing in the gulf which on account of its restlessness and the many waves which are always there, is called Golfo de las Yeguas [*i.e.,* "Gulf of the Mares"], two sailors fell overboard from the flagship—an accident which often happens when they are working in confusion at a critical moment. The flagship—not being able to help them, since it was carried on and separated from them by the wind—gave a signal, by discharging a piece, to the ships that followed it that they should try to pick up the men. As none of the other ships was able to go to their help, that one on which were the bishop and the religious hove to; but, on account of the excitement of the moment, they failed to do so with proper caution and prudence. The rudder was brought over with all the sails up so that the head of the ship was brought down dangerously, and the whole bow as far back as the foremast went under water. That there might not be one accident only, the violence of the wind and the burden of the sails and the force of the waves jerked the tiller [*pinçote*] from those who were at the helm, and swung it across fast under the biscuit hatchway, leaving the ship without means to steer it when that was most needed. The hatchway was closed, and no key was to be found. The ship was going to the bottom, being submerged in the water, and the waves, which were like mountains, were beating on its sides, so that the mariners in alarm were shouting, "We are lost, we are going to the bottom and cannot help ourselves, for want of a rudder and direction." "Let us turn," said the bishop, "to our Mother and Lady, the mother of God, and let us promise to fast in her honor for three days on bread and water if by her help we may receive our lives." The religious did so, and, falling down in prayer, they supplicated her for aid; and instantly—a proper work for the divine pity and that of the Mother of Compassion—the tiller, or stem of the rudder, came out, of itself, from the hole into which it had gone. This was contrary to the common expectation in the ordinary course of similar cases; for the hole was very small, and therefore it was very difficult for anything which had once entered it to be brought back again. Four men quickly caught it, and, bringing it across with great strength, turned the ship back into its course. The seamen were in amazement at this extraordinary event; and, as they had had experience in like cases, they regarded it as the favor and benefit of our Lady who had been invoked by her afflicted and unhappy chaplains. Therefore to her the religions rendered devout and humble thanks, and with great joy fulfilled the vow which they had made.

On its voyage the fleet touched at the island of Guadalupe for wood and water. This island was inhabited by a barbarous and inhuman race, bare of any sort of clothing, and (what is worse) bare of any sort of pity; for they had no pity upon those who, without doing them any harm, came there to get water which would be wasted in the sea, and wood for which they had no use whatsoever. There were in the fleet the Marqués de Montes Claros, going to be viceroy of Nueva España, and, as commander, Don Fulgencio de Meneses y Toledo; and on the eve of our father St. Dominic, twenty-five soldiers having gone ashore as a guard with an ensign in command, all those on board the fleet went ashore and mass was said as the religious had desired. After that, the religious and all the rest went to wash their clothes and to bathe themselves, of which there was great need. The sailors went to get wood and water. Being all more widely scattered than was proper, they failed to keep a proper lookout, when they ought to have been more on their guard against the peril which menaced them. The islanders, taking advantage of the opportunity to carry out their evil purpose, came down close to them, being hidden in the thick undergrowth of the mountain. They began to shoot arrows at the Spaniards when the Spaniards were not keeping a lookout, and when they themselves had the advantage. This they did so rapidly and in such numbers that it seemed as if it rained arrows. When the Indians were perceived many were already wounded, and much blood had been shed. The surprise and confusion threw the crew into a panic, and huddling together in a frightened group they fled, each man striving to put himself in safety—one leaping into the boat to go back to the ship; another throwing himself into the sea, which was then regarded as more pitiful than the land; still another hiding himself among the trees and letting the savages pass as they shot their arrows at those whom they found ahead of them, and letting them pick up as spoils the clothes which he had been washing, or which were now being dried after the washing. Those who could do least to resist the attack of the islanders were the religious; and hence many of them fell wounded and others dead, for it was easier to draw their souls from them than to draw out the arrows. Three of them hid themselves in a thicket, where the Lord delivered them from a shower of arrows which were shot after them as they went to hide. Holding a little [image of] Christ in their hands, they begged him earnestly that he would blind the savages that they might not see them and might pass them by. The Lord heard them, and thus, though the islanders saw them hide themselves and shot many arrows after them, yet the arrows did not strike them; and the Indians, who are keener than mastiffs in discovering people, could not find them, though they passed the place where they were.

The wounded were: father Fray Juan Luis de Guete, a son of the convent of Preachers in Valencia, in whose spine an arrow was fastened, being stopped by the bone; father Fray Juan Naya, a son of the convent of San Pedro Martyr at Calatayud, who escaped with a wound in his arm where an arrow had passed through it; and father Fray Jacintho Calvo, who was struck twice. He was a son of the convent of La Peña de Francia, where in course of time he hung up one of the arrows. The wounds were not so penetrating as to take their lives; but they made the fathers very happy because here, with this blessed beginning, they had begun to shed their blood for the Lord who had redeemed them with His own, and for the gospel which they were going to preach in His service. The religious who died there were six. They were so picked and selected among all the rest that, as they were the cream of all the others, it was plain that that which the islanders had done *en masse* was, so far as concerned the Lord, a most particular providence of His who had directed the arrows against the best and the ripest of the religious that they might be offered as early fruit on the table of the supreme Father, as something in which one may safely assert that He takes much pleasure. Three of these holy martyrs were children of the most religious convent of Preachers in Valencia, which, as it is so prolific in saints, naturally had here the greater share. The first was father Fray Juan de Moratalla, a native of Murcia, a religious of noble example, great mortification, silence, modesty, and composure. [He was devoted to prayer and solitude, and to the good of others. The second was father Fray Vicente Palao Valenciano, a religious very precise in his observance of the rules, and such as a priest ought to be. The third was Fray Juan Martinez, a priest, an Aragonese, a religious of purest and holiest life. The fourth was Fray Juan Cano, a native of Burgo de Osma, a son of San Pablo de Valladolid, young in age, old in virtue. The fifth religious was Fray Pedro Moreno, a deacon, a native of Villalba, a son of the royal convent of Sancta Cruz at Segovia, and a member of the most illustrious college of San Gregorio at Valladolid. He was devoted to prayer and to silent meditation. At his death the Lord wrought a miracle by enabling him to make his way to the seashore, where he died in prayer, and was afterward found beneath the water in the attitude of prayer. The sixth religious was Fray Jacintho de Cistenes, a son of the convent at Valencia, and a native of that noble city. He was young in age but venerable for his virtue. The Lord had revealed to him that he should die on the day of St. Lawrence, as he actually did, after suffering for some time from his mortal wound.[39]]

Chapter LIX

The erection of some churches, which took place at this time

The religious who were coming to the province, although they had been diminished in number by the savages of Guadalupe, were of great use. They were fourteen in number, and, that they might immediately begin that which they had sought over so many seas and through so many hardships, they were assigned to their duties. The newly-elected provincial took with him four for the province of Nueva Segovia, where at that time the conversions were going on rapidly, because the country was large and nearly all the inhabitants were heathen. When they reached the cape known as Cabo del Bojeador, a place which is ordinarily a difficult one, the provincial saw that a small cloud which covered the peaks of some mountains near there was moving toward the sea, which began to be unquiet and rough. The pilot thought it best that the sails should be lowered somewhat, in order better to resist the attack of the wind and the waves which threatened them. While he was striving to do this, the tempest anticipated him; and the wind came with such force that wind and wave turned the vessel on its side, and the water entered over the sides of the ship. It was necessary for the religious to put their hands to the oars, while the rest went to work, with great difficulty, to get in the sails—nothing being left but the courses, in order to make it possible to steer. Although the amount of sail was so small, the wind was so powerful that, lifting the vessel on one side, it forced the other under the water. The religious repeated the exorcisms against the tempest, upon which it subsided a little; but when the exorcism was completed it came back with as much force as at first, almost capsizing the vessel, and making it ship water. When the exorcism was renewed, the tempest moderated itself anew; but when the exorcism was completed, its fury returned as before. Thus they perceived that this tempest was not merely a tempest of wind and of waves, but was aided by the devil—who at the words of the exorcism lost his strength, and as soon as that ceased received it again, to hinder the ministers of the gospel. Four times they repeated the exorcism, and four times the same thing happened, upon which the father provincial, recognizing the author of this evil, said: "Since I see that ministers are to be given to the villages of the heathen, and that the devil, who unjustly keeps under his tyranny, is about to be banished from them, I promise to build a church under the patronage of the guardian angels, that they may aid us against this cursed enemy who is so clearly making war against us." As soon as he had made this promise, it seemed that the guardian angels took upon themselves the protection of the fragata; for the tornado began to disappear, and they continued their voyage. On the following day they rounded the cape, by rowing against a slight contrary wind which had arisen; and when this wind had quieted down, the fragata came to some billows where a number of opposing currents met. The waves were so high that the little boat put its side under water. A religious threw into the sea some relics of St. Raymond, repeating the glories of the saint, and the sea was immediately calmed—just as when water boils too violently in the kettle, and a little water is poured into it; and by the kindness of the saint a fair wind was given to them, with which they continued their voyage.

When they reached Nueva Segovia, a minister was provided for the village of Nasiping, which had been accepted ten years before, but for which it had been impossible previously to provide a minister because the supply of them was so scanty. Even now there was so much requiring the attention of the religious, and they were so few, that half a miracle was necessary for the missionary to be given. Father Fray Francisco de la Cruz, or Jurado,[40] was taken dangerously ill. He was a religious of much virtue, of whom they had great hopes. The father provincial, fearing to lose him, promised to give a minister to Nasiping if the sick man recovered. Father Fray Francisco recovered, and the provincial fulfilled his vow and named the church after St. Michael. This village is on the banks of the great river [*i.e.*, of Cagayán], five or six leguas higher up than the city of the Spaniards. In the year 1625, twenty-one years after it received ministers, there had been baptized in it more than three thousand four hundred persons, as is certified by the baptismal records; and, in addition to this, many were baptized in sickness who, because of their immediate death, were not entered on the records. To this village there came an Indian from Tuguegarao, which is distant two days' journey by water. He very earnestly desired the religious to confess him, and to give him the other holy sacraments. The religious confessed him and gave him the communion, more that he might assist his devotion than because he supposed he was in danger. He had come on foot and seemed strong, so that it seemed that he was very far from being in such a state of necessity; but after he had received the sacrament he died. This was something at which the religious wondered, and which aroused in him great devotion and joy when with his eyes he saw so plainly the power of divine predestination, carried out in ways so hidden and mysterious. Father Fray Pedro Muriel,[41] who is still living, has testified as an eye-witness that when he was minister in that village, in the year 1631, the locusts were more in number than the natives had ever seen before. In the fields of that village they were in such numbers that they spread over a space three leguas in length and a quarter of a legua in breadth, covering the earth and the trees so that the ground could not be seen, so thickly did they cover it; and they ravaged the fields as if they had been burnt. [The Indians did what they could to frighten away the locusts, but in vain; and the Lord heard the prayers of one of the Indians that He would drive away the locusts during the night. At dawn, when he expected to find all of his fields desolated, he found that just half of them had been eaten, and that all the rest had been left. The Lord showed a similar grace to a poor woman who prayed for His aid in protecting her field of maize.]

In this same year, 1604, the provincial sent three religious to the estuary of Lobo and the country of Ytabes,[42] in the province of Nueva Segovia. All those Indians are heathen; and though by nature they are very tractable and easy to deal with, simple and free from malice, and concerned with nothing but their agriculture, still the outrages of those who took tribute from them were so great that they enraged the natives and obliged them to take up arms, to the great loss of the Spaniards. As they were few and the multitude of the Indians many, the few, although they were very courageous, came to their death by the hands of the many; or, rather, the unjust came to death by the hands of divine justice, which in this way was pleased to chastise and end their injustices. And as we very seldom reckon rightly, the chastisement which God wrought by the hands of these Indians was attributed by the Spaniards to the courage and valor of this tribe; and thus they were very fearful of them until the holy gospel declared by the Dominican religious changed them from bloodthirsty wolves to gentle sheep—the Lord aiding by manifest miracles to give credit to His faith and to His ministers, to the end that they might be able to do that which without this or similar assistance from the Lord it would have been impossible to achieve. One of the three religious who entered these heathen villages to undertake their conversion said, in giving an account of what happened: "Since the hand of the Lord has been so plainly succoring these Indians by the hands of those religious who dwelt among them, their reformation has been great and marvelous. They have gone from one extreme to the other, almost without any intermediate stage, since the religious took them under their care. Before that they were so free, so completely without God or law, without king or any person to respect, that they gave themselves up freely to their desires and their passions. Evidence of this is found in those wars which they were continually waging among themselves, without plan or order; and in the drunkenness and the outrages of which they were guilty, without regard to God or man. He who was most esteemed among them was the greatest drunkard, because, as he was the richest, he could obtain the most liquor. He who slew the greatest number of men was regarded as superior to all the rest. They married and unmarried daily, with one or many wives. In a word, they were a barbarous race, given up to all sorts of shameless conduct. In spite of all this, when the missionary came among them they were as docile as if they had during all their lives been learning to obey, which is something very difficult even in religious orders. This was true, although the religious instantly laid a general interdict upon all their ancient vices; obliged them to consort solely with their lawful wives; even forced many to abandon their land and their old villages, that they might come where teaching was given them; and, in a word, compelled them to enter all at once, and in a body, into ordered ways of living, in matters both divine and human. They had not a thought of opposing a single command; and this has been achieved without stripes or penalties, but simply by kindness and gentleness. The result has been that those who did not understand anything except killing, and drinking till they could not stand, and running without any restraint after every sort of vice, now never think of doing these things—as I have seen in these first three villages in this district of Ytabes. The day we went among them we found all the men lying about the streets, dead drunk; since that day there has not been one drunk enough to lose his senses. The same reformation has been achieved in all other matters, for they were not compelled to do all this by fear of the Spaniards. Quite otherwise; the Spaniards regarded these Indians as so indomitable and intrepid that, for fear of them, they did not dare go up the river as far as their villages; but after the religious went among them, they were gathered into large villages that they might be more easily instructed in the faith, having been previously scattered among many small ones, like so many farmsteads [in Spain]. There were three villages thus formed: one of about five hundred tributes, named Taban, the church of which was called San Raymundo; and the other two of more than a thousand tributes each—one called Pia, its church Santa Ynes de Monte Policiano, afterwards known as San Domingo; and the last one, named Tuao, the church of which was dedicated to the holy guardian angels because of the incident referred to above. Thus all those people were brought together and united, to reduce them to settlements, and to a civilized mode of life and government; and to the church; but this result was obtained at no small cost to the religious. Of three of them, two immediately fell very sick, and the third still more so, for he died as a result of the illness. This was father Fray Luis de Yllescas, a son of the convent of Sancto Domingo at Mexico, a very humble religious, very obedient and beloved by all. He received the holy sacraments for his departure with great devotion; and went away to enjoy, as may be presumed, the reward of his labors, which had been many in a short time. Yet neither this death nor the failure of health in the rest caused them to withdraw their hands from the work upon which they had begun. On the contrary, the great good which they beheld, wrought by the Lord among these Indians, served as medicines and remedies for the ills from which they suffered; and for their convalescence, though they had no worldly luxuries, that fruit was much better which, more and more every day, was borne by this new plant of the church. From it they recovered health, strength, and new courage to carry on the work which they had begun. To give them still greater spirit, the Lord came to them working miracles. The first mass which was celebrated in the village of Pia took place on St. Bartholomew's day, the twenty-fourth of August. [Before the end of the month, a sick person who wished to be baptised beheld some fierce and abominable forms which dissuaded him from baptism, and reminded him of the rights and customs of his ancestors, charging him not to change the faith in which his fathers and grandfathers had lived. These dreadful forms were driven away by three persons, clad in black cloaks with white garments beneath. The sick man was often asked if he knew these three persons who had delivered him, and he said "no." When he was asked if they were religious of our order he also said "no," because he had never seen any of the religious wearing their cloaks. He always declared that he had been awake and not asleep; and the narrative was accepted as certain. At one time, a religious who was himself in poor health was left in charge of thirteen newly-converted Christians, who were all confined to their beds by sickness. Being unable to give them the care which he desired, he placed upon the abdomen of each of them a little roasted rice-bran, very hot, begging the Lord to make up by His pity for the lack of medicine. When he came back the next day to visit them, all but two were well, and had gone to work in the field; and the others soon recovered. The same treatment given by another Indian or by the sick man to himself had no effect; and thus it is plain that the healing was due to the desire of the Lord to honor and to give authority to the hand which applied the remedy. The Indians themselves observed that, after they had religious, far fewer died than before they had them. In their ancient days of superstition, when a man fell sick he generally died, because he was treated only by the witchcraft of the aniteras, whose sole purpose was to get gold from the sick persons by false promises. The sorcerers did them no good and indeed rather harmed them, since cures came from our worst enemy, the devil; while now the Lord was giving them, by means of the religious, health that was health indeed. One of the religious in this region, father Fray Juan Naya,[43] fell ill, and grew worse so rapidly that he was given up as a consumptive. By the advice of another religious, he made a vow to our Lady to serve in that province among the heathen, if she should be pleased to grant him sufficient health for him to carry on this work. He made the vow for seven consecutive years from the day of the Visitation, July 2, 1605. During all this time he had his health; but at the end of the seven years he was attacked by a very severe and dangerous illness, which left him when he renewed his vow for four years more. Similar experiences have been frequent among the religious. It has even happened to some who were not very devoted to this work, and who desired to go to other provinces where the Lord might be served with less severity and with somewhat greater comfort, that they have been afflicted with diseases, which gave place to miraculous health as soon as they made vows to remain and minister to the Indians whom they wished to leave. In this region the Lord manifested His goodness and gave authority to his ministers, curing a sick woman who was at the point of death, by means of the sacrament of holy baptism. In this same village it happened to father Fray Juan Naya that a poisonous snake entered his shoe without any evil effect. An Indian in this same village called upon God in his illness, and, when it did not seem good to the divine Providence to heal him, he called upon the devil whom he had previously served. The Lord punished him with dreadful visions, from which he was delivered upon praying to the Lord for His protection; and he was finally cured, after making his confession. A child was miraculously healed in the town of Pia at the time when father Fray Juan Sancta Ana was vicar there. A woman who did not seem to be dangerously ill prayed so earnestly to be baptized that the father granted her wish. She died almost immediately after, the Lord having shown her a marvelous kindness in causing the religious to baptize her immediately.]

Chapter LX

What our Lord wrought, by the intercession of our Lady of the Rosary, who stands in a shrine between the two villages of Pia and Tuao.

[In the church of the village of Pia there was an image of our Lady on one of the side altars. It had been made in Macan, and had been first set up in the church of our order in the city of Nueva Segovia, whence it was taken to the church of Pia. Here the image was greatly beloved; and when father Fray Juan de Sancta Ana gave it away to another village, after having received a second image of much greater beauty, the people begged so earnestly to have it returned that the vicar was obliged to have another painted on canvas and sent to the village of Tuguegarao (to which he had given the one for which the Indians begged), and to have the first image brought back. While the father was considering where it would best be put, the idea occurred to him that it would be well to establish a shrine on the road between Pia and Tuao, at a distance of about a league and a half from each of the towns. This shrine was set up on St. Stephen's day in 1623. On the day on which the shrine was consecrated more than ten thousand persons were gathered together from the neighboring villages. One of the women of the highest rank in the village of Pia undertook the care of the shrine, placing a lamp to burn constantly before the holy image. This Indian was named Doña Ynes Maguilabun. The Virgin was not slow to reward her for this devotion, for once when Doña Ynes took with her to the shrine her little nephew, a child of five years, who was suffering from a large swelling under his left arm—a disease among the Indians which runs into an abscess, and, being so near the heart, is very dangerous indeed, because of the lack of medicines and of medical science among these Indians—the little one was left in the shrine, and fell asleep on the steps of the altar. While there he had a vision of the Virgin, and, when he awoke, the swelling was entirely healed. Other miracles were wrought by the same image. One particularly worthy of mention happened in the year 1624. There being a severe drouth, the father who was at that time in the village of Tuao, Fray Andres de Haro,[44] and father Fray Juan de Sancta Ana, decided to make some processions and offer prayers to the Lord for His mercy. They accordingly arranged to make processions on a certain day from each of the villages to the shrine. The Indians of Pia confessed their sins, that the burden of them might be removed from the land; and on that same Sunday it rained so copiously in the region of this village of Pia that it seemed as if the village would be drowned and as if the floodgates of heaven were open. On the day appointed for the processions, the father of the village of Pia told the Indians that it was not necessary to make the procession, but that he would say a solemn mass of thanks to our Lady, which could be done in the church. They, however, insisted; and when they reached the shrine they found there all the people of the village of Tuao, where not a drop of rain had fallen, because the inhabitants of Tuao had not thought of confessing. They immediately began to prepare themselves for confession, and all that day the inhabitants of Tuao and Pia confessed their sins, revealing some which, from lack of faith, or pusillanimity, or shame, they had concealed. When they reached home in the evening it began to rain in both villages and in all the fields around them; and it rained so hard that it was impossible to bring back the ornaments which had been taken to the shrine for the saying of mass. On several other occasions our Lady showed mercy by granting rain in answer to the prayers of those who besought it before this holy image.]

Chapter LXI

The venerable father Fray Miguel de Venavides, one of the first founders of this province and archbishop of Manila.

Among the great kindnesses and benefits which our province, and indeed all these islands, have received from the Lord, one of the greatest was His having given them father Fray Miguel de Venavides as one of the first who came to establish this province of the Holy Rosary, and as second archbishop of this city. At a time when its inhabitants suffered great tribulations, and found themselves suddenly besieged by a number of enemies much larger than their own—enemies from within their houses and their homes—they found in him a true father for their consolation, and a prelate acceptable to God, who could placate His ire by interceding for his people. He was born in Carrion de Los Condes, of noble parents, well known in that region because of their descent and their virtue. When he was not more than fifteen years old he assumed the habit of this religious order, and learned by experience how true is the saying of the Holy Spirit that it is well for a man to carry the easy yoke of the service of God from his youth. He received the habit and professed in the distinguished convent of San Pablo at Valladolid. He immediately began to display the subtilty of his mind, which was very great; at the very beginning of his studies he seemed like an eagle soaring above his fellow-pupils, distinguishing himself by special marks or acuteness, so that most of the students and the learned were astonished. He was, accordingly, soon made a member of the college of San Gregorio in that city, a crucible in which is refined the metal of the finest intellects which the order has in the provinces of España and Andalucia. Here he had as master him who of right was the master of the theology of España—the most learned father Fray Domingo Bañez. The two were so completely suited to each other in virtue and ability that father Fray Miguel could not fail to be the beloved disciple of such a master. So much did the great teacher love him that, when he saw him advance so far in both virtue and ability, he was accustomed to say *Hic est discipulus ille* [*i.e.*, "This is that disciple"], giving him by antonomasia the name of his disciple, out of the many, whom he regarded with so great praise. He taught the arts in his convent, and theology in many houses of the province; and finally returned to be lecturer in theology in his convent of San Pablo. It was while he was engaged in this duty and exercise that he was taken captive by the voice of father Fray Juan Chrisostomo, who was seeking for religious for the foundation of the province of the Holy Rosary in the

Philippinas. The province was to be founded for the conversion of the many heathen who were in those islands, and for the purpose of entering upon the preaching of the gospel in the most populous kingdom of China, if the Lord should open the door to it, as well as in that of Japon and the other kingdoms neighboring to the said islands. Being seized by a fervent desire and a holy zeal for the redemption of the souls of the many heathen in these islands, he gave up his position as lecturer, and the honors and degrees which were waiting for him; and esteeming it a higher task to labor for Christ and for his fellow men he made up his mind to go with those who were preparing for this holy journey. The Lord thus ordained because of the serious problems which were to be met, in which his character, ability, knowledge, and talents would be very necessary to overcome the many obstacles which confronted this holy foundation as soon as its founders reached Nueva España, and also in the royal court and in the Roman court; for in all these places there were many impediments. Against all of them father Fray Miguel was the defender of truth; and by his speeches and writings he came off always victor. Afterward, when the difficulty which was met with in Mexico was overcome, he came, with the rest of the fathers who founded the province, to the city of Manila on the day of the apostle St. James; and on the day of our father St. Dominic, which came immediately afterward, he presided in the great church over some theological discussions. This he did to the admiration of his listeners, who were not accustomed to have anything so remarkable in these regions. The good bishop of these islands, Don Fray Domingo de Salacar, was bathed with tears of joy when he heard, to the great refreshing of his spirit, such superior preachers of the gospel in his bishopric—men who were not only fit to be teachers of these heathen races, but to teach others who might be the same, and this more excellently than he had ever expected to see in those regions. Among the many various heathen nations who come to this country that which excels in intelligence, civilization, and courtesy is that of the Chinese; and, much as they excel in these qualities, they likewise excel in their multitude and number. For there are very many who come every year to attend to their large and rich business, and to serve the city in all the trades which can be expected in the best regulated of cities; for they learn everything with the greatest ability, and succeed in everything that they undertake.

Some of the Chinese, though very few, were Christians; and it was believed that many would be converted if there were someone to preach in their language. But this is so difficult that, although many desirous to undertake that conversion had endeavored to learn it, no one as yet had succeeded; and thus no religious order had taken up this ministry, being afraid of the difficulty of the language. When father Fray Miguel arrived, he instantly undertook this enterprise—for the Lord had created him for great things; and this ministry was given to our order, the bishop asking each and everyone of the religious orders who were there before to undertake it, and not one of them accepting it because of the reason given. Father Fray Miguel immediately began with all his energy to study this language, and succeeded with it. What is more, he learned many of the letters of it, which are much more difficult. Father Fray Juan Cobo joining him immediately, they began to teach the Chinese, amazing those people that anyone should have been able to succeed with their language and to preach to them in it. Much greater was their amazement, however, at the extraordinary virtue and charity which they beheld in these two religious. They did not content themselves with the labor of teaching them—which was not small, for soon many were converted and began to be baptized; but they proposed to build a hospital where the sick poor could be cared for. The number of these was great, because their sufferings were great in this foreign land, where they were neglected by all, and suffered the extremity of need, which is sickness and death. The fathers began their hospitals; and, poor religious as they were, they had no better house than that which they were able to make, almost without money, out of beams and old planks—the habits and cloaks of the religious often serving as beds, because they had no other bedclothes. The religious sometimes brought in the sick whom they found lying on the streets, without power to move themselves and with no one to pity them. In this way the fame of the virtue of father Fray Miguel and his companions was very widely spread, and there were many of the Chinese heathen who were converted and baptized. The fragrance of this great charity spread so far that it reached Great China and proclaimed in trumpet tones what was done for their sick in the Philippinas. There was one man who came from China to look upon so rare a thing as caring for the sick—poor, and cast out by their own nation and kinsmen; but admitted, sought for, and cared for by persons who were not known to them, and who were not only of another nation, but of a different law and faith, and who labored without any expectation of temporal profit, but merely for the salvation of souls. Hence the Lord was favorable to them, and this work was constantly growing better in all things. It is today one of the most glorious things in Christendom, not because of its income and its building (though in these respects it is very good), but because of the many who at the hour of death are baptized in it with many indications of going hence to glory, as being newly cleansed of their faults and their sins by baptism.

The rich harvest which was reaped in the conversion of these Chinese, as well by preaching to those in health as by the care and instruction of the sick, was so sweet to father Fray Miguel that it caused in him glowing desires to go to

Great China. It seemed to him, and with reason, that there, without abandoning their own country and the company of their fathers, sons, wives, and kinsmen, which here are great impediments to their conversion, the Christians converted would be many more, and far better ones. Hence he was always making plans to go to that great realm, where the devil is so strongly fortified that he does not even permit the entrance of those who might, by preaching the gospel, cast him from the throne which he unjustly holds among that people. He was finally successful in making his entry into that kingdom, and went there with father Fray Juan de Castro, who was the first provincial of this province. They suffered the hardships which have been described in chapter twenty-six, together with the marvelous miracles which the divine pity wrought in their favor for the preachers of the gospel. When they returned to Manila from China, where they had suffered so much, the orders of their superior directed them to undertake another longer and more painful voyage, which was to España. They were to accompany and assist the bishop, Don Fray Domingo de Salaçar, who was going to discuss very important business with his Majesty; and were also to endeavor to bring back religious from España, to aid in the great labor which rested upon the religious of this province in the conversion of the heathen of these lands, He did not take for this journey money or anything else, or even more clothes than those which he wore, so that he did not have a change of clothes in the whole voyage, which lasts for six months. A ship is so much an enemy to cleanliness that, when he reached Mexico, his habit was in such a condition that the father prior of the convent in that city was obliged to give him clothes wholly out of charity. During the voyage he fell into the sea and was miraculously brought back to the ship by the Lord at the prayer of the good bishop—who afflicted by the accident, prayed the Lord briefly but devotedly for the remedy of it; and he gained what he desired, for the Lord is very quick to listen to the prayers of His servants. The time between the end of this voyage and that which follows afterward over the Mar del Norte [i.e., Atlantic Ocean] was spent by father Fray Miguel in the convent which offered him hospitality, but without the dispensations which the reception of hospitality usually brings with it. He was the first in the choir and the refectory, and in all the other labor of the convent. In particular he helped in the infirmary, in caring for the sick and serving them, whenever he had an opportunity. This was a charge which he took upon himself when, at the coming of the first founders to the Philippinas, they were guests in this same convent. As at that time he had done well in this service, daily exercising many acts of humility and charity, virtues which are supremely pleasing to God, he would not cease this same conduct on this second occasion; on the contrary, as one that had grown in virtue, he did it better than before. What he did here for the sick religious was not a heavy task [for him], for he had become accustomed to do much more in his hospital at Manila for the Chinese heathen, who are by nature filthy and disgusting. Father Fray Miguel reached España, and was present before the royal Council of the Indias, endeavoring to obtain religious for this province as its procurator-general. One of the counselors, incorrectly informed by persons who resented the sermons of our religious, said: "If the matter were in my hands, the Dominican religious would not be in the Philippinas." The rest desired him to restrain himself, and he went on with what he had to say. Father Fray Miguel answered, showing his cloak, which was very old and patched and full of holes: "So far as concerns ourselves, we have no need to go to the Indias; what we endeavor to do by going there, this cloak tells well enough." So well did the cloak of rough, mended serge speak that all were highly edified, and he who had offered opposition was abashed and corrected. In the convent of San Estevan he gave to be washed his inner tunic, which served him in place of a shirt. This was of serge so rough and hard that one of the religious of the convent of novices, who put it on over his habit, was unable to bend any more than if it was a bell; and they all gathered around to look at it as if it were a bell that was sounded. That which began as jest and ridicule so powerfully supplied the place of father Fray Miguel in winning religious, that many determined to go to the province where the religious treated themselves so rigorously and observed such poverty.

Father Fray Miguel found an evil doctrine spread abroad in the court, which a member of a religious order[45] had taken pains to introduce. He had come from the Philippinas with documentary authorizations from the bishop and the two cabildos [*i.e.*, ecclesiastical and civil], before the province of the Holy Rosary was established there, and before there were any Dominican friars in the islands. After having carried on some negotiations at Roma he had returned to the court, and endeavored to bring it about that the preaching of the holy gospel in heathen countries should be begun by soldiers, who by force of weapons and musketry should make the country quiet and subject the Indians, in order that the preachers might do their office immediately without resistance. This doctrine is very well suited to human prudence but is contrary to divine Providence, to that which the Lord has ordained in His gospel, and even to the very nature of the faith, which demands a pious affection in those who hear it. This is not to be acquired as the result of the violences, murders, and conquests wrought by soldiers. On the contrary, as far as in them lies, they make the faith to be hated and abhorred; and hence the Lord commanded that the preachers should be as sheep among wolves, conquering them with patience and humility, which are the proper arms to overcome hearts. Hence not only the apostles, but all the other apostolic preachers who had followed them, have by these means converted all the nations of the earth. This father saw all this very well; but it seemed to him, as indeed he said, that these were old-fashioned arguments and that the world was now very much changed; and that no conversion of importance could or would be made unless soldiers went before to bring into subjection those who were to listen to the gospel, before the preachers preached it. He painted out this monster with such fair colors of rhetoric and with arguments so well suited to our weakness, our little spirit, and our less readiness to suffer for Christ and His gospel, that these lords of the Council were firmly established in this his doctrine—a new doctrine, as its author himself affirmed, and, as such, contrary to the gospel and to the works of the saints who acted in conformity therewith. To overcome this error, much was done by the bishop of the Philippinas and by father Fray Miguel. The latter, being younger, was able to exert himself more; and being so great a theologian and so subtile of mind, he was able to adduce such superior arguments, and so clearly to reveal the poison which was hidden in the arguments of this religious, that the king our lord and his Council were firmly persuaded of the truth. They came to regard it as a great inconsistency to say that our Lord Jesus Christ had acted with so short a view as a legislator that, when He made a law which was to last to the end of the world, He had announced a method which was to be followed only at the beginning by the preachers of it who were present before Him, and not under the same conditions by those who should follow after—just as if His providence were unable to apprehend that which was distant and future. It will further be seen, if we consider it well, that the gospel received much more opposition at the beginning than it does at the present time; and if it was not necessary at that time to subject kingdoms by war, in order to preach the gospel to them, much less will it be so now. Hence grave scandal would arise in the church if, when the Lord commands that gentle sheep shall be the ones to introduce His gospel, the introduction of it should be entrusted now to bloodthirsty wolves. Afterward, by the activity and diligence of father Fray Miguel these black clouds which promised thunderstorms of arquebuses and soldiery were dissipated; and there were left for the promulgation of the gospel the gentle clouds of the preachers, which with the soft rain of teaching, example, and patience have carried the gospel to the most savage and hardened heathen. On this occasion father Fray Miguel displayed such force, and such were his arguments, that the Catholic king directed a most important council to be held, at which were present the president of Castilla, the father-confessors of the princes, the auditors of the Audiencia, the lords of the Indias, and many distinguished theologians. In this conference it was determined that there should be soldiers in the Spanish towns for the defense of the country, but that these soldiers should not go as escorts to the preachers, and that they should not go in advance of them subjugating or killing Indians; for this would be changing into a gospel of war that gospel which Christ our Lord delivered to us—a gospel of peace, love, and grace. So great was the reputation for learning and sanctity which father Fray Miguel gained in these matters that, in the arduous and difficult undertakings which afterward came up, his Majesty directed that he should be consulted and his judgment should be followed, as that of a learned man despising all things which were not of God, and zealous for the good of souls. There was issued at this time a brief of his Holiness to the effect that the bishops of the Indias should have authority to make visitations to the religious who ministered to the Indians, in all matters connected with this ministry, as if they were parish priests. Father Fray Miguel, understanding the bad results which would follow such a plan, presented a very learned memorial, signed by all the procurators of the Indias, to the prince-cardinal Alberto, who gave audience and decided causes for his Majesty. Nothing more was necessary to cause the brief to be recalled, and not to be put into execution. Father Fray Miguel was directed to give the Council of the Indias his advice with regard to the repartimientos of Indians for mines, estates, and the like. He gave it, and it was so sound that they esteemed it highly, the more on account of the character of him who offered it. Hence, when the time came to appoint bishops for these islands he was appointed the first bishop of Nueva Segovia, although such an idea had never crossed his mind, and it was necessary to force him to accept the bishopric. The Council even went so far as to ask him to indicate to them those who seemed to him suitable for the other bishoprics; and those whom he thus indicated were appointed. He sent out religious to the province three times. The first company he sent with father Fray Alonso Delgado, the second with father Fray Pedro Ledesma, and the third, whom he accompanied himself, went under the direction of father Fray Francisco de Morales as vicar, who was afterwards the first minister of our religions order in Japon, and a holy martyr. That he might better prepare the religious for the journey, he went twice from Madrid to Sevilla when he was already a bishop traveling on foot with his staff and his hat like a poor friar; so the people who came to find him and did not know him asked him if he had seen the bishop of Nueva Segovia. He, to avoid vanity, answered them that the bishop was on his way to Sevilla, concealing the fact that it was himself. For the advantage of the inhabitants of Manila, he brought it about that commerce with Nueva España was opened to them and that the money which came from their trading was sent back to Manila up to the amount of five hundred thousand pesos in money or silver bullion. Up to that time, they had license only to receive the principal back again; while the profits were retained in Mexico, or were brought back without a license, at great expense. For the Indians he obtained, by a memorial which he offered, that the natural dominion and chieftaincy which they had over their villages should be left to them, with all their lands, mountains and rivers, and the other rights which they had from of old; since the fact that they had become subjects of his Majesty ought not to cause them to lose the natural right which they had inherited from their ancestors. Further, since the conquest of these Philipinas Islands had not been carried out conformably to the holy instructions which the conquerors carried with them, and which they were bound to observe, but had been carried out in exactly the opposite manner and with the most serious acts of injustice, he gave information with regard to these things to his Majesty and to his royal Council of the Indias. It was decreed that the consent and voluntary obedience and allegiance of all the Indians should be asked for anew. The new bishop, Don Fray Miguel, very earnestly undertook to attempt to carry this decree to execution, and accordingly it was made. When the bishop was desirous of embarking, there were so many rumors of enemies, and the damage inflicted at Cadiz was so great, that it was impossible to have any fleet that year; and there was no other vessel for him to travel in except a small patache with a single deck. The cabin in the poop which he occupied was so low that it could not be entered exception on one's knees, while for the twenty religious whom he was taking there was no accommodation at all. He tried, by putting up an awning, to protect them from the sun and the water; but the only one on the ship was full of patches, and very small. The Lord made matters better for them by causing the voyage which they were obliged to take to be very calm, for the patache was not built to encounter storms. It did not rain more than twice, so that they were at least able to lie on the deck at night, though by day they were compelled to suffer the heat of the sun, which was extreme and very oppressive in their little patache. For this the religious gave thanks to the Lord; but the bishop was so accustomed to hardships that this fair weather grieved him; and he said that the Lord had forgotten them because He did not send them hardships, which are the best things which in this life He gives to His friends. "For my sins," he said, "the Lord deprives us of hardships, and of the merit which they bring with them when they are borne with patience for the love of the Lord who sent them. Not so did we sail on our first journey when so devoted servants of God were going; but we traveled in great and continual afflictions—tempests, fire, and fears of enemies. That we should now lack all this, and travel with such fair weather when we are not such as they, is not for our good. In me is the fault; it is well that I should feel it and weep over it." When he went ashore, he traveled on foot all the way to Mexico, and from there to the port of Acapulco, a distance of more than a hundred and fifty leguas. Thus he afforded the example of a poor religious, even when his state as a bishop would have excused him from such poverty and hardship. However, he did not seek for excuses, but for opportunities for poverty and religious devotion, though at the expense of so great an exertion, and in his advanced age. He reached Manila at a time when there happened to be a procession from our convent to the cathedral, because of an occasional need. He disembarked there, at a gate which was near our convent on the shore, and the procession began by receiving him. This caused much joy, on account of the high esteem and regard in which he was held by both religious and laymen. He accompanied the procession to the cathedral, and when the time came he went into the pulpit, taking the sermon from him to whom it had been committed. He preached most eloquently; and, though he came down bathed in perspiration, he did not change the heavy tunic of sackcloth which he wore. On the contrary, he went direct to the sacristy and robed himself to say mass, though he said it very slowly, and with so much feeling that it was a great effort for him. These were acts, and this was an entry, which promised an extremely good bishop and superior. The promise was not falsified, but fell short of the truth, so much did he surpass it. He went straight to his poor bishopric to care for his flock. In the principal part of his diocese, the province of Nueva Segovia, they were nearly all heathen. There were only about two hundred baptized adults, those who were not so being innumerable; for it was only a very short time since our religious had begun to preach the gospel to them. When the new bishop was once among his sheep, he began to watch over their welfare, and to defend them from the alcaldes-mayor and the encomenderos, who abused them like wolves. The bishop's conduct forced him to hear rough words and violent insults from those who had fattened themselves with the blood of the Indians. They feared lest they should grow lean if the shepherd, coming out to the defense of the flock, were to force them to be satisfied with moderate returns, without flaying the sheep. The bishop was not intimidated, and did not desist from this just and due defense; nor did he cease to strive for the good of his Indians against the outrages which he beheld. On the contrary, he strove to give his remonstrances their due effect and if he was unable to succeed there in securing the rights of the Indians, he was accustomed to write to the governor and the Audiencia, without taking his hand from the work until he had brought it to the perfection which he desired. Though he aided the Indians, he did not neglect the Spaniards, who lived in the principal towns of his bishopric less edifying and exemplary lives than those whose Christianity is ancient ought to lead in towns of the newly converted. They are under obligation to be shining lights, to give light to those who are either blind because of their heathen belief, or who know little of God because they have been newly baptized. He stirred them up to live as they ought, and aided them in their necessities like a loving father; if he could not make them such as he wished, he improved them as much as possible. At the death of the archbishop of Manila, he was obliged to go to that city, and saw in it so many things contrary to the divine Majesty and to the human one that he found himself under the necessity of writing to his Majesty a letter very full of feeling, which begins: "I have twice visited this city of Manila since I came to these islands as bishop. The first time was last year, ninety-nine, because I received reliable information that the governor and the auditors were in such bitter opposition that there was fear of a serious rupture. Now, learning that there was no archbishop in the city, it seemed desirable" (and was so without doubt) "that I should be present and prepared for any contingency." He gives an account of what had happened, and says: "I am obliged to speak as my position and the condition of affairs require, very clearly, without caring who may be affected by my words; for God, your Majesty, and the common weal are of more importance than any smaller things." The truth of what he stated, and the clearness with which he spoke, are plain in the rest of the letter, which to avoid prolixity is not inserted here. He strove to settle the state of the church in these islands; and when he saw some bad customs introduced without any foundation, and contrary to reason and theology, he was greatly grieved. What he was not himself able to remedy, he wrote of to the supreme pontiff. Since the competency of the bishop was so well known in España, he was appointed archbishop as soon as the vacancy was known, although he had no procurator there; for, being a poor and peaceful bishop, he did not expect to carry on any suits, and hence did not care for a procurator or agent at court. Since his poverty was known, his Majesty caused the bulls to be drawn, and directed the royal officials of Manila to collect from the bishop the expense of drawing them when it should be convenient for him to pay it. The bishop hesitated long, and asked the advice of many, before he accepted this promotion, having seen and experienced the difficulties, the opposition, and the dissensions which accompanied this dignity, at such a distance from the eyes of his Majesty and of the supreme pontiff, to whom in difficult cases (of which there were many) he might have had recourse. Yet finally, since all thought that it was desirable for him to accept the office, he was compelled to take it for the public good, although he saw that for his private advantage it would be very injurious. Becoming an archbishop did not change that poor and humble manner of living which he had followed as bishop and as religious. He continued to wear the same habit of serge and tunics of wool. His food was always fish, unless he had a guest, which happened seldom; or unless he was afflicted by some infirmity. Whenever he had a journey to take on land—for traveling in these islands is usually carried on by water—he was accustomed to go on foot; and, that he might travel with more abstraction from the world, he used to walk uttering prayers. He sent the others forward in hammocks or on horseback and he followed after alone, commending to the Lord himself and the undertakings in which he was engaged, in order that they might turn out more satisfactorily. If, when he was indisposed, he was forced by pleadings to go into a hammock—something which is much used in this country, and which is carried by Indians—he used to get out again as soon as he left the town, and sometimes earlier, if he heard any of the carriers groan; for this groan so penetrated his soul that it was not possible for him to travel any farther in this manner. His bed was the same which he had when a poor friar, a mat of rushes or palm-branches on a plank. The small income of his archbishopric he spent in alms; and he used to delight in giving them with his own hands, kissing the alms with great devotion as if he were giving them to Christ, who has said that He receives them when they are given in His name to the poor. That the principal door of his house might not cause embarrassments to persons who had known better days and who were under the necessity of asking alms, he had another door for these persons which was always open, so that they might come at any time to tell him their troubles, and that he might relieve them as well as possible. In this way he spent all his income, and therefore had very little expense or ostentation in his household. He never had a mule or a chair to go about with, avoiding all this that he might have means to give to the poor. He was most devoted to the ministry and instruction of the Indians and the Chinese; and, whenever he had an opportunity for doing so, he used to aid in it with great pleasure. He envied much those who were occupied in so meritorious an exercise, as he wrote in the last year of his life to those whom he had left behind in Nueva Segovia, in a letter which reads as follows: "To my fathers and brethren, the religious of the Order of St. Dominic in Nueva Segovia. A poor brother of your Reverences, very weak in health and very full of troubles and of his own wretchedness, has written this to your Reverences, his truest brethren, who are walking about in those places of rest and new fields of the true paradise, feeding the flocks of the Great Shepherd and rejoicing your souls with the sports and the gambols which the new-born lambs are making upon the hill-sides at the dawn of the true sun. May your Reverences refresh yourselves and feed upon that celestial milk which creates manna covered with honey upon those mountains. May you rejoice in the fair season that now is; for I once tasted the same pleasures—

144

though the fair weather lasted but for a short time for me, because of my sins and my pride; and now I see myself wretched as no one else is wretched. Happy the father provincial, who, having seen as from the parapet of a bull-ring something of the wounds and the bulls here, has returned so soon to the delights of that region, and is among his sheep. I refer you to him; let him speak the love which I have for every one of your Reverences and the esteem which I feel for you all. Pay me with the money of love and pity. *Valete in Domino, viscera mea, felices valete in aeternum.*[46] To all the Indians, a thousand greetings; and I beg their prayers for this poor soul." His life was continually burdened with scruples which sometimes are more cruel enemies than those who are openly declared as such. They were not born in him from ignorance, but from his great depreciation of himself and from his looking upon the greatness of God, both of which caused him to be always timid. This, as he said, was the counterweight with which the Lord burdened him that he might not be puffed up by the great blessings which the Lord had granted him. He preached continually, that he might the better advise and direct his sheep. He grieved for the poor much; and over sinners he was a Jeremiah, weeping for what they failed to lament, that he might make them weep. He was deeply versed in sacred scripture, and with it he filled his writings, and even the ordinary letters which he wrote. In the opinions which he gave, everything was founded upon and approved by the divine authority, which was his rule and his arms, both offensive and defensive. He was accustomed to read with great care the sacred councils and canons of the church. In them he found stated with the greatest precision everything of which he had need for the government of his church, as well as for the satisfactory decision of the questions with regard to which they asked his opinion, and of the disputes which arose among learned persons. When there were different opinions among such persons, he was accustomed to say, "*Veritas liberabit nos* [*i.e.*, "the truth shall make us free"], and this will make clear to us that for which we seek; let us follow it and strive for it." This confidence was always justified; for on many occasions when it seemed that the whole world was in a tumult, and that justice was certain to be clouded over and obscured, he was then accustomed to say, with the greatest confidence, "The truth shall make us free," and finally it turned out so. Because of the love which he had for truth, he could not endure to hear new opinions; and if they were opposed to the doctrine of the ancient saints, he attacked them like a lion set on fire, though he was in all other things as gentle as a lamb. For the same cause, he was most devoted to the teaching of St. Thomas—who, like a mystic bee, made the honeycomb of his works from the flowers of holy scripture, sacred councils, sacred canons, and the works of the saints whom the Lord gave to His church as teachers and guides for its direction. In order that in the Philippinas so sound and safe a doctrine should be read, he strove greatly that in the province, although the numbers were so few, there should always be some one to read St. Thomas. As soon as he entered upon his archbishopric, he asked for a religious of our order to read in the cathedral to those who had been ordained; and carefully took pains to encourage and favor those who went to listen, so that the rest should imitate them. This desire he retained up to his death; and hence in his last sickness he gave the little which he had, asking the order to build a college for this purpose. With this beginning, which was of the value of a thousand pesos, was established the college which we now have in Manila under the advocacy of St. Thomas, in order that from their first letters the students may feel an affection to this holy doctrine, and may follow him afterward when they are further advanced. The devotion which Don Fray Miguel felt for our Lady was so great that in everything which he did or said he commended it to her, saying an *Ave Maria* before he began. So scrupulous was he that he was unable to say the *Ave Maria* unless he understood all the circumstances; and even if it occupied a considerable time for him to repeat it, still, in spite of this, he always said it. One day the dean of his church, Don Francisco de Arellano—a man whom, on account of his virtue, the bishop loved and esteemed—asked what was the beginning of this devotion, and whence it was derived. He answered that our Lady herself, to whom at first he had said the *Ave Maria*, was the beginning, and that she it was who had taught him this devotion. The dean remained in wonder, and did not dare to ask him more on this point; nor did the good archbishop ever make any further declaration. Hence the mode in which this happened was never known; but the great attention which he gave to it was seen. Whenever there was anything to be done the *Ave Maria* always preceded. It was said before he answered or put a question, or took any medicine, or gave alms, or did anything else. Thus always all his acts were actually referred to God our Lord, and to His most holy Mother. This was a custom of the highest virtue; but when the business was of unusual weight, he was not contented with an *Ave Maria*, but recited a rosary. Thus he did in China, when the judges caused him to write a petition in their presence in Chinese characters—something which far exceeded his powers, but not those of the Virgin. Accordingly he wrote a miraculous petition, to the satisfaction of the judges. They believed that which they saw to be impossible, as it really was; for though father Fray Miguel knew some of the commoner Chinese letters, he did not understand those which were necessary for what was then required of him, since they were extremely peculiar and were in the judicial style, with which he was not acquainted.

Hence this was doubtless a miraculous event, worthy of the compassion with which this great Lady comes to the aid of her afflicted devotees. The sufferings of the archbishop from storms at sea, as well as from the opposition of clergymen and laymen with disrespectful words and acts, were very great, but were the cause of great happiness. As was affirmed by his confessor—a religious of great virtue, a man who had known him for many years and who was familiar with the secrets of his soul—when the sufferings were at their greatest, and in his sorrow and affliction he went to God, our Lord himself visibly consoled him and gave him strength, not once, but often. To this was attributed his habit of looking sometimes with his eyes fixed on heaven, with flames of fire, as it were, shining upon his face. On such occasions he was heard to utter some words which, without his striving or having power to say more, he spoke in affectionate converse with God. This caused great devotion in those who heard; and as it was so, it is no wonder that he so much desired other sufferings in addition to the weighty cross of his scruples, because their absence was much more painful to him than the necessity of enduring them. Hence he showed much more sadness and melancholy when he was exposed to no hardships than when they were heaped upon him; for in the latter case he was sure of the consolation of heaven, which was lacking when he had no sufferings.

The end of his days finally approached; and as he lay on his bed it was plain to him that this was his last sickness, and he began to prepare for this important journey. At his departure he was much afflicted to leave without a minister the Indians of Marivelez, which is situated at no great distance from Manila. Since these Indians were few and by themselves, he had found no one who was willing to accept the charge of them. Taking advantage of the present occasion, he sent for father Fray Miguel de San Jacintho, who at that time was provincial of the province, and most energetically begged him to urge on his religious to give instruction to these poor Indians. When the provincial promised that he would do all he could for this purpose, the bishop remained in great content, as if there were nothing now to cause him sorrow. He divided his poor treasures, sending part of them immediately to his church, and giving part to our Lady of the Rosary, and part to the poor. In his illness he did not complain or ask for anything; and when he was asked if he wished or longed for anything, he answered, "I desire to be saved." His face was very full of joy, and the words which he uttered came forth kindled so by the love of God that they showed plainly what a fire of love was in the breast where they were forged. He asked them to dress him in his habit; and on the coming of the festival of the glorious St. Anne in the year 1605 he asked them to get ready his pontifical robes, as if he were preparing to go out on that festal day. This was as much as to say that his departure was at hand. He was surrounded by his friars, and though they saw him joyful they themselves were very sad to perceive that they were to be deprived of such a superior and such a religious. He consoled them with loving words, and, perceiving that his departure was at hand he called fervently upon his special patroness, the Virgin, his guardian angel, our father St. Dominic, and the other saints of his devotion, with whom he spoke as if he were already with them in heaven. His countenance appeared to be celestial rather than to belong to earth; and amid loving converse with God, with His most holy Mother, and with the saints, his soul departed to his Lord, leaving his body, as many said, fragrant with the odor of roses. By the voice of all, he was given the palm of a virgin, as if all had heard him in confession and felt the certainty which his confessor had and manifested in this respect, although this declaration was made after that in which the palm had been given to him as to a virgin. When the fathers of St. Francis came, father Fray Vicente Valero, who lived and died with the reputation of sainthood, went up to the dead man, saying, "This body is holy and should be regarded as such," and kissed the feet. After this all of his religious did the same thing, and they were followed by the others, for in this way the Lord honors those who faithfully serve Him. His interment was performed with all possible solemnity in the cathedral, on the epistle side near the high altar. The archbishop left behind him some writings of much erudition, and full of Christian teaching, which are very helpful to the ministers of the holy gospel.

Chapter LXII

Of some religious who died at this time

[At this time there were taken away by death a number of the most superior religious, the lack of whom was greatly felt. In the year of our Lord 1604 one of the definitors in the provincial chapter was father Fray Pedro de San Vicente. He was elected as a definitor in the general chapter, and also as procurator of the province at the courts of España and Roma. There was no one at either court at that time, and a procurator was necessary, especially for the purpose of bringing over religious from España, without whom this province could not be maintained. He set out to undertake the duties entrusted to him, in the ships which sailed that year for Nueva España, and died on the way, the same ships in the following year bringing back the news of his death. Father Fray Pedro was a native of Zalamea. He assumed the habit in the convent of San Esteban at Salamanca, whence he came to this province in the year 1594. Here he was engaged in the ministry of Bataan, and afterward in the ministry to the Chinese of Binondoc, being much beloved and esteemed in both these offices. He always thought well of all, and never spoke ill of anyone. He was twice superior of Binondoc, to the great spiritual and temporal augmentation of that mission. He set sail on the voyage without taking a real or a piece of silk, or any other thing, either for the journey or for the business which fell to his charge, trusting solely in the divine Providence. He even refused to take for his convent some articles of little value here, but esteemed as rare and curious in España, and such as it is customary for a religious to take as a mark of affection to the convent where he assumed the habit. When he died he made the following testament or declaration: "I, Fray Pedro de San Vicente, declare that I die as a friar of St. Dominic, without having in my possession gold or silver, or anything else, except one old blanket with which I cover myself at night. I pray for the love of God that this may be given to a boy who travels with me, named Andresillo." Let it be remembered that father Fray Pedro was in the Philippinas ten years, for the greater part of the time minister to the Chinese and for four years their vicar, and that he was very much beloved; that they are of their nature inclined to make presents; that many in this town are very rich, and are ready to give much on small occasions; and that when they saw him about to go to España they were much more likely to show generosity, without his needing to put forward any effort. Any one who will consider these things, and who will observe that he went from among them so poor, without money or anything

149

else, will clearly recognize his great virtue, and see how justly he is entitled to the great praise of the Holy Spirit, who says, "Happy is he who does not follow after gold, and who does not put his trust in the treasures of money; who is he? let us praise him because he has wrought marvels in his life."

In the province of Nueva Segovia there died at this time father Fray Jacintho Pardo, a learned theologian and a virtuous religious. He was a native of Cuellar and took the habit in San Pablo at Valladolid. He was so much beloved in the convent that the elder fathers strove to retain him; but it was shown in a vision to a devout woman that father Fray Jacintho was to serve among the heathen.] He was sent to Nueva Segovia, where there were very many heathen to be converted; for at that time missionaries had just been sent there, and nearly the whole of the province was without them. The natives were fierce, constantly causing alarm from warlike disturbances, and were much given to idolatry and to the vices which accompany it. The good fortune of going thither fell to him; and he immediately learned the ordinary language of that province so perfectly that he was the first to compose a grammar of it. Since the village of Tuguegarao (where he lived) in La Yrraya had, although the inhabitants understood this common and general language, another particular language of their own, in which it pleased them better to hear and answer, he undertook the labor of learning that also, and succeeded very well. He acted thus as one desirous in all ways of attracting them to Christ, without giving any consideration to his own labor, and to the fact that this language could be of no use outside of this village. They were a warlike, ferocious, and wrathful tribe; and, being enraged against their Spanish encomendero, they killed him, and threatened the religious that they would take his life unless he left the village. Being enraged, and having declared war against the Spaniards, they did not wish to see him among them. But father Fray Jacintho, who loved them for the sake of God more than for his own life, desired to bring them to a reconciliation and to peace; and was unwilling to leave the village, in spite of their threats. To him indeed they were not threats, but promises of something which he greatly desired. Under these circumstances he fell sick, and in a few days ended his life. The Spaniards, knowing what the Indians had said, believed that they had given him poison so that he should not preach to them or reconcile them with the Spaniards; and this opinion was shared by the physician, because of his very speedy death. If this were true, it was a happy death which he suffered in such a holy cause. He died on the day of the eleven thousand virgins, to whom he showed a particular devotion; and it might have been a reward to him to die on such a day, since the church knows by experience the great protection which these saints offer at that time to those who are devoted to them.

[In the district of Bataan died Father Juan de la Cruz, a son of the convent of San Pablo at Sevilla. He was one of the first founders of this province, in which he lived for eighteen years. He was small of body, and weak and delicate in constitution; but his zeal gave him strength for the great labors which accompanied the beginning of this conversion. He was one of the first workers in the field of Pangasinan, where he suffered all the evils and miseries which have been described in the account of that conversion. He very rapidly learned the language of these Indians, which they call Tagala; and succeeded so perfectly with it that father Fray Francisco San Joseph, who was afterwards the best linguist there was, profited by the papers and labors of father Fray Juan de la Cruz. Father Fray Juan even learned afterward two other Indian languages, those of the Zambales and the Pampangos. Father Fray Juan, being the only linguist among the fathers, was called upon constantly to hear confessions; and therefore suffered even more than the rest from the exposures of traveling from place to place in this district. These hardships broke down the health even of strong men like father Fray Christobal de Salvatierra, who suffered from a terrible asthma. Father Fray Juan was afflicted by an asthma so terrible that it seemed as if every night must be his last; and he felt the dreadful anxiety which accompanies this disease. He also suffered from two other diseases even more severe, colic and urinary ailments, which afflicted him even more than the asthma. He was so patient and so angelic in nature that all these diseases and afflictions could not disturb him or make him irritable. His body he treated like a wild beast that had to be tamed, weakening it with fasts, binding it with chains, mortifying it with hair-shirts, and chastising it with scourgings. He was chosen as confessor by the archbishop of Manila, Don Fray Miguel de Venavides. Immediately after the death of the archbishop he returned to his labors among the Indians, but did not survive long. When a religious of the Order of St. Dominic is about to breathe his last, the rest of the convent gather about him to aid him to die well; and to call them together some boards are struck or a rattle is sounded, he who strikes them repeating, "Credo, credo." Father Fray Juan de la Cruz, desiring to follow the usual custom of the order, taught an Indian to strike together these boards, although the father was alone in the village; and this was the last farewell of this noble religious. He had refused repeated requests to return to Manila for care; and he was buried, as he desired, in the church of those Indians for whose spiritual good he had spent his life.

In this year 1605 the religious of our order had been three years in Japon. They were not a little disturbed by a brief which at this time reached Japon and which had been obtained by the fathers of the Society of Jesus. This brief directed that all the religious and secular clergy who desired to preach in

Japon might go thither by the way of Eastern India, but that no one should have authority to go by way of the Western Indias. The brief directed that all who had come in that way or by the Philippinas should depart, on penalty of major excommunication, *latæ sententiæ*. The religious of the other orders, when this brief was shown to them by the fathers of the Society, replied that the brief had been presented in the previous year to the archbishop of Manila; and that the fathers of the various orders had laid before the archbishop reasons for supposing that his Holiness had been misinformed, and had appealed to the supreme pontiff for a reconsideration. They declared that it was unreasonable to expect them to leave Japon until the reply of the supreme pontiff should be received. The brief was annulled by his Holiness Paul V in 1608, only three years after the petition; and this repeal was confirmed afterwards by Urban VIII. In the interim the fathers of the Society of Jesus did things which annoyed the other religious, but were not sufficient to drive them from Japon. After the repeal the superior sent fathers Fray Thomas del Spiritu Sancto, or Zumarraga, and Fray Alonso de Mena to extend the mission from Satzuma to Vomura [*i.e.*, Omura]. It was a time of great disturbance and of much feeling against the Christians. The fathers of the order did what they could for some fathers of the Society of Jesus who were imprisoned in a church. They went on to the kingdom of Firando—the lord of which[47] had in 1587 begged for religious of St. Francis, but was now strongly opposed to Christianity. Among his vassals they found some who were Christians in secret, and encouraged them and gave them the sacraments of the church.]

Chapter LXIII

The conquest of Maluco by the intercession of our Lady of the Rosary; the foundation of her religious confraternity in this province, and the entry of religious into it.

On April 16, 1606, an intermediate chapter was held in Manila, at which notice was given of the brief of Pope Clement VIII, *De largitione munerum.* Directions were given to observe this brief with rigorous exactness, in all things which it commands to all religious orders and religious. It was ordered and directed that all memorable things, worthy of being placed in history, which had happened in this province should be diligently gathered together. In accordance with this, the father provincial gave a formal precept to all the religious of the province that they should write down, each one of them, what he knew in regard to this matter with all accuracy and truth. In this way something of that which has here been recounted was brought together; but there continues to be much which remains buried in oblivion. Some difficulties were resolved; and it was decreed that devotions to some saints should be offered, whose devotions had up to that time not been offered in the province.

On the first of April in this year occurred the glorious victory which Don Pedro de Acuña, knight of the Habit of St. John, knight-commander of Salamanca, governor and captain-general of these islands, gained in the Malucas, restoring them to the crown of España, as for many years had been desired and intended but without effect. This memorable victory was won by the intercession of our Lady of the Rosary, who was the sole source of it. This important stronghold remains incorporated in the government and province of the Philippinas, to the immortal reputation and glory of the great soldier and devout cavalier who gained them during his government. He deserves this glory not less for his devout Christian zeal, love of God, and devotion to our Lady of the Rosary—in which from his tenderest years he was bred by his most devout and prudent mother—than for his great military skill and prudence, which he and all his valorous brothers acquired from his father, a distinguished and most fortunate captain, as also he saw all his sons become. The great favor which our Lady of the Rosary showed to our army in this conquest was very well known and celebrated. That the evidence of it might be more clearly made known to those who were not present [at the victory], a formal narrative of the matter was made before the treasurer Don Luis de Herrera Sandoval, vicar-general of this archiepiscopate in the year 1609.

Many witnesses being examined, all agreed that this fort was gained by the miraculous aid of the Virgin, though the soldiers did not on that account fight the less valiantly. It was plain, in many things that happened, that sovereign assistance was given by this Lady, as may be seen by referring to the statement of the first witness, the sargento-mayor of that army, Christobal de Azcueta Menchaca, who was present throughout the whole matter; and, who on account of his position, had better knowledge of what occurred than anyone else in the army. His statement is as follows: "In the month of February, 1606, the governor was at Oton, four leguas from the town of Arebalo, in the bishopric of Zebu, on his way to the conquest of Maluco—where the Dutch had built a fort, and had made treaties of peace with the king of that country against the Castilians and Portuguese. It was also said that they had invaded the country of the king of Tidore, our ally. The governor mustered his forces at Oton; and with those who had come from Mexico in June, and those who had been added in these islands, the total number was thirteen hundred Spanish infantry, and six hundred Indians from the vicinity of Manila, who fought courageously under the protection of the Spaniards. Religious of all orders accompanied the troops, and among them was a certain father Fray Andres of the Order of St. Dominic, with another lay religious. As if by legitimate inheritance from their father, all the friars of this habit had in their charge the devotion to the Holy Rosary; and hence father Fray Andres suggested to the sargento-mayor that her holy confraternity should be established in this army, that this our Lady might open the door to the difficult entrance they were to make. The sargento-mayor spoke to the governor in regard to the matter, and to the holy bishop of Zebu, Don Fray Pedro de Agurto. The sargento-mayor received permission to discuss it in the army, and the captains and soldiers all agreed with great heartiness; and they determined that the holy confraternity should be immediately established, with all its ceremonies and ordinances, so that this important enterprise might begin with some service done to our Lady the Virgin. The governor ordered the image of our Lady of the Rosary to be embroidered on the royal standard, that she might guide the army. He was the first to pledge himself as a member of the confraternity, and was followed by the master-of-camp, Juan de Esquivel, and the captains, the soldiers and sailors, and the members of his household—all of them promising alms when they should be provided with money on account of their pay. It was then proposed to establish the confraternity in the first city which should be gained from the enemy, and to call it "the City of the Rosary." For this purpose a canvas was painted, having upon it a representation of our Lady with her son Jesus in her arms, distributing rosaries to the governor, the master-of-camp, the captains, and the rest of the soldiers. They confessed and received communion, and went in procession, as is customary when the confraternity is established. The bishop celebrated pontifical mass, giving dignity to this solemn act with his holy presence. According to the ordinances, a Dominican friar is obliged to preach if any be present. Since Fray Andres had little skill in this office, and spoke with little grace, he tried to arrange that the bishop should preach; but matters turned out so that the religious was obliged to preach the great things of the Mother of God and of her rosary. As all this had been guided by God, and the preacher chosen by His own will, God controlled the preacher's tongue in such a manner that all should be fulfilled which concerned His purpose. Thus the father amazed those who were present—the bishop to such an extent that he said aloud to the whole congregation: "Gentlemen this blessed father has preached in such a manner that it seems the Holy Spirit has been dictating to him that which he has said; and I do not know what account to give of the same except to praise God, for it is He who caused it." The fleet sailed to Tidore; and when it reached there the forces spent Holy Week in confessing and receiving communion. While they were there an eclipse of the moon occurred, which was taken by the augurs of the island as a bad omen, and they uttered presages of evil, and cried aloud; but the Spaniards took it as an omen of victory. They did not find in Tidore the king, who was friendly. They discovered two Dutchmen who had a factory there; and they and that which was in the factory were held for the king of España. On Friday of Easter week, which was the last day of March, the fleet cast anchor a cannon-shot from the fort of Ternate; and on Saturday the artillery from the ships and galleys was fired, to clear the field. The sargento-mayor made a landing with the army, drawing them up along the creek between the fort and the sea. The vanguard was held by the master-of-camp, Gallinato, lookouts being posted in the trees. While he was planning to make gabions, the tumult of the army, as if the voice of all, declared that they should not doubt the victory; that on that very day they were going to capture the fort and the country, for it was Saturday, a day dedicated to our Lady. They began with great readiness. It was about midday, an hour little suited for an attack in so hot a country, for the sun beat down on them. In addition, on one side they were harassed by falcon-shots fired from the fort of Cachitulco; it was a very effective weapon, although at first they shot their balls too high. After lowering their aim somewhat, they struck seven Spaniards. The companions of the governor forced him to move to another place, as balls were constantly striking where he was. At the very moment when he left the spot, his shield-bearer, stepping into his place, was struck. On this account the sargento-mayor endeavored to hold back the forces until they could hear what the lookouts said, or receive an order from the governor. From among the body of the troops he heard a voice, calling upon him to attack without doubting of the victory; that the mother of God purposed that on that day her holy confraternity should be established in this country. The sargento-mayor turned his head and asked in a loud voice: "What devout or holy person has said this to us?" There was no answer, and it was not known from whom the voice proceeded; but it seemed to him that it spoke to him from within, and that it came from heaven. It inspired in him such spirit and courage that he turned to the captains and said: "Gentlemen, the mother of God wills us to gain this fort today." Captain Cubas reached the fort, from which his troops were somewhat driven back by the Moros, and his foot was wounded by a pointed stake [*puia*]. Some beginning to call "Sanctiago!" and others "Victory!" they all began to run on boldly and proudly without any order. So quickly was the fort taken that the captain-general did not even know it when the soldiers had actually surmounted the wall. They went on to where the king was fortified, with many arquebuses and culverins; and with four pieces of ordnance (*pieças de batir*), and with a high wall, from which the enemy did much execution with bucacaos[48] and fire-hardened reeds anointed with poison. But none of these things availed him; and, seeing that the day was lost he fled with some of his followers, in a caracoa and four xuangas, to the island of the Moro, or Batachina [*i.e.*, Gilolo], to which they had sent their women and children and their wealth. On account of this the sack did not bring very much gold or money, but amounted to only two thousand ducats and some cloth and cloves. The rest of the prize was artillery, culverins, arms, and ammunition. After the victory, the sargento-mayor went to ask the governor for the countersign, and found him on his knees before an image of our Lady, saying: "I beg humility of you, our Lady, since by you this victory has been gained." On the following day, Sunday, the second of April (which was, accordingly, the first Sunday in the month), the governor ordered an altar to be prepared, and directed that the painting we carried of the mother of God of the Rosary, with the governor, the captains and the men at her feet should be placed thereon, so that mass might be said. They brought from the mosque a pulpit, in which father Fray Andres preached. That which had previously been a mosque was from that day forth the parish church and mother church—the religious living in one part of it, and administering the holy sacrament. The confraternity was established, and it and the city and the principal fort received the name of El Rosario [*i.e.*, "The Rosary"] that this signal mercy might remain in the memory of those who were to come. In these events there were many things that appeared miraculous. The first of them was the voice which the sargento-mayor heard, with regard to which he declared upon oath that he could not find out who spoke it, that it appeared to speak to him within, and that the words inspired in him great confidence, as has been said. The second miraculous element is the speed with which victory was attained; for when the governor went away to speak, with the king of Tidore, who is friendly, the report that the fort had been gained reached him so quickly that the governor was amazed, and the king did not believe it. The third was the few deaths which occurred on our side; for only fifteen died in the war, and twenty were wounded. The fourth is that when a Dutchman—or, as others say, a man of Terrenate—was trying to fire a large paterero to clear a straight path where a great number of our soldiers were marching up hill in close order, he tried three times to fire it with a linstock, but was unable to do so. When the Moros told him to hasten and fire it, he said that a lady with a blue mantle was preventing him with a corner of the mantle, and sprinkling sand in the touch-hole. So, throwing away the linstock, he began to run; and the Spaniards came up with him and killed him.

At the beginning of August in the same year, large reenforcements of religious came from España; and so great was the need which there was of them that they came at a very fortunate time, especially since they were picked men in virtue and learning. The first who volunteered for this province were five members of the college of Sancto Thomas at Alcala, which event attracted so much attention in the convent of San Estevan at Salamanca that, when the vicar of the religious reached there, thirteen members of that convent volunteered. Among them was the preacher of that distinguished convent, father Fray Diego del Aguila. To these, others from other convents added themselves, and a member of the college of San Gregorio, of whose great virtue an account will immediately be given. When the time for beginning the voyage arrived, the thirteen members of the order from the convent of San Estevan at Salamanca prostrated themselves on the floor of the church, after thanks had been returned for the meal which had been completed, and asked for the blessing of the superior that they might begin their journey. This act aroused great devotion among those who were present. When they had received the blessing, they went in procession to the convent of novices, where they took their cloaks and bags; and intoning the devout hymn of the Holy Spirit, they began with His divine support upon this journey, with their staves and hempen sandals, after the manner of persons who go on foot. They were led by father Fray Diego del Aguila, the preacher of that convent at the time, and an example of virtue in that city where he had preached with great reputation for the four years preceding. Hence to see him walking on foot, and on his way to regions so remote, was a thing which caused great tenderness and devotion in those who knew him, and who saw so devout and so humble an act, so determined a resignation, and such contempt for the world. He labored much in the ship, hearing confessions, and preaching and teaching; for as in voyages there are so many kinds of people, there is need of all of these things, while many of the people need them all at once, because they do not know the doctrine which it is their duty to know and believe, and do not take that care of their souls which they ought to take. Some of them do not even desire to have such things spoken of, that their ignorance may not be known; and hence there is much labor in teaching them, and it is a great service to God not to refuse this labor.

[The member of the college of San Gregorio at Valladolid who came with the rest of these religious was Fray Pedro Rodriguez, a native of Montilla and a son of the convent of San Pablo at Cordoba. His departure caused much grief. His parents loved him tenderly, for he was, like Benjamin, the youngest and was very obedient and docile by nature. The religious of his convent were grieved because they had seen in him so notable a beginning in virtue and letters. In spite of the efforts of fathers, kinsmen, and religious, father Fray Pedro maintained his resolve. His virtues were very great, and he mortified himself constantly. His last illness befell him when the vessel had already come among these islands; and they were already at the port of Ybalon, and were carrying him ashore that he might receive the viaticum, when he lost consciousness. He had desired to be left in the islands of the Ladrones, that he might serve as missionary; but he was not permitted to do so, on account of the great difficulties which he would have met with because of ignorance of the language. It may be that father Fray Pedro would have overcome them; but such things ought not to be left in the hands of a single person. The evil results which follow are morally worse than the gain which may be expected, as has been found out by experience since religious of the seraphic father St. Francis have remained there. His body was taken to be buried in the church of Casigura. He left behind him among his brethren the name of saint.]

Chapter LXIV

Other events which happened at this time in Japon and the Philippinas

[The circumstances in Japon were such that many of the converts were obliged to spend six, or eight, or even fifteen years without confessing, while some of them had not seen a confessor within forty years. Hence the fathers Fray Thomas and Fray Alonso were anxious to go up into the country to continue the good work which they had begun. The vicar-provincial, Fray Francisco de Morales, sent father Fray Alonso de Mena to the kingdom of Fixen,[49] where there had been no church up to this year 1606. A certain captain, Francisco Moreno Donoso, had taken some Franciscan fathers with him on a journey, and on the voyage had been delivered from great danger by the intercession of our Lady of the Rosary. He was therefore devoted to this our Lady. Although the kingdom of Fixen is very near Nangasaqui, the king had always been unwilling to admit preachers of Christianity; but this king had a great regard for Captain Moreno Donoso, who went to visit the king with father Fray Alonso; and the captain made the king many gifts, refusing to accept anything in return except a chain. The king showed him such favor that the captain took advantage of the opportunity to ask permission that father Fray Alonso might establish convents and churches in the kingdom. The king was pleased to grant it, insisting only that the sanction of a great bonze, named Gaco, should first be secured; he was a native of Fixen, and was the most highly regarded man in Japan because of his learning. The king sent his own secretary to go before the bonze, to tell him of the poverty, the penitence, the contempt for the things of this world, the modesty, the humility, and the courteous behavior of the father. The bonze, seeing that it was the pleasure of the king, said that such a man might very well receive this permission. In conformity with it three poor churches and houses were built— one in Famamachi under the patronage of our Lady of the Rosary; the second in the city of Caxima [*i.e.*, Kashima]. named for St. Vincent; and, after some time, another one at the king's court [*i.e.*, Saga], for which at that time permission had been refused. Father Fray Alonso and his companion, when he had one, got the little they needed for their support from Portuguese and Castilians in Nangasaqui, that they might avoid asking for alms from the Japanese, and might thus give no opportunity for the bonzes to complain against them, and to find a pretext for sending them out of the country. Father Fray Alonso remained in this kingdom; and the order persevered until the persecution, when all the religious who had been hiding there were ordered to depart from Japon. Father Fray Alonso found in this kingdom some Japanese who had been baptized in other kingdoms, but had not been well taught in the faith, or who had forgotten the good teachings that they had received at their baptism. They were guilty of much irregularity in their marriages; and some of them had assumed to baptize others without knowing the essence of the baptismal form, so that it was difficult to determine which of them had received valid baptisms. These imperfectly prepared converts had also done harm by endeavoring to sustain arguments against the opponents of Christianity, and, being insufficiently grounded in the faith, they had spread false impressions of the Christian religion. Notable cases of conversion occurred, there being some instances well worthy of remark in the court; and finally the sanctity of the life of the missionaries caused them to be called *xaxino padre*, "fathers who despise the world." The father Fray Juan de Los Angeles, or Rueda, came to live at Fixen in the following year, 1607.

In this year 1606 of which we have been speaking, there died at sea father Fray Domingo de Nieva, who was on his way to act as procurator of the province. He had labored much and well among the Indians of Bataan and among the Chinese. Father Fray Domingo was a native of Billoria in Campos, and a son of the convent of San Pablo at Valladolid. He was a man of ability and of good will. When nearly all the lecturers in theology from that convent, together with the lecturers in arts, and many of their most able and learned disciples, determined to go to the Philippinas, father Fray Domingo joined his masters. He suffered his life long from headache. Being sent to Bataan in company with three other fathers, he, as the youngest, had to carry a very heavy burden of duties. He was fortunate enough not to suffer from any further diseases, the Lord being pleased not to add any to his constant headache. His mortification, fasting, and discipline were very great. He wrote some devout tracts in the language of the Indians, and some others in that of the Chinese. He had printed for the Chinese in their language and characters an essay upon the Christian life, with other brief tracts of prayer and meditation, in preparation for the holy sacraments of confession and the sacred communion. He wrote a practically new grammar of the Chinese language, a vocabulary, a manual of confession, and many sermons, in order that those who had to learn this language might find it less difficult. He was prior of Manila; and in the third year of his priorate the news arrived of the death of father Fray Pedro de San Vicente, who was going to España as definitor in the chapter general and as procurator for this province. Since it was necessary to send another in his place, father Fray Domingo received the appointment to the duty. Like his predecessor, he died on the voyage from the islands to Mexico.]

Chapter LXV

The foundation of Manavag in Pangasinan and the deaths of some religious

In the year 1605 the missionaries to Pangasinan, not contented with the fruitful results of their labors in the level region of that province, took under their charge the village of Manavag, situated among the mountains at a considerable distance from the other villages. The first entry into this village was made by the religious of our father St. Augustine in the year 1600; they built there a church named after St. Monica, and baptized some children. The village was so small, however, that it was not possible for a religious to find enough to do there to justify his continued residence; and accordingly it was visited from Lingayen, the capital of that province, which was at that time in their hands. It caused them a great deal of labor, since they were obliged to travel three days if they went there by water, and two if they went by land; and therefore it was seldom visited, and little good resulted to the village. Inasmuch as the whole population were heathen, they required much persuasion to lead them to baptism, and a great deal of attention to their religious instruction. On this account, those fathers placed a juridical renunciation of the said village in the hands of the bishop, Don Fray Diego de Soria. The bishop, being a religious of our order, asked his brethren to take charge of this village, since there were in it many baptized children, and no other body of religious could care for and guide them. The bishop, in asking the religious to take this matter in charge, was laying upon them no small burden; yet the need was almost extreme, and the great labor brought with it great reward—for, as the apostle says, each man shall be rewarded at the last judgment in proportion to his labors. Hence they determined to assume the charge, and the superior sent there father Fray Juan de San Jacintho,[50] a devoted religious and an indefatigable laborer in the teaching of the Indians. He went to Manavag in the year mentioned, and the fact was spread abroad among the neighboring villages. On account of the great love which they had for the order, and especially for the religious who was there (for he was like an angel from heaven), some other hamlets were added to that one, and the village of Manavag was made of reasonable size. The Negrillos and Zambales who go about through those mountains were continually harassing this village, partly because of their evil desires to kill men, and partly for robbery. They often came down upon it with bows and arrows, and with fire to burn the houses and the church which was practically all of straw. They committed murders, and robbed women and children. Those in the village being thus terrorized, and the men being unable to prevent the evil, since their enemies came when they had gone out into the fields, it was determined to take as patroness the Virgin of the Rosary, that she might aid them in this need. They accordingly dedicated a new church to her, and solemnized the dedication with many baptisms of adult persons. Within a few months, there was not a heathen within the village—a clear proof that the presence of heathen in the country is due solely to a lack of missionaries. Wherever the missionaries are, all are immediately baptized; and not only those of that village which has the missionaries, but some of their neighbors also, participate in the teaching of the religious, and in the favors of our Lady of the Rosary. This is plain from a miracle which occurred a few years after, and was verified before the vicar-general of this country, who at that time was father Fray Pedro de Madalena. It happened thus. Four leguas from Manavag, in a village of Ygolote Indians who inhabit some high mountain ridges, there lived an Indian chief, a heathen, by the name of Dogarat, who used sometimes to go down to the village of Manavag, and to listen out of curiosity to the preaching of the religious. Since the matters of our faith are truly divine, the Indian began to incline toward them, and even toward becoming a Christian. He therefore learned the prayers, and knew them by heart; and the only thing which held him back was the necessity of leaving his vassals and his kinsmen if he was baptized, and going away from the washings in a river of his village, where they used to gather grains of gold, which come down with the water from those hills and ridges where they are formed. God our Lord, to draw him to the precious waters of baptism, brought upon him a severe illness. When he felt the misery of this disease, he sent to call the religious who was at that time in Manavag, father Fray Thomas Gutierrez, who came to his village, called Ambayaban, and visited the sick Indian, giving him thorough instruction in the matters of our holy faith. When he was thoroughly prepared he baptized him and named him Domingo. By the aid of the Lord he recovered, and used to attend church on feast days. He asked for a rosary, which the religious gave him with a direction to say the prayers of the rosary every day, that the Sovereign Lady might aid him. He went out hunting once; and in order that the rosary, which he always wore about his neck, might not interfere with him or be broken by catching in a branch, he took it off and hung it on a tree, and with it a little purse in which he was carrying a trifle of gold. It happened soon after that some Indians set fire to the mountain to frighten out the game. The fire kindled the tree where the rosary was hanging, and burnt it all to ashes. Some time afterward Don Domingo came back for his rosary, and discovered the destruction which the fire had wrought, and the tree in ashes. As he was looking among them he found his rosary entire and unhurt, while everything else was burnt up, and the purse and the gold were consumed, though they were close to the rosary, which did not show a sign of fire. The Indian, amazed, went and told his story to father Fray Thomas, who for a memorial of this marvel kept the miraculous rosary among the treasures of the church, giving the Indian another in its place. There it remained, in token of the esteem and respect which our Lady willed that the fire should pay to her holy rosary.

[In the month of June, 1607, father Fray Juan Baptista Gacet ended his labors happily in the convent of Sancto Domingo at Manila. He was a son of the convent of Preachers at Valencia, and a beloved disciple of St. Luis Beltran, whom he succeeded in the office of master of novices at Valencia. When St. Luis returned from the Indias, the Lord moved father Fray Juan to go to them, as he desired to reap a harvest of souls, and feared that they might strive to make him superior in his own province. He received the approval of St. Luis, and went to the Indias at the time when master Fray Alonso Bayllo went out from his convent of Murcia, by command of our lord the king and of the general of the order, to divide the province of Vaxac from that of Sanctiago de Mexico. Being threatened with a superiorship in the province of Vaxac, father Fray Juan did what he could to avoid it. When a company of religious under the leadership of father Fray Pedro de Ledesma passed through Nueva España on their way to the Philippinas, father Fray Juan decided to accompany them, though he was already of venerable age; and he reached Manila in 1596. Here he was greatly honored, and, being too old to learn the Indian languages, was retained in the convent of Manila to act as confessor and spiritual guide to a number of devout persons in the city. He was made definitor in the first provincial chapter, and was later obliged to accept the office of prior—having no other country to flee to, as he had fled from España to the Indias, and thence to the Philippinas, to avoid this elevation. He was given to devout exercises and to prayer, reading often from some devout book, usually from St. John Climachus, and afterward discussing the passage, and making it the basis of devout meditation. After leaving the office of prior, he returned to his life of devotion and abstraction.

On the twentieth of July in the same year, father Fray Miguel de Oro ended his life in the province of Nueva Segovia. He was a native of Carrion de Los Condes; and he took the habit and professed in San Pablo at Valladolid. He afterward went to the religious province of Guatemala, where he remained for some years, but afterward returned to España. In 1599 the plague attacked all España and raged with especial violence in Valladolid. Father Fray Miguel, with four other religious of our order, devoted himself to the care of those who were plague-stricken. After the plague he retired to the convent of La Peña de Francia; but his memory was constantly stirred by the recollection of his service among the Indians, and in 1601 he went with some other religious to Manila. He was assigned to the province of Nueva Segovia, where, although on account of his great age he was unable to learn the language, his holy example was of great value. He was of great help and comfort to the minister whom he accompanied, doing all that he could to make it possible for the minister (who knew the language) to work among the Indians, and to write in the Indian language compositions and spiritual exercises, which were of service to the ministers that came after them. He used to wear next his skin a thick chain, weighing ten libras; and, that the other brethren might not perceive the marks of it on his tunics, he used to take care to wash and dry them apart. He died as a result of a fever caused by the heat of the sun. Father Fray Miguel was of swarthy complexion, with black and very prominent eyes which inspired fear. After his death he remained handsome, fair, and rosy, which caused those present to wonder-all supposing that these were signs of the glory which his soul already enjoyed.]

Chapter LXVI

The establishment of two churches in Nueva Segovia

In the month of August, 1607, at the octave of the Assumption of our Lady, a church was erected in the village of Nalfotan, the chief village among those which are called the villages of Malagueg [*i.e.*, Malaúeg] in Nueva Segovia. This church had the name and was under the patronage of St. Raymond. The Indians of these villages were and are courageous and warlike. Hence before the coming of the faith they were constantly at war among themselves and with their neighbors, being men of fierce mind and lofty courage, and highly prizing their valor, strength and spirit, an inheritance left to them by their ancestors. Thus they and their neighbors of Gatarang and Talapa, with whom they were very closely related, gave the Spaniards a great deal of trouble, and were feared and still are feared by the other Indians of that large province. In the village called Nalfotan the chief and lord at this time was a young man named Pagulayan, to whom our Lord, in addition to high rank, great wealth, and courage, had given a quiet and peaceful disposition. He was a friend of peace and of the public weal—[seeking not only] his own advantage, but that of his people, and striving to secure what he recognized as good; and in him ran side by side the love of peace, and military spirit and courage—in which he was distinguished and eminent, and for which he was therefore feared by his enemies. God our Lord, so far as we can judge, had predestinated him for Himself; and this he showed by the great affection with which he listened to matters dealing with the service of God, even when he was a heathen and was living among barbarians, idolaters and demons, such as were all his vassals. When he heard that the Ytabes Indians, his neighbors, had religious of St. Dominic who taught them a sure and certain road to salvation, and to the gaining of perpetual happiness for the soul in heaven by serving God in peace and quietude, he strove with all his heart to enjoy so great a good. He discussed the matter with his Indians, and with their approval went down many times to the city of the Spaniards to carry out his religious purpose, endeavoring to have the father provincial, Fray Miguel de San Jacintho, give him a religious for his village. The provincial would have rejoiced to give him one; but those whom he had were so busy, and he had already withdrawn so many in response to such requests, that he was unable to satisfy this good desire, except with the hope that a missionary would be provided there as soon as the religious had come whom he was expecting from España. The good Pagulayan, although he was somewhat consoled, did not cease to

166

complain, with feeling, that he had been unable to bring to his village the good which he desired for it. As he was unable to obtain a religious, he took with him a Christian child from among those who were being taught the Christian doctrine in the church, that the boy might instruct him until a father should come who could complete and perfect his teaching. Nay, more: he and his people, having confidence in the promise which had been given them, erected a church in their village that they might influence the religious [to go there], and have that stronger reason for supplying a minister to them rather than to other villages which had no church. All this greatly affected the religious; and finally, in August of this year [1607], father Fray Pedro de Sancto Thomas[51] went there and found the church already built, and the whole village—men, women, and children—gathered on purpose to receive him, as they did with great joy and the exhibition of much content. This caused like content in the soul of father Fray Pedro, who giving many thanks to the Lord, whose work this was, firmly resolved to labor with all his strength in this vineyard which seemed to bear fruit before it was cultivated. Father Fray Pedro was very well suited to begin a conversion like this; for he was so simple and affable that the most remote barbarians, if they talked with him, were compelled to love him. He was of a very gentle nature, and extremely open-hearted, being entirely free from any duplicity or deceit, and acting in all things with the bowels of charity. This is the greatest snare to catch love which may be set for men. Hence they received him as if he came from heaven, and at the beginning they listened to him and obeyed him with great zeal. The devil at these things suffered from rage and the worst pains of hell, as he saw himself losing, all at once, villages which had been his for so many ages. Hence by the means of a sorceress, a priestess of his, named Caquenga, he began to disturb the Indians, to whom this wicked woman said such things that many determined to follow the rites of their ancestors and not to receive the teaching of the divine law. So devilish was this cursed anitera that she kept stirring up some of them against the religious, while at the same time with those who wished to keep him she pretended to be on their side; thus she deceived them all, especially those who were influenced by their zeal for ancient superstitions. Hence they themselves killed their fowls and the swine which they had bred, tore down their houses, and cut down their palm-groves, in which their principal wealth consisted; and, crying out, "Liberty!" they fled to the mountains. Here they joined those who had hitherto been their enemies, that they might be more in number and might bring a greater multitude of weapons against a solitary friar who went unarmed, and whom they had invited to their village with such urgency, and received with such joy; and against whom they had no complaint except simply that he preached to them the law of God and the gospel of peace, at their own invitation, and that a most earnest invitation. Pagulayan, with some of his vassals, was constantly at the side of Fray Pedro—who, being secure in his own conscience, was not intimidated, but strove to bring back those who had revolted. Seeking for means of speaking to them, he determined to send an Indian who should arrange in his behalf for a conference; and who should promise the chief of the revolted ones, whose name was Furaganan, that the Spaniards who were ¡n the city of Nueva Segovia would not punish him for what he had done. That the Indian might feel safe and might believe him, he gave the man a relic of St. Thomas to carry; for among them there was no one who knew how to read or write, because they had no letters of their own, so that he was unable to give him a letter, or any other token better known as coming from the father. This, however, sufficed to cause Furaganan to listen to the messenger without ill-treating him; and he agreed to meet the religious at a certain place and on an appointed day. As a token of fidelity and peace, Furaganan sent his bararao—a dagger with which they stab close at hand, and can easily cut off a head—that it might be put in the hands of the religious. They met on the assigned day; and the Indian, annoyed with Caquenga, who had caused the disturbance among them, immediately joined the party of the religious against whom she had caused them to rebel. Furaganan asked them to give him this Indian anitera as a slave, alleging that she had been a slave of his mother, and that in this way and no other could quiet be restored, because he could not suffer that this intriguing slave-woman should, merely through her crafty acts, be more esteemed by the Spaniards than were the chiefs. She was, he said, full of duplicity, having remained with Pagulayan that she might be able to say afterward to the Spaniards that she was not at fault for the uprising—although, in point of fact, she had been the cause of it. Fray Pedro promised to look after this business with great diligence, and to do what should be best. The Indian departed, apparently in peace; but the others did not continue in that frame of mind. At midnight, while the religious was reciting the matins, on the first Sunday of Advent, and when he had come to the first response, the insurgents set fire to the church, thus alarming those who had remained in the village, and causing them to take flight. Pagulayan came to father Fray Pedro, and, acting as his guide, put him on a safe road, carrying him at times on his shoulders across creeks and rivers on the road which they followed. At dawn they halted in a thicket, whence the father went to a little village farther down, because the place where they were was not safe. Here Pagulayan carried the robes from the sacristy, and father Fray Pedro put them as well as he could into a chest, being obliged to leave out a canvas of our Lady, which on account of its size the chest would not hold.

Leaving it there, he went on to the village of Pia, where there was a religious with many Christians, and where the people were peaceful. The insurgents went straight down to the village where the chest and the picture were; and, opening the chest, they took out the ornaments, the chalice, and all the rest, and profaned everything. They cut the ornaments of the mass into pieces, to make head-cloths and ribbons. They tore the leaves out of the missal, and drank out of the chalice, like a godless race governed by the devil. Taking the image painted on the canvas, they set it up as a target for their lances. One of them blasphemously said: "This, the fathers tell us, is the mother of God; if this were truth, our lances would draw blood, and since she sheds none, it is all trickery and deceit." The savage said this when he was throwing his lance at the image, and his audacity did not remain without its punishment, for he was soon after condemned to the galleys; and here, in addition to the ordinary hardships suffered in them, he was maltreated by all the other galley slaves when they learned that his crime had been committed against our Lady. They struck him, buffeted him, kicked him, and abused him with words as an enemy of the Virgin; and in this state he died, passing from the wretched life of the galleys to eternal death in hell.

In this same year the Indians of Zimbuey, in the level part of La Yrraya in the same province, rose and murdered their encomendero Luis Henriquez, angered because he had treated them during the previous year with more rigor than was proper. There was no religious here. The Indians, in fear of like severity during the present year, had mutinied against the encomendero and thrust him through with a lance. Out of his shin-bones they made steps to go up to the house of their chief—a piece of savagery such as might be expected from enraged Indians. Information of these two risings was sent to the governor of Manila, who sent out the sargento-mayor Christobal de Azcueta with a sufficient number of soldiers. He ascertained the facts in both cases and brought out the truth clearly—namely, that the excesses of the dead encomendero had caused the Indians of his encomienda at Zimbuey to rise, and that the intrigues of Caquenga had roused the Indians of Malagueg. The latter, conscious of their fault, came to the city of Nueva Segovia to beg that the religious might return to them; and father Fray Pedro de Sancto Thomas returned with them. He had greater confidence in the many hopes which he had, for many of them, that they would be good and faithful Christians, than resentment for the wrongs which he had received from others. All this disturbance came to an end, and he built convents and churches and baptized many. In course of time all those people were baptized. Pagulayan was named Luis, and one of his sisters was named Luysa Balinan. They were always very brotherly and sisterly in all things, especially in following virtue. They

169

remained very firm in the faith, and have aided much to bring their Indians to embrace it. They lived according to the teachings of the faith, giving a noble example in this respect, and obviously surpassing all those of their land in everything that has to do with virtue and the service of God. They were, during all their lives, the support of the mission, the comfort of the religious, and generous honorers of their church—upon the adornment of which they spent freely in proportion to their means, giving silver lamps and other very rich ornaments for the service and beautifying of the church. Nor did they forget the poor, not only of their own village, but of the others, who very often come to this one to find food, since this is generally the village where food is most abundant. Don Luis Pagulayan died while young, in the year 1620. His death was much regretted and deplored, as it still is both by the religious and by his Indians, and much more by his sister, Doña Luysa Balinan. She is yet living, and perseveres in holy customs and in laudable acts of all the virtues; for she wears hair shirts underneath her dress as a married chieftainess, is constantly in the church, and is very frequent in her confessions and communions. She is very careful that not only those of her household (who are many) but all of the village—which is one of the largest in the province of Nueva Segovia—should carefully observe the law of God and hear and learn the Catholic doctrine. This she herself ordinarily teaches, and teaches well, for she has had much practice in this office, so that she greatly aids the ministers. A few years ago, there was in this province a great famine; and Doña Luisa having very fertile land, from which she might have made a great profit, preferred to offer it to Christ through His poor. Hence she spent it all upon them, directing all the poor to come every day to her for their food, as was done. In any tumult or disturbance that may arise, she is one from whom the religious learn with perfect certainty the truth of what has happened; and by her assistance (for she is very prudent) the remedy is obtained. The Lord watches over her and prospers her in all things—not only spiritual, in which she surpasses, but also temporal, for she is one of the richest persons that there are in this province. When some superstitious performances were carried on here by some of the chiefs, she immediately informed the religious. When he asked her if she dared to declare the matter before the guilty persons, that in this way the evil might be demonstrated and cured, she replied that she would venture, even though they should give her poison; for they were unable to avenge themselves in any other way, and she had reason to expect them to do this. Such is the spirit and courage with which she serves the Lord and strives for the good of her fellow-men; and so little does she esteem life when there is an opportunity for her to venture it for such a noble end. In the year 1626, the names of those entered in the records of baptism in this church of Nalfotan were counted. The total was found to be four thousand six hundred and seventy, in addition to those baptized in sickness, who were many; and all this rich harvest was reaped in a village which eighteen years ago was composed wholly of heathen.

At the end of this year, 1607, another church was built in December, on Innocents' day, in a village of the same province named Yguig, two days' journey up the river from the city of the Spaniards. The encomendero had collected his tribute from these Indians with great care; but he had given no attention to providing them with Christian instruction, as God and the king commanded him. The Lord, who overlooks many other grievous sins, was unwilling to let this pass without chastisement; but the punishment which He gave the encomendero was that of a kind father, and was inflicted outside of his clothes—that is to say, it fell only upon his wealth, which, when it is guiltily acquired, shall not profit. This encomendero lost all; and when these misfortunes came upon him, one after the other, he perceived that they did not come by chance, and saw what it was with which the Lord might be angry. This was his supporting idolatry and the service of the devil in this village, by his mere failure to provide Christian instruction in it, as was his duty. He repented of what he had hitherto done, and vowed to provide in this village the teaching of the true God, and a religious to preach and teach it. In this year he asked for the religious from the father provincial, Fray Miguel de San Jacintho, and one was given him. Since there was a discussion as to what patron this new church should be given, many slips with the names of saints upon them were placed in a vessel. Three times the name of Sanctiago, patron of the Españas, came out; and hence the church was given this name, which has been retained in this village of Yguig. This has been done in spite of the fact that, on account of great inundations and floods of the river, it has been necessary to build the church on four separate sites—the first three having been overflowed, although it did not appear possible that the river should reach land situated so high. This river, however, is very large; and its floods are so extreme that they overflowed these eminences, until the church was finally placed where it now is, which is upon a very high hill. Here it enjoys without disturbance the fresh breezes, and is safe against any flood. Among all these changes and difficulties, this tribe would have been scattered and their village destroyed, if the religious had not sustained them with alms and charities. They received much assistance from the Indian chiefs, in particular from one who far surpassed the others in Christian zeal and in fidelity to God, the church, and the Spaniards. The Lord has wrought him great and apparent benefits for this. One was as follows. He went for many days under a temptation of the devil to kill another Indian chief, who had wrought him a great wrong; and could not rest by day or by night for thinking how he might obtain satisfaction against the guilty man. Now he thought of these plans, now of those, and was in such disquiet that he could not conceal the matter. The religious came to a knowledge of this, called him aside, and rebuked him earnestly, for his guilt and the great sin which he was designing, which was entirely contrary to the laws which should govern a Christian, such as he was, who is bound to love his enemies. It was even contrary to the principles of his rank and his chieftainship for him to desire to commit a murder. Don Ambrosio Luppo (as this Indian was named) responded, weeping freely: "Would to God, father, that you might see my heart, in order that you might understand well how much I suffer from the deed of this man, and might also see plainly how great an impression your teachings have made upon me. If I had not looked to God for some way of following your teachings, would this man have had his head on his shoulders so long? But I pardoned him because God pardoned me; and from that time I have been calm, and more devout than before." He received another benefit. He and his wife much desired to have children, but, though they had lived for many years together, they had now passed their youth, and had no children. They communicated their desire to the father, and he advised them what they ought to do, saying: "When good Spaniards feel these desires, they offer particular devotion to the mother of God and to other great saints"—naming some who are of most signal assistance in such cases—"and they go to the churches and offer prayers before their images, that they may intercede with God who can do all things. In this way they many times attain what they desire." "All this will we do very willingly," answered husband and wife; "but what shall we say in our prayer after we have recited the *Paternoster* and the *Ave Maria*?" The religious taught them what they ought to say and what prayers they ought to make to our Lady, briefly indicating to her the desire which they had, and offering to her service the fruit of the blessing which they might attain by their prayers. This they did, going with their petition to the Lady of the Rosary which was in their church. A year later they had a son, to whom the religious, in memory of that which had been agreed upon, gave the name of Juan de Sancta Maria. The parents recognized him as a gift from our Lady. Afterward this same Lady, by means of this same religious, restored the child to complete health in an instant, when it was almost at the point of death. This she did for the comfort of the parents, for it seemed as if they would follow it out of sorrow. On many other occasions she has come to their help; and the Lord has rewarded them with a generous hand for the faith and the good services which, since they became Christians, they have done and are doing.

Chapter LXVII

The election as provincial of father Fray Baltasar Fort, the martyrdom of the holy Leon, and events in the province.

In April, 1608, the electors, assembled in the convent of Sancto Domingo at Manila, chose as provincial father Fray Baltasar Fort, minister of the holy gospel in the province of Pangasinan. He was by habit and profession a son of the convent of San Estevan at Salamanca, and adopted into that of the Preachers in Valencia, his native land, whence he came to this province in the year 1602. He was at this time prior of the convent. He was of a character such that all necessary qualities for so high an office were united in him; and hence his election was very agreeable to all, both religious and lay, because he was greatly loved and reverenced by all—not only of his own religious order, but also of the others. In this chapter were accepted the houses which had been newly formed in Japon, Pangasinan, and Nueva Segovia, an account of which has been given in the two preceding chapters. What had been at other times ordained and commanded was recalled to mind—namely, that in our conversations we should speak constantly of God, a subject which is never exhausted, is never wearisome to a good man, is edifying to all, and keeps the religious in the fulfilment of the obligations that belong to their estate.

[At this time the fathers who were laboring for the good of the natives of Japon had a joyful day in seeing the martyrdom of a person who had been brought to the faith, instructed, and baptized by their ministry; and in whom the faith had struck so deep roots that he yielded fruit an hundred fold, according to the gospel, by suffering martyrdom within four months after becoming a Christian. Having been baptized on July 22, 1608, he was decapitated for his confession of faith on the seventeenth of November in the same year, in the kingdom of Satzuma, his native country. There were laws of the emperor, and also of the actual king of that region, that no soldier or person of rank should be baptized, since it was believed that the strength of these persons would be weakened if they gave up their obligations to those deities from whom victory was expected. In spite of this law, many soldiers and persons of rank were baptized, among them Xichiyemon, a youth of high rank. He received baptism from the hands of father Fray Joseph de San Jacintho, who warned him of the tumult which his baptism would arouse, and of the destruction of his soul which would follow if he were to renounce his baptism. He was so determined and courageous that the father baptized him by the name of Leon. His devotion was such that his conversion could not long be hidden; and, when it was known, the valiant Leon was obliged to resist the supplications of his superior officers, his friends, and his relatives, who represented to him the shame which he would bring upon his family if he should die by the hands of the executioner. This is a thing above measure infamous in Japon, because all malefactors of rank who are condemned to death cut open their own abdomens, and wound their bowels with their own knives [*catanas*], and thus kill themselves, that they may not die at the hands of another."[52] His obligations to his wife and children, and his duties of obedience as a soldier, were insisted upon; but he remained resolved to die as a Christian, not taking his own life, but offering it. He was not imprisoned, and visited his spiritual father, Fray Juan Joseph de San Jacintho, in a little village a quarter of a legua from Firaça. At the appointed time he dressed himself in new white clothes, washed his head, and gird on two swords. He then went to the cross-roads where he was to suffer, and died with a rosary in his hand and a little picture of the descent from the cross on his bosom. His holy body was exhumed by the Christians, and was kept by the fathers of St. Dominic, who afterward, when they were driven from the country, took it with them to Manila and placed it in the chapel of the relics. The tyrant commanded that Leon's wife and eldest son should suffer death, because they had been unable to persuade him to recant. Pablo, Leon's friend, who was accused at the same time, was not so happy as he, but was merely banished from the kingdom of Satzuma.

On the eleventh of April in this year (*i.e.*, 1609) there arrived at Manila some religious from the number of those who were brought from España to this province by father Fray Gabriel de Quiroga. He died on the voyage before he reached Mexico, and most of the others were scattered, and remained in Nueva España. Father Fray Gabriel was a son of our convent at Ocaña. He was a great preacher, and had come to this province in 1594. He was in the ministry to the Chinese; being unable to learn the language on account of his advanced age, and being in ill health, he returned to España. Here he felt scruples at having left the province of the Philippinas, and asked permission of the most reverend general to return to it with a company of religious. In 1607 he gathered a company in Sevilla, but was unable to come for lack of a fleet. Later in the same year, learning that six patches were being prepared for the voyage, he arranged to reassemble the religious and to take them in these vessels, though he had already been appointed bishop of Caceres. He quickly got together thirty associates, taking the risk of sailing in December. The storms were so furious, and the asthma from which the bishop suffered was so severe, that he departed this life on the way. Of all those who came with him only eight completed the voyage which they had begun.

The success of the religious in Satzuma during the six years which they had spent in that kingdom aroused the tono, who was persuaded by the devil and his servants the bonzes to expel the fathers from his country. The case of the holy martyr Leon contributed to influence the tono. It was said in that kingdom that no one ever failed to do what his lords commanded him, and hence such disobedience as that of Leon was regarded as dangerous to the state. The bonzes particularly were bitter against the Christians, who despised the deity whom they worshiped.[53] All the cases of misfortune and all the downfalls which had happened to Christian princes within a few years were referred to their belief, although the misfortunes of the heathen princes had been much more numerous. As the king of Satzuma was at this time actually preparing for a war of conquest against the islands of the Leuquios,[54] he was greatly impressed by these reasonings. He was also disgusted because no vessels had come from Manila to this country, the desire for trade having been his chief object in sending for religious. The king of Satzuma sought for some pretext for expelling the father, without finding any. In the month of August, he sent word to them that the emperor complained because the Spanish religious in his country had never appeared before him. This was only a pretext to get the religious out of the country. There were at that time in all Japan, outside of Nangasaqui, not more than three churches licensed by the emperor: one in Meyaco, of the fathers of the Society; a second in Yendo, of the Franciscan fathers; and a third in Ozaca, of the Society. All the rest were practically in concealment, and had license only from the tonos or kings. The emperor, though he knew this, paid little attention to the matter. The fathers, however, were able to say that father Fray Alonso de Mena had visited the emperor, and had received license from him for the stay in Japan of the rest of the fathers. Still, thinking that they might do well to appear before the emperor, they decided to follow the suggestion of the tono, and father Fray Francisco de Morales went directly to visit him and was kindly received. Before father Fray Francisco returned, the tono gave commands that all the Christians should recant, and exiled those who refused to obey, confiscating their goods. When this happened, there were in Satzuma only the fathers Fray Joseph de San Jacintho and Fray Jacintho Orfanel. Father Fray Joseph went directly to appear before the old tono, and was received with much apparent courtesy, which was a mere cloak for the evil which he was preparing to execute. The father also desired to go to visit the young tono, but was advised that he could do no good; and therefore he went from village to village, strengthening and encouraging the converts. He and father Fray Jacintho, happening to be both at once within the convent, the governor forbade the religious to leave the church, and prohibited the Christians from going to it, hoping thus to prevent the religious from receiving any support. There was only one half-leprous boy, named Juan, who succored them at this time. When he went to buy what they needed, the people paid no attention to his coming and going, because of his being afflicted in this way.]

Chapter LXVIII

The religious, being exiled and expelled from the kingdom of Satzuma, are admitted to other kingdoms.

[The kingdom of Japon is subject to constant changes and novelties, as may be known by those who have lived in it, and by those who have read what historians have to say of it. Although the plague of inconstancy is very common among all heathen, the Japanese are particularly subject to it. It is not to be wondered at that the king of Satzuma, after all that he had done to bring religious from St. Dominic to Manila, should have expelled them without any cause. The natural inconstancy of this race is sufficient explanation for his conduct. St. Francis Xavier was expelled from the same kingdom of Satzuma, as he was afterwards from the country of Yamaguçu,[55] whence he fled to the kingdom of Firando. As early as the year 1555, the heathen Japanese believed that so soon as the faith should enter their country the kingdom would be destroyed; and in the following year the city of Amaguchi was destroyed, and there was a great persecution. In the year 1564 there was another persecution, even more severe, in Meaco, the imperial court. Father Cosme de Torres was obliged to leave there and to go to the kingdom of Bungo. In Firando the churches were overthrown, and the emperor Nabunanga imprisoned Father Argentino[56] and his associate, refusing to release them until he received, as a ransom, from the most noble and Catholic Don Justo the fortress called Tayca Yama.[57] In 1599 the Taico [*i.e.*, Iyeyasu] banished by public edict all the religious there were in Japon (all of whom were then Jesuits), declaring that all Christians were his enemies; but soon after he granted to father Fray Juan Cobo—a religious of St. Dominic, who had come from Manila as ambassador—that he, and religious of the Society or of any other order, might preach and make converts in Japon. The sons of the seraphic father St. Francis went, under this permission, in 1593, and were kindly received; but very soon afterward commands were given to crucify them, as preachers of the gospel. Father Fray Francisco de Morales felt that conditions were such that it was necessary to comply, and began by taking down the church and looking for boats to carry it in; for it was fitted together with grooves, without nails, and could be, used elsewhere. They removed for a time to Meyaco, and soon afterwards to the city of Ozaca. In the erection of both churches they were bitterly opposed by the members of the other religious orders, although the others could not serve the twentieth or the thirtieth part of the people of those cities. The Japanese banished from Satzuma suffered greatly. Among this people banishment is often worse than death, which is not greatly feared by them. Banishment is generally accompanied with a loss of their goods, so that those who are noble and rich are by it instantly reduced to poverty and drudgery. The fathers carried away their vestments, the timber of the church, and the body of the holy martyr Leon, removing them to Nangasaqui. Father Fray Francisco also carried with him the lepers of the hospital which he had before his house, that they might not be left in the power of wolves. In the meantime, the affairs of Christianity went on prosperously in the kingdom of Fixen. In July, 1609, father Fray Juan de Sancto Thomas, who sent the first religious to Japon when he was provincial, came to Japon as vicar-provincial, bringing with him as his associate brother Fray Antonio de San Vicente. He labored much and successfully in Fixen, and the Lord showed the fathers grace by enabling them to baptize many whom He had predestinated at the point of death. There were especially many cases of baptism of new-born children, whom the parents intended to kill, or left to drown in the river.]

One day's journey up the river from Abulug, in the province of Nueva Segovia, there is a village named Fotol in the midst of a number of other smaller villages, as is customary among the mountains. When these villages were visited for the purpose of collecting tribute, the religious was accustomed to go along that he might be there conveniently to give them some knowledge of the law of God, and strive to bring them to a love of the faith by which they might be saved. This diligence, although it was exercised so seldom—only once a year—was yet not in vain; for the words of the gospel sown in the hearts of these heathen took root and caused them to go down [the river], voluntarily, for the purpose of seeking a preacher to live among them, to teach, direct, and baptize them. Father Fray Miguel de San Jacintho, vicar of Abulug, sent there father Fray Diego Carlos.[58] The Spaniards did not dare to visit the village when they collected the tribute, except in numbers and with arms. On this account, and because they were surrounded by mountaineers who were heathen, untamed, and ferocious, it seemed to the Christian Indians of Abulug that the religious ought not to go without a guard to protect his life; but since the order given by our Lord Jesus Christ is not such, but directs that His preachers should go as sheep among wolves, father Fray Diego would not receive the advice given him by these Indians, though they were friendly; and departed alone with his associate, as a preacher of peace and of the law of love. All the Indians, great and small, came out to receive them with great joy; and the religious immediately began to preach to them and to teach them. In a short time they did a great work, and baptized not only those of this village, but also those who dwelt near there.

They left their old sites and, gathering in this one, formed a new settlement. The church was built under the patronage of our Lady of the Rosary, and here the Christian faith went on flourishing until the devil, hating so much good, disturbed them and caused them to fall away for a time—to their great harm, spiritual and temporal; though afterward, recognizing their error, they returned to their obedience to their Creator, as will be told hereafter. Almost in the same manner, and following the same course, another church was built at this time in the high region at the head of the great river, six days' journey from the city of the Spaniards, in a village named Batavag. Here father Fray Luis Flores, who was afterward a holy martyr in Japon, gathered together seven little hamlets, making one very peaceful one. He preached to them, taught them, and baptized many, without receiving any other assistance in all this than that which the Lord promises those who, for love of Him and from zeal for souls, go alone, disarmed, and in gentleness among heathen. To such no evil can happen, since, if the heathen hear the teaching and are converted, all is happiness and joy both in heaven and for the preachers, since the sinners are converted; while if they refuse to admit them, or if, when the preachers are admitted, the heathen do not become converts, the preachers have a certain reward, as the Lord has promised. This reward will be much greater if the heathen, in addition to refusing to be converted, treat them ill, or take their lives from them, for the sake of the Lord whom they preach. Therefore in this as in all the other conversions the religious have always gone alone, unarmed, and in poverty, but sure that they are to suffer no evil. The results in Batavag were very good, although they did not last many years because, desirous of a greater laxity of life than the divine law permits, the natives went up into the neighboring mountain, apostatizing from the faith which many of them had professed in baptism.

In the mountains of Ytui, which are not far from Pangasinan, father Fray Juan de San Jacintho went on a journey at this time, accompanied by only two Indians. Here he taught, settled their disputes, and brought them to the faith. These people were a race of mountaineers, among whom other religious had not been safe even with an escort of many soldiers; but the gentle manners of father Fray Juan caused them to become calm, and many of them came sometimes to Pangasinan to ask that religious might be given to them. Many years passed before it was possible to provide them with religious; but the father provincial had, as minister of Pangasinan, seen their pious desires and wished to give them the religious. For this he requested the sanction of the ordinary, and asked the governor for the royal patronage. When the fathers of St. Francis learned this, they came and said that this conversion belonged to them, because it was very near to the ministry and the convent which they had in Baler. The order (which needed religious in other regions) instantly yielded without any dispute, permitting the fathers of St. Francis to take charge of these Indians. This they did, but very soon abandoned them, since the region was not one to be coveted, but was very unhealthy. As a result these Indians remained for some time deprived of the ministry of the holy gospel; and, what caused greater regret, they were morally certain to apostatize, like many other Christians among heathens, since they were children among idolatrous parents and kinsmen, without religious and without instruction.

[In this year, 1609, father Fray Juan de Anaya departed this life. He was a native of San Pedro de las Dueñas, two leguas from Segovia, and was a professed son of the convent at Valladolid, whence he came to this province in 1598. He was sent immediately to Nueva Segovia, the conversion of which had just begun. He learned the language very quickly, and so wrought with them that he not only taught them the gospel and the Christian life, but also civilization. He showed them how to build their houses, and how to work their fields; and taught them all other matters of human life, not only by instruction, but by example. He sought out the Indians, and brought them down from the mountains and the hiding-places where some, deluded by their sins, had gone to hide from grace. Father Fray Juan was not content to ask where they were and to send for them; but, trusting in his natural strength, he went to look for them and brought them down from the mountains, traveling through the rough and thorny places among the thickets where they hid. He compelled them to enter upon the path of their welfare, not by the violence of a tyrant, but by the force of love and charity. When he was vicar of Pilitan, some of the poor Indians lost all their harvest from an overflow of the river. Not daring to wait for those who were to come and get the tribute, and indeed through fear of starvation, they left the village, and many of them fled to the mountains. Father Fray Juan was deeply afflicted because of the danger which their souls ran. This grief and his many labors affected his health, and finally brought on a flux, from which he died. Another religious, a subordinate and companion of Father Juan, father Fray Vicente Alfonso, died eight days later. He was a Valencian by birth, and had been a sailor up to his twenty-fourth year. He assumed the habit in the convent of Preachers in Valencia, and set a good and humble example as a religious. He was very charitable, giving away even his clothes to the poor. In the province of Pangasinan, in the month of August, 1609, there departed from the miseries of this life father Fray Francisco Martinez, a native of Zacatecas, and a son of the convent of Mexico. He came to Manila in 1598, and was assigned to Pangasinan, where he learned the language of the natives with great perfection. He was constant in labor and in prayer. To defend the Indians, he did not shrink from suffering or fear the perils of the sea. On one occasion, when he had gone to Manila on this account, he fell into the hands of Japanese pirates on his way back to Pangasinan, and was several times in danger of death, with the pirate's knife at his throat, who intended by such terrors to increase the ransom. Death called him from his labors and sufferings. He rejoiced, and died a most holy death.]

In this year the most reverend general of the order, seeing how many great things were wrought by the medium of the divine grace through the religious of this province, and condemning the silence with which they hid and covered them, without giving any account of them even to the general head and superior of the order, issued a mandate to the provincials that they should every year, on pain of incurring mortal sin, give him information of what took place in this province of the Philippinas, Japon, and China in the conversions of the heathen and the extension of the holy Church, the service of the divine Majesty, and the edification of the people of Christ. In addition to this, they were to give an account of the state of our order in each province, declaring how many and what convents it included, how many religious it possessed, and of what virtue, sanctity, learning, and good example they were; telling if any of them, after having done illustrious things, had died gloriously; and recounting all other matters which might be an honor to God, a source of comfort to the religious, and an adornment and decoration of our religious order. Together with this mandate, he wrote with his own hand the following letter, from which may be seen the high esteem in which he held this province. The letter is in the archives of the convent of Manila.

"Very reverend Father Provincial: Father Fray Alonso Navarrete has given me good news of the great devotion, spirit, and continual preaching in this new province. In this I have felt very great satisfaction; but it would be desirable that I should receive more detailed reports with regard to matters there, and particularly with regard to what has been done for the conversion of the heathen, by the grace of our Lord, in those kingdoms of China and Japon. This knowledge would be of great service to our Lord, great edification to our fellow-men, and great honor to our holy religious order. On this account and in order that you, very reverend Father, may have the merit of obedience, it has seemed good to me to send you the enclosed mandate. This is sent, however, still more that it may serve as a memorandum for the fathers provincials who may succeed your Reverence in that province, because I know that there may be some carelessness in this respect. Orders have already been given that friars religious shall go to that province to preach and assist your Paternities in the conversion of the heathen. Would that it might please our Lord that I might go with those for whom our Lord has prepared so great rewards in heaven. Your prayers, very reverend Father, and the prayers of all that province I beg for myself and for my associates. Palermo, June 18, 1609. Your Reverence's fellow-servant in God,

FRAY AGUSTIN GALAMINIO,

master of the Order of Preachers."

Chapter LXIX

The venerable father Fray Bartolome de Nieva, and brother Fray Pedro Rodriguez

[Death fell heavily upon our fathers in this year, seizing the best on every side. In Manila it cut short the thread of the life of father Fray Bartolome de Nieva. Father Fray Bartolome was a native of Nieva in Castilla la Vieja. While still a layman, he went to the Indias in the search for wealth. He spent some years in Mexico; and in spite of the great wealth of that country, the luxury of life there, and the agreeable climate, he could not be satisfied or find peace. Hence he determined to change his course of life, that he might find the calm for which he sought. Though he was already a grown man, he became a child in following the duties of a religious order. He assumed the habit in the convent of Sancto Domingo in that illustrious city, and began not only upon the elements of the religious life, but upon those of grammar. He did well in the studies of arts and theology, and by the aid of the Lord he came forth a religious of great spiritual qualities—prayer, penitence, and prudence, both spiritual and temporal. He joined a company of religious who passed through Mexico in the year 1594, on their way to the Philippinas. He was too old to learn the language of the Indians, but he accompanied the brother who taught and baptized the Chinese in the hospital for that people; and thus assisted the other minister, whose duty it was to live in the hospital. When he determined to go to the Philippinas his companions in Mexico strove to prevent him, because he suffered from several infirmities, and the labors in the Philippinas were known to be very severe. The Lord, however, gave signs that He desired him to go. He showed especial devotion to the holy Virgin and was a useful and devoted minister. The Lord gave father Fray Bartolome wonderful powers of spiritual conversation, and of insight into character; and even some powers of prophecy, of which a number of illustrations are given. Through him the Lord healed not a few sick. A letter of his is reported at length, in which he incites a sinner to give up his evil way of life, and shows a knowledge of the man's heart which could only have been given him by God. Other instances of the same sort are cited and an account of the holy death of father Fray Bartolome is given.

At the same time there died brother Fray Pedro Rodriguez, a companion of the first founders of this province. He was most closely associated with those who taught and baptized the Chinese. During his whole life he had sole charge of the temporal affairs of the hospital. Father Fray Pedro was not content with receiving those who came, but had persons to inform him if there were any sick in the orchards or quarries, or other places where the Chinese who live about Manila were gathered for work; and immediately sent to have them brought to the hospital. He often went in person to bring them, and, no matter how offensive or disgusting their diseases, he cared for them with his own hands. He waited upon them at all hours of the day and night, caring for their bodies; and he strove to teach them the things necessary for the salvation of their souls, as soon as their sickness gave him an opportunity. He suffered greatly from asthma; but, in spite of this affliction, he constantly employed the discipline of stripes—not upon his flesh, for he had none, but upon his bones, which were covered with nothing but skin; insomuch that some Spaniards came to look at him, regarding it as a marvel that such a living image of death should be able to stand. His head was like a skull with eyes in it, but so sunken that it seemed almost as if he had none. The truth is that he ate no more than sufficient to sustain him in this condition; yet he was so attentive and careful to provide dainty food for a sick man that the religious were sent there to him during their convalescence. He had no greater pleasure than this and his unexpected success in converting some heathen. The Lord provided him with these pleasures, which served him as food and drink to sustain his life. To the two hours of mental prayer observed in the whole province he added two others daily, continuing them after that which follows matins, and prolonging them till dawn. As soon as daylight appeared he left the work of Mary to go to that of Martha in caring for his sick, giving them breakfast after their own custom—which is followed in all the care that is given them, and in everything done for them. In spite of all these labors he thought so humbly of himself that one day when a religious heard him uttering heavy groans and deep sighs, and asked the cause, being unable to refrain from doing so, Fray Pedro answered that it was because he was so evil that, though he had so many times prayed to the Lord for a trifle of His love and charity, he had not gained it. The superior desired to try him as to his obedience; and seeing that he labored with such delight at the hospital, and took such joy in serving the sick, he determined to find out if there were some self-love hidden in all this. He therefore directed him to leave the hospital, and to come to the city and take up the office of sacristan in the convent. Fray Pedro immediately obeyed, and, going into the sacristy which was entrusted to him, he fulfilled his duty with cleanliness, neatness, and good grace in all things, just as if he had exercised it all his life, and had never been occupied with the other. He was accordingly directed to return to the hospital, where he was more needed. The governor, Don Juan de Silva, went to visit the hospital; and when he saw this brother with nothing but bones and skin, and when he

183

heard the things which they said of him, he felt such reverence for him that he kissed his hand, and offered him his favor for all things of which his hospital had need, and arranged to grant him all that he wished, for the governor looked upon him and venerated him as a saint. At the time of his death, about three thousand who had died in the hospital had received baptism. In the intermediate chapter which took place in the following year honorable mention was made of this religious.]

Chapter LXX

Father Fray Luis Gandullo, his entrance upon the religious life, and his coming to this province

[The events which happened in the case of this father are such as God rarely manifests, even in the case of those who are nearest to Him; and I should not dare to bring them to the light if they were not attested by three notable circumstances. The first is that he never formed his own judgment about what happened, but submitted the matter to a learned and spiritual man. The second is, that father Fray Luis kept such silence about these things that he only revealed them under the solemn mandate of his superior. The third is the innocence of his life, and his marvelous virtue. A formal certificate as to these three circumstances is given at length; it is by Fray Juan de Sancto Thomas, and is dated at Manila, August 10, 1615. Father Fray Luis Gandullo was a native of the town of Aracena in the archbishopric of Sevilla, and was born of a rich and noble family. At the age of fourteen he made a vow to assume the habit of the Dominican order. This vow he was unable to carry out for eight years, because of his duties to his widowed mother and his two sisters. While still a youth, he was favored with a vision of the Virgin, which was followed soon after by a vision in which the devil appeared to him. After his two sisters were settled in life a certain trouble befell him in his own country, which obliged him to leave it and to go to the Indias. He dwelt for some time in Nueva España, where he lived with some freedom, the Lord preparing to drive him, by the very thorns which he should find in this road, to the religious life. His ancient desires to become a friar of St. Dominic returned to his mind, and he began to arrange with the prior of the convent of the city of Puebla to assume the habit. The prior and the friars of the convent, being asked by him if a secret business pledge which he had made had any validity, declared that it had no force in conscience, and would not hold him in a court of law if the party concerned would tell the truth of the case. He assumed the habit and waited for fourteen months to be professed. While he was looking for his profession to take place his creditor entered the convent, declaring that they were taking away his money by permitting the novice to enter the profession, since he could earn what he owed in the secular life. Upon this, the superior commanded Luis to lay aside the habit; but the Lord punished the creditor by burning a great deal more of his property than the debt amounted to. Luis, who knew that the obligation was merely a confidential agreement, refused to pay it because he did not owe it. He was ordained as priest, having determined to become a secular clergyman. Under this condition he prayed God to help him fulfil his vow; and afterward had visions, among them a dreadful one of the devil in the form of a snake. Being constantly attended by visions, he determined to carry out his vow, and one night heard a voice calling to him, "Luis!" He answered, "Lord!" and the voice went on to say, "Rise, and go to Mexico to assume the habit." It seemed to him that it was the voice of his dead brother. His conduct when he came to the convent was such that the brethren there decided to grant him the habit and the profession together, since he had already completed his novitiate. When the founders of this province went through Puebla, father Fray Luis desired to accompany them, but was unable to carry out his wish at that time. He received intimations from a holy woman, a penitent of his, that the Lord favored his desire to come to this province; and to this intimation were added other supernatural signs. A great scandal having arisen because of violence shown by the viceroy to a superior of a certain religious order,[59] father Fray Luis felt called upon to preach against the viceroy; he was condemned to exile in the Philippinas, and received the sentence with joy. He accompanied father Fray Juan Cobo, who was exiled for the same cause, as is narrated in chapter twenty-four of this history.]

(*To be concluded.*)

1

i.e., "The holy synod commands parish priests and other preachers to the Indians to instruct them often and earnestly in the doctrine of this mystery;" and, "To those whom the parish priest shall regard as sufficiently instructed, and made fit by the correctness of their lives, he shall not fail to administer the holy eucharist, on the first Easter following."

2

Francisco Blancas de San José was a native of Tarazona, and entered the Dominican order at Alcalá de Henares. He came to Manila with the mission of 1595, and was sent to Bataán; afterward he spent several years in the Manila convent, preaching to Indians and Chinese, as well as Spaniards. He also gave especial attention to the instruction of the negroes and slaves there, of whom there were many thousands. He also labored in Cagayán and (1609) in Mindoro and Balayan. In 1614 he sailed for Spain, but died on the voyage, before reaching Mexico. (*Reseña biográfica*, i, pp. 172–177.)

3

Jacinto de San Jerónimo came to the islands with the mission of 1604. The rest of his life was spent mainly in the missions of Cagayán; near its end, he went to the new mission of Ituy (now Nueva Vizcaya), where he died in 1637. (*Reseña biográfica*, i, p. 327.)

4

Probably referring to the expedition sent from Mexico early in 1559, to conquer Florida, under command of Tristan de Luna y Arellano; it included 500 Spanish soldiers and a considerable number of Indian allies. This attempt proved unsuccessful, and most of the Spaniards were slain by the warlike Florida Indians.

5

The sketch of Salazar's life given in *Reseña biográfica* (i, pp. 35–49) states that he obtained permission to carry twenty religious with him to the Philippines, all of whom he procured from the convent at Salamanca. But twelve of them died (apparently from ship-fever) before reaching Mexico; and the others were so prostrated by sickness that they could go no farther.

6

i.e., "Reprove, entreat, rebuke, in all patience and doctrine."

7

Cantaro (from Latin, *cantharus*): the name of a large earthen or metal receptacle for liquids, hence for the amount contained in it; also, a measure for wine, varying in different parts of Spain. The cantaro (or alquiére) of Portugal is equivalent to nearly 2⅕ or 3⅓ U. S. gallons in Lisbon and Oporto respectively.

8

Referring to the cultivation of their rice, usually in fields more or less under water.

9

i.e., the fifth Sunday in Lent.

10

These were Dominicans and Franciscans (VOL. IX, pp. 161, 172). One of the latter was named Gregorio da Cruz; a letter from him to Dasmariñas may be found in VOL. IX, p. 197. Huerta, however, says (*Estado*, pp. 672, 673) that the early Franciscan missions lasted only from 1583 to 1586, and were not resumed until the year 1700.

11

See Morga's account of this expedition and its results, in VOL. XV, pp. 78–89, 130–160, 187–190. Cf. letters sent from Manila to Camboja, and papers connected with the embassy sent to Dasmariñas, in VOL. IX, pp. 76–78, 86, 87, 161–180.

12

The island (and group) of Lubang, southwest of Manila; a dependency formerly of the province of Cavite, but now of Marinduque.

13

Pulo Obi—that is, Obi Island; it lies near Cape Camâo (sometimes called Cambodia), the southernmost point of Cochinchina.

14

It is difficult to identify this town with exactness, but it is probably the same as the modern Pnom-penh (Panomping) on the great river Me-khong (also called Cambodia). The usurper of Langara's throne was Anacaparan (see Morga's account, in VOL. XV).

15

That is, the usurper Anacaparan. According to Morga, he resided at Sistor, which probably was the modern Udong.

16

Tiuman (Timoan, Timun) Island is off the eastern coast of the Malay peninsula; it is about ten miles long and five broad, and is a mass of rock, rising into heights of 2,000 to 3,000 feet.

17

Pedro de Ledesma, although an old man when he came to the islands, lived until 1625, after having filled several offices in his order—mainly at Manila, where he died. He brought seven missionaries with him (1596).

18

For meaning of this title, see VOL. XV, p. 88.

19

See Morga's account of this expedition (VOL. XV, pp. 160–168). Another relation (unsigned) is presented in a MS. document conserved in the Archivo general de Indias, with the pressmark: "Simancas-Secular; Cartas y expedientes del gobernador de Filipinas; años 1600 á 1628; est. 67, caj. 6, leg. 7."

20

According to the MS. mentioned in preceding note, this officer was Pedro de Beaztegui (probably for Verastegui).

21

Spanish, *Avia yo andado todas estas estaçiones*: an allusion to the "stations" which represent, in a Roman Catholic church, the stages in Christ's sufferings; and to the devotion which consists in making the circuit of these stations.

22

See Vol. XV, p. 206.

23

Apparently meaning here, "the country of the Irrayas," rather than the name of any distinct district. The Irrayas are in modern times a heathen tribe, of mixed Malay and Negrito blood, dwelling in the southern part of Isabela province, Luzón, on the western slopes of the Palanan range, and on tributary streams far up the Rio Grande de Cagayán.

24

The Angatatan River, on which is situated the hamlet of Magaldan; it falls into Lingayén Gulf.

25

Thus in Aduarte's text, but misprinted for Guadaira. Alcala de Guadaira is a small town in the diocese of Sevilla.

26

Prauncar, the son of Langara; he had been replaced on his throne by the Spanish adventurers. See Morga's account of Joan de Mendoza's expedition to Camboja, and the death of these two Dominicans, in Vol. XV, pp. 183–190, 244–247.

27

According to Morga's account, this friar was a Dominican.

28

The Dominicans made their first establishment at the City of Mexico in 1526; nine years later, their houses were organized into the province of Santiago de Mexico. In 1550, Chiapas and Guatemala were separated therefrom, and formed into a new province; and in 1592 permission was given to cut out still another, the province of Oajaca. Alonso de Vayllo was its second provincial (1594–97). See account of the Dominican order in Nueva España in the sixteenth century, in Bancroft's *Hist. Mexico*, ii, pp. 724–733.

29

i.e., "Christ became, for our sake, obedient even unto death."

30

Tomás Hernández was sent, soon after his arrival at Manila (1602), to the Japan mission; but at the end of four years he returned with broken health, which compelled him to cease his labors. He lingered, however, until 1642, when he died at Manila.

31

See list of these missionaries in *Reseña biográfica*, i, pp. 307–319. Thirty-one arrived at Manila, besides the two who died on the way.

32

One of the year-periods used in Japanese chronology (see Vol. VIII, p. 263). The Keicho period is 1596–1615.

33

All these priests became martyrs, except Hernandez; the fate of the lay brother is unknown.

34

One of the Koshiki Islands, lying west of Satsuma, and belonging to that district.

35

Konishi Yukinaga Tsu-no-Kami, a noted general, was converted in 1584, and took the name of Augustin. In 1592 he commanded the main army (composed mainly of Christian Japanese) sent by Taikô-sama for the conquest of Korea. Konishi won renown in that enterprise, in which he was engaged until Taikô-sama's death (1598) caused the recall of the Japanese troops from Korea. Opposing Iyeyasu, Konishi was among the prisoners taken at the battle of Sekigahara (1600), and was beheaded at Kioto. See Rein's *Japan*, pp. 284–288, 290, 299.

36

Owotomo Bungo-no-Kami (called Franciscus by the Jesuits), the most powerful feudal lord in Kiushiu, was one of the first daimiôs in Japan to accept Christianity, and was the main support of the missions in their early years. He died in 1587. The family of this prince were deprived, under Iyeyasu, of their possessions, which were divided among the latter's adherents. See Rein's *Japan*, pp. 273, 519.

37

This was a soldier named Joan Diaz (Vol. XV, pp. 189, 279). Cf. Morga's account of this Dominican mission (Vol. XV, pp. 279, 280).

38

Jerónimo de Belén, a Portuguese by birth, came in the mission of 1595, from Puebla de los Angeles, Mexico. He ministered at Bataán, Manila, and Cavite respectively; in 1603 went on the Camboja mission, and on its failure returned to Manila. He died in 1642, in Pampanga.

39

Sketches of the lives of all these friars are given in *Reseña biográfica*, i, pp. 320–327.

40

This friar came in 1604; he died at Nasiping, July 16, 1611.

41

Pedro Muriel came to the islands in 1615, and was sent to the Cagayán missions, where he seems to have spent most of his remaining years. He died at Manila, about 1642.

42

Itaves is a district south of central Cagayán, on the waters of the Rio Chico de Cagayan (or Bangag River). It has over 15,000 inhabitants, contained in more than a hundred villages; these people are mainly Calauas, and are heathen Malays. See *U. S. Gazetteer of Philippine Islands*, p. 561; also Smithsonian *Report*, 1899, p. 535.

43

Juan de Naya spent most of his missionary life in Cagayán. Finally being ordered to Mexico, he died on the voyage thither, January 27, 1620.

44

Andres de Haro, a native of Toledo, made his profession at Cuenca in 1613. He came to the Philippines in 1615, and spent more than forty years in the Cagayán missions. At various times he filled important offices in Manila, among them, that of commissary of the Inquisition. He died in that city, September 19, 1670, at the age of seventy-six years.

45

Apparently a reference to the Jesuit Alonso Sanchéz, who had gone in 1586 to Spain (see VOL. VI) as envoy from the various estates of the Philippine colony.

46

i.e., "Farewell in the Lord, beloved of my heart; may you fare well and happily forever."

47

This was Matsura Shigenobu Hô in, the daimiô of Hirado (Firando) and Iki. He succeeded his father in 1584, and died in 1614, at the age of sixty-five. He was an officer in the Korean campaigns under Konishi, and served during 1592–98. See Satow's note regarding him, in *Voyage of Saris* (Hakluyt Society's publications, London, 1900), p. 79; also his portrait, p. 80.

48

The same as bagacay or bacacae; see VOL. XVI, p. 55.

49

Hizen is one of the most notable provinces of Japan, commercially and historically. Its chief city is Nagasaki, which about 1586 was wrested from the daimiô of Omura by Taikô-sama, and declared the property of the central government. The Dutch maintained a factory there, although under humiliating conditions and restrictions, from 1639 to 1859. Another notable town in Hizen is Arima, where the Christians were so cruelly persecuted in 1637. The daimiô of Hizen, mentioned by Aduarte, was probably Nabeshima, prince of Saga, who was a favorite with Iyeyasu.

See Rein's *Japan*, pp. 300, 520–523.

50

Juan de San Jacinto made his profession in the Dominican convent at Salamanca, in 1594. He came to Manila in the mission of 1602, and ministered to the natives in Pangasinan and afterward in Ituy. He was finally compelled by ill-health to retire to Manila, where he died in 1626. See *Reseña biográfica*, i, p. 316.

51

Pedro de Santo Tomás came to the islands in the mission of 1602, and labored twenty years in the Cagayán missions—especially among the Irrayas, whom he pacified after their revolt against the Spaniards. He died at Lal-ló, June 29, 1622.

52

The Japanese custom of *hara-kiri*, or *seppuku*; see description Rein's *Japan*, pp. 328, 329; cf. Griffis's *Mikado's Empire*, p. 221.

53

The bonzes are the priests of the Buddhist temples; but they belong to various sects under the general appellation of Buddhism.

54

This daimiô was Shimadzu Yoshihisa; he was commissioned to subjugate the Riu-Kiu Islands, which were then added to the province of Satsuma.

55

i.e., Yamaguchi, in Nagato; the latter is the province at the southwest extremity of Hondo (or Nippon) Island, and lies opposite Kiushiu Island (in which are Satsuma and Hizen).

56

Father Organtinus (Sommervogel can find no distinctive Christian name) was born at Brescia in 1530, and entered the order in 1556. He set out from Lisbon for India in 1567; and soon went to Japan, where he spent the rest of his life, dying at Nagasaki in May, 1609.

Murdoch and Yamagata's *History of Japan, 1542–1651* (Kobe, 1903), gives this Jesuit's name as Organtino Gnecchi (or Soldi), and the date of his arrival in Japan as 1572; and furnishes considerable information (partly derived from Charlevoix) regarding Gnecchi's labors in Japan.

57

Takayama (called Justo Ukondono by the Jesuits) the governor of Akashi, in Harima; at Adzuchi-yama, on Lake Birva, he built a house and church for the Jesuits, and otherwise favored them. About 1615, he was, with other Christians, banished to Manila.

Nobunaga became, about the middle of the sixteenth century, the most powerful feudal lord in Japan. He strove to govern the country in the name of the Mikado, but aroused the enmity of the other feudal lords and of the Buddhist priesthood, and was treacherously slain in 1582. See Rein's *Japan*, pp. 267–273, 306.

58

Diego Carlos was a native of Guatemala, and made his profession at Puebla de los Angeles in 1592. Six years later, he came to the Philippines, and spent the rest of his life in the Cagayan missions, where he died in 1626.

59

Probably referring to the act of Villamanrique in sending to Spain ignominiously (1588) the Franciscan commissary Alonzo Ponce (Bancroft's *Hist. Mexico*, ii, pp. 717, 718).

.

Lightning Source UK Ltd.
Milton Keynes UK
UKHW010037070223
416578UK00002B/237

9 783734 078514